FACE OF DEATH

It stood in the shadow thrown by the birdhouse, its huge, black eye sockets staring toward him. The head glinted white in the moonlight, the black horror of its gaze trailing rivulets of muddy river water down across the protruding cheekbones and into the wide, toothy grin of its mouth like dark blood running.

There was no scream left in Kevin. His voice was a dry, soundless echo of the cat's cry.

Clearly he could see the long, pale fingers of the left hand, and the right, curled around the handle of the knife. He could see the hand begin to rise, so slowly at first that it seemed only part of his imagination.

In slow-motion acceptance of what was happening, Kevin saw it coming toward him, the knife in striking position.

He whirled and ran, fighting his way through the darkness toward the kitchen door, feeling beneath his bare feet the rough brick of the walkway, and feeling it hold him back as if each small rise in the bricks had become mountains for him to cross.

All his nightmares combined had not prepared him for the terror in this moment, in knowing that right behind him came the *thing*, the thing that was more horrible even than its purpose, which was to kill him, as it had killed Carl. As it would kill them all once it got into the house. . . .

WAIT AND SEE

BY RUBY JEAN JENSEN

ZEBRA BOOKS
KENSINGTON PUBLISHING CORP.

ZEBRA BOOKS

are published by

Kensington Publishing Corp.
475 Park Avenue South
New York, NY 10016

First printing: June 1986

Printed in the United States of America

PROLOGUE

1959

They met in the afternoon. One after the other they crossed the sun-baked field between the Childress house and the river. When he ducked beneath the willow leaves she was waiting, her clothes thrown to one side, her voluptuous body pale bronze, tanned from long, lazy hours in the sun. She lay on her back, her arms stretched languorously out. She looked up at him from under thick lashes, sultry eyes almost hidden behind them. Her lower lip drooped damply away from the upper. One stray thought flitted through his mind: Two years ago at this time of the summer they were having water fights in shallow parts of the river. Then, she was just Charlene, the cousin he saw each summer. He never dreamed, then, of this.

He kneeled, love slave to worship Aphrodite.

He held her face between his hands. "You are so beautiful. Your eyes are like the sky at midnight, your hair is the sunset. I love you so much."

"First we have to talk," she said aloud.

He drew back, dismayed by the tone of her voice. "What?"

"You act like everything is just like it always was. It's not. When I got pregnant everything changed."

"But . . ." When she talked to him like this he wanted to run away. But Charlene had kept him her slave since their first summer together when they were seven years old, and he was still her slave at fifteen. He shivered at the look in her eyes, the wild strangeness that could excite him unbearably, or chill him, as now.

"I won't live like that," she said. "Look at Mama. Trapped here in Grandpa's house because she got pregnant without being married and had me when she was just seventeen. I'm not going to live like that, Daniel."

"We—we could get married."

"*Married!* Cousins don't marry. It's against the law. We've broken the law, Daniel. And besides, I don't want to get married. I don't want to have a baby when I'm just fifteen. I don't want one ever."

She edged nearer him. Though not quite touching, he felt the electric pull of her body. Her voice changed, became softer, almost a whisper. Her eyelashes drooped again. The way they always did when she became persuasive, when she was out to get what she wanted. He felt helplessness returning, knowing he would do whatever she wanted, even though he knew it was wrong.

"I've got it all figured out," she said. "I've been concentrating on changing our realities. There's

6

more than one level of existence. I've read all about it. If we weren't trapped in our bodies we could fly through the air, go right up to the tops of the mountains, go down into the river, go over the trees, the rooftop—" She raised her arm, her palm flat, fingers together to demonstrate their weightlessness. "We'd be the way we are, forever, only free. We'd be freed from this reality."

He stared at her, hypnotized by the strangeness on her face. She brought her hand down suddenly and reached behind her. Sunlight glinted on something double-edged and sharp.

"I took it from the knife drawer in the kitchen three days ago," she said. "There are so many Mama hasn't missed it. I honed it, and it's sharp as a razor. Feel."

Daniel extended a finger and felt the fine edge of the knife. The blade was perhaps five inches long and tapered back from the point to one inch in width. He could hear her breathing, an excited, quick little gasp that was almost like when they made love. Behind them the river flowed, splashing aggressively against the grassy bank. A quiet wind rustled the leaves of the willow tree that drooped low around them, shutting them off from the field, the house and barn across the field, the road beyond, the small town.

"What—are you going to do with it?" he asked, afraid of her answer.

She looked at him, her eyes meeting his without a waver. There was a half smile on her lips. A touch of contempt.

"Not me, Daniel. *You.*"

He jerked his hand away from the knife.

"We'll do it," she whispered, "One more time. And

when we're through you'll plunge the knife into me, right here. And then you'll do the same to yourself. And we'll be free, Daniel, *free*, like the bats that fly at night, and the moths, and the very wind itself. You don't have to be afraid."

Her breath was hot on his face, and yesterday it had been sweet as the honey in Calvin's beehives, but it was tinged now with something dark and unknown, as though somewhere in the sweetness had come a rot that was eating her and eating him.

"That's crazy, Charlene!"

"No. It's not. I've been thinking, and that's the way we'll do it. I'll help you." She laid the knife on the crushed grass between them and pulled his face to hers, her hands against his ears. There was the sound of the rushing river in his head, and her whisper sounded far away, though it came into his mouth. "Kiss me now, Daniel. I'll tell you when it's time."

With her kisses hot on his mouth he gave in. A terrible trembling consumed his body as his hands felt freely of her.

An arm's length away the water of the river made its own sounds in a protected cove, brushing in against the muddy bank, sweeping out earth grains beneath the roots of a massive cottonwood tree.

Her body began convulsing against his. Her thighs clutched his and held him prisoner. Her eyes were closed now, her neck arched back. Moisture from his own mouth glistened on her open lips.

"Now, now," she cried, "do it now. *Kill me now.*"

He reached for the razor-sharp knife and raised his body away from her. He looked at the spot on her left breast where she had told him to plunge the knife and froze.

"Now," she demanded, opening her eyes. They were darker than usual beyond the shadow of her lashes. "Me, then you."

She rose up slightly, and her hands closed over his on the knife handle. Her breath rasped through him. He felt his hand raise with her strength and come down, creating its own sounds of sharp, swift movement. He heard it tear into her flesh and sink, a sound such as he had never heard before. Somebody cried out softly. It was himself, he thought. Charlene was stronger than he. She was not the coward that he was. He jerked his hand back from her hot palms and the handle of the knife.

Her eyes flew open widely and stared at him. Her body bowed in reverse, drawing convulsively away from him as though to burrow into the earth. Blood appeared suddenly in the corners of her mouth. She made watery sounds in her throat as she said, "Now you, now—you." But her hand was gripped tightly around the knife handle, and though it gave a movement of the wrist as though to pull the knife out, it remained where it was, embedded deeply in her purpling flesh.

In horror he watched her stare fade and suddenly realized what they had done. As the blood pumped one last time through her body and made thin trails from her mouth and nose down over her softly tanned cheeks, as her eyes glazed and seemed to look beyond him, he gathered her up in his arms.

Naked, she lay across his lap, her left arm limp, her right hand still clutching the knife, her head drooping as if her neck were broken. Her eyes stared past him.

- *"Charlene. Charlene,"* he cried, his voice breaking from its low, masculine tone and squeaking high again, as if he were still a child after all.

He wept over her, his tears falling to her chest and making tiny watery trails through the blood that had oozed from around the deeply embedded knife. Her flesh grew strangely cold, and he drew back from her, horrified and repelled, and let her body slide into the grass.

On his knees he bent over her, eyes open and staring through the drying blur of tears. His trembling hand reached out to unclinch her fingers from the knife handle, but he couldn't touch her. He couldn't bear the thought of pulling the knife blade through her flesh. He was terrified of hearing that sound again, that soft sound of metal against flesh.

I didn't do it. I didn't do it. I couldn't have!

He had never killed any creature. He had never liked even to step on an insect. How could he have helped do this to Charlene?

Through the lacy leaves of the willow tree that grew beneath the cottonwood he could see the field between the river and the barn. The red tile roof of the house rose beyond it among the trees in the yard and reminded him of the others, of Grandma and Grandpa, and Aunt Winifred. Had Aunt Winifred seen Charlene leave the house? Charlene had told her mother that she was going to walk to town, and Aunt Winifred had given her a small grocery list. He, waiting on the end of the long front porch, had watched Charlene go down the lane toward town, and she had gone out of sight around the bend, hidden by the English walnut trees that lined the road. There, he knew, she had crawled through the fence and gone through the grape vineyard and almond orchard back to the river. She had planned their meetings carefully.

Aunt Winifred would think Charlene was in town.

He began to search frantically among the small pile of clothes for the note paper with the grocery list. He found it in the pocket of Charlene's blue shorts. It was a tiny back pocket, stitched in red. He remembered vaguely, as from a fading dream, how it had set him on fire to watch that little hip pocket move when Charlene walked. He would have done anything for her. Hadn't he always?

He crumpled the note in his hand and almost threw it into the river. He drew it back just before his fingers would have released it forever from his control. The water might destroy it, cause it to disintegrate, and the little fish might then pick it permanently apart. But what if someone found it before that could happen?

He put it back into the hip pocket of the brief blue shorts with red stitching.

The water splashed against the bank, carried by a wave from the swift middle. Although it was dingy with mud it was slow moving at this point, curving as it did in among the tree roots that kept it from eating away the land. Far out in the middle where the river grew deep and strong a small whirlpool raged, swirling slowly at the outer edge and sinking in the center to a swiftly moving vacuum from which, he had been told when he was a boy swimming in the safer parts of the river, nothing would ever emerge.

If Charlene were there—in the vortex—

He couldn't finish the thought, yet he saw himself in a brief vision swimming out into the river with Charlene. He washed it away with a swift jerk of his head.

The red roof of the house caught his eye again, and even though he knew he would not take Charlene out to the whirlpool, he had to do something. To leave her here on the riverbank to be found made him feel naked to his soul, as if all the secrets between him and Charlene would then be revealed. All the kisses, all the deliciousness—all the—sins.

Aunt Winifred had never liked him much anyway. He had always felt that she dreaded the summers and looked forward to school starting so that he would be gone again. Even back when he was seven years old and just starting his summers on his grandparents' ranch, she hadn't liked him. She had always acted like Charlene was going to get too dirty when she played with him. They'd come into the house, he remembered, and Aunt Winifred would ignore him and look critically at Charlene's clothes, her hands, and her face, and would take her into the washroom to clean her up. It always left him feeling as if he had rolled in dirt. Which, to tell the truth, sometimes he had.

He couldn't face Aunt Winifred.

Not with this.

He had stopped crying, and now he noticed that blood was smeared on his hands and on his naked belly where he had held Charlene against him. He groaned out his revulsion and pushed away, as if by that method he could rid himself of the blood. The sound of the water drew him and, grasping the root of the cottonwood tree, he slid into the river. With his free hand he washed away the blood.

He lowered his head into the water and opened his eyes, looking back into the murky darkness beneath the exposed tree roots. The water here was quite deep. He could see the bank curving even farther back under the roots, almost an earthern cave, with the bottom lost in the darkness. He shivered, waves of cold water rushing into his soul. The roots reached out, still clinging to the soil of the ground above, like a cupped hand with many fingers. It was a perfect place to hide a body. He could tie her here, beneath the tree, beneath the ground, in the dark stillness of the water, and later he could bring down from the barn the short length of chain he had seen there. Her body would never wash ashore. So long as the tree stood, so long as the roots remained, so would the body.

He pulled himself out of the river and, working quickly, with only an occasional glance over his shoulder to make sure no stray fisherman came along the bank or boated along the river, he pulled Charlene into the water and wedged her body in the darkness beneath the tree. He tied her blouse around her left wrist and a root that curled down and back up, a strong root that would hold forever. Her body floated, sinking slowly into the water and rising again, now looking white and fishlike, as if all her summer tan had drained out with her blood. Her long, copper-bright red hair swept out strand by strand like a large silk fan.

He was glad to get out of the water.

He didn't know what to do with her shorts. He rolled them up and looked for a stone to weight them with, and found none. He would have to swim down into the bed of the river to find a stone, and the thoughts of going back into that water, where her body was floating, white ghost beneath the tree, chilled him to the depths of his being. Later he would have to go in again with the chain, but he would face that when the time came.

He decided to hide the shorts somewhere in the barn, in a place that was never used anymore. There were hundreds of those. The tool boxes of the old tractor that had rusted to a permanent hulk of metal; the feed boxes in the milk barn that were never used anymore now that Grandpa no longer kept cows; other places, many other places in the big barn between the river and the house.

He dressed quickly, then with the rolled shorts tucked under his arm, he hurried along the riverbank. He went stooped into the grape vineyard, where there was more protection, and from there to the barn lot. He went through an open gate in the wooden stockade fence. He hastily hid the shorts in the dark, webby silence and took down from a cluster of chains in the tack room a chain about eight feet long. He took a padlock from a tool box. He retraced his steps to the river and slid into the deep water beneath the tree. He wound the chain three times around her waist and twice around the root, and padlocked the ends together.

He noticed that her eyes were wide open and staring at him. Her cramped fingers held the knife against her chest.

When he swam away he did not want to look back at her but saw her in his mind: her body floating, twisted up toward the root, held by her chains, her left arm reaching out beyond her head, her fingers tangling the ends of her floating, silky red hair—*as if she were reaching for him.*

He had to face going to the house. He had to face Aunt Winifred and the others and act as if he didn't know anything at all about Charlene.

He would have to hang around another week or two before he dared leave for home. He would have to answer questions about Charlene's disappearance, he was sure.

And he had to keep his face free from emotion when he answered the questions.

I don't know where she is. The last I saw of her she was going to the store for Aunt Winifred.

As he walked away from the river for the last time, he heard a whisper behind him.

You, Daniel. Now you. I'll help you.

He began to run.

It's your turn, Daniel.

He stumbled, fell, got up again, terror turning the sun's warmth to ice on his back.

I'll wait for you. . . .

1

They were coming at last. She had waited all these years with revenge in her heart.

Winifred hadn't seen Daniel in almost twenty-six years. Vivid in her mind was the way he had looked in the last days she had seen him, a slender boy of fifteen, his handsome face pinched with the worry they all felt. Charlene, her precious Charlene, had been missing for one day, two, three; then Daniel went home to Chicago, and she never saw him again.

Scarcely a moment had passed during the years that Winifred did not think of her daughter, Charlene. As she did her chores around her parents' home, she thought of Charlene. As she cooked the small meals for her parents, as she cleared the table and cleaned the kitchen she thought of Charlene. As the years limped by, on and on, as her parents died, first Dad, in 1970, at age eighty, then Mother, in 1983 at age eighty-eight, Winifred wept for Charlene. At age fifteen Charlene had grown into a beautiful young woman, fully mature, with long red hair that Winifred had brushed and curled lovingly. It was Charlene she missed. She hardly realized when her parents were gone. The house became more quiet. There was less to do. But she had stopped communicating actively with anyone in 1959 when Charlene had disappeared. Her thoughts always turned inward toward the question: *What happened to my baby?*

In the first years after Charlene was gone, she searched for her body. She looked into every dark corner of the old barn, in the dusty mangers, up the ladder into the dark loft. She searched among the hay bales that had been left over. She looked into the feed bins at the ends of the milk stanchions downstairs and in all the other rooms.

She searched through the harness room, moving aside squeaky old leather things that hid nothing behind them but spiders and their webs.

She couldn't displace the feeling that Charlene was dead, and her body hidden somewhere within reach. And she knew who had killed her. Her hatred grew until she could think of nothing else. When she thought of Charlene she also thought of Daniel.

The one time she had expressed her conviction, that he had killed her and hidden her body, both her dad and mother criticized her furiously, damning her for uttering such blasphemy against their grandson.

"How can you say that?" her father, John Childress, cried, his face void of color and quivering loosely, his eyes bright and snapping with horror at her accusation. For days and nights he had been with groups of local citizens searching the countryside for

Charlene, tracing and retracing her last path down the curving country road to the small town one half mile away ón the banks of the Sacramento River, going through town from building to building, asking questions of anyone who might have seen her.

Now, exhausted, he faced his daughter. But Winifred was exhausted, too, and there was one possibility the others had not considered. She screamed out the accusation again: "She's dead! I know she's dead. She was killed and hidden, I know that. And who could have done it but Daniel? Haven't you seen the way he's been looking at her this summer? Like a rutting bull he's been after her!" Her father moved toward her and stopped helplessly, his hands motioning and dropping tiredly to his sides.

"Don't ever say that again, Winifred, as long as you live. Don't ever say that again. Charlene has been leading the boys on since she was thirteen years old. She's run off with somebody, that's all. And it wasn't Daniel."

All the energy he had left was in his voice.

There was only one consolation. After Charlene's disappearance, Daniel never again came to the northern California ranch; not even for his grandparents' funerals. She was glad he stayed away. She couldn't bear to look at him.

However, as the years passed and her desire for revenge grew, she realized her mistake, and she began to ask her relatives about Daniel. Through letters she began to follow Daniel. He married a young girl when he graduated from high school and divorced her soon afterward. He entered college and left it and married again, another wasted year. He became a

19

sales representative for something, and he married Ronna Ivans Knight, who had been married before and had a daughter, Kim, who was now fourteen. Winifred had no interest in Kim. It was Daniel's children she wanted. Kevin, who was nine now, and Sara, six.

There was another child, a few months old. His name was Ivan. His mother's family name, obviously, passed on to her son.

No matter. It wouldn't save him.

One by one they were going to die. Daniel would know how it felt to lose a child.

Kim felt as if she were still half asleep. She dreamed through her eyelashes, the scenery moving past in waves of green, bronze, blue, her brain lulled by the slight jiggle and sway of the car. When she allowed herself to think about it, the driving was beginning to seem like it would never end. Day after day.

Behind her Kevin's seat belts made their restraining noises as he began to squirm again. "Mom, I'm hungry."

Their mother, at the steering wheel, changed positions slightly as if Kevin's voice had jarred her out of a trance imposed by the long straight double lanes of the interstate. They had started at dawn this morning, without breakfast, from their motel in Nevada. Before they had settled in last night the five of them, all of them, had gone to a small market and purchased fruit and snacks in preparation for the day. They couldn't afford to stop more often than was absolutely necessary, their mother said, and especially they couldn't afford to stop at restaurants. Their dinners, all during the trip, had been eaten in fast food places, which, of course, pleased everyone but Mom well enough. Especially Kevin. If he'd had his way, there would be hamburgers and fries for breakfast, too. But Kim could remember that she had been much the same way when she was nine, too. Now, though, she wasn't as interested in food. There were times when she wouldn't even bother to go eat if she didn't have to remember that Kevin and Sara needed something, and their mother was sometimes too—well, worried, Kim guessed, and almost forgot. Did forget, sometimes.

Kim drew a reviving breath and started to undo her seat belt.

Ronna said, "Kim, hand Kevin an orange."

"I don't want an orange," Kevin said, on the edge of a whine. The farther they drove, the closer to whining he got. "I don't like oranges very well. They're sour. Or their juice runs down my arm. It's sticky. It itches."

"An apple then," their mother said. "And—do you want a banana too, Kevin?"

A long sigh issued from the back seat, and more squirming. "Well, okay." Then he added, "How come we didn't get any cookies or something like that?"

Kim got onto her knees and leaned over the seat. She fixed her stare on Kevin's blue eyes. "Hush, Kevin. You know we don't eat cookies for breakfast."

She silenced him with her eyes: It was the morning that she had served them cookies and milk, the morning after Dad had walked out on all of them.

21

But that was an unusual time. Their mother was in bed crying, Kim suspected, and Kim had tried to keep the kids from hearing or seeing anything. Keeping them quiet kind of entailed giving them a special treat. Sara, who was always like a little mouse, was no problem. If she had her dolls, she was satisfied. But Kevin and the baby, both of them boys, which probably had a lot to do with it, were a little harder to settle down. To keep them from bothering their mother, Kim had brought out the cookies. But that was three months ago, and she wanted Kevin to keep his mouth shut now.

He blinked under her fierce stare and said nothing. Kim reached down into the grocery sack that had been tucked into the only free space in the car, in front of Ivan's car seat. His legs were so short they simply stuck out in front of him, leaving plenty of room on the floor. She had to stretch to reach the sack because the baby's car seat was always left in position behind their mother on the far side of the back seat. Sara, sitting in the middle of the back seat, was almost lost. She was only six, and not a very large six. She had a lap full of small dolls that she was dressing and undressing. Sometimes she hummed. Sometimes she made conversation for her dolls as they talked to one another.

Kevin leaned as far forward as his seat belt allowed and tried futilely to see into the sack. "Why can't I get my own, Mom? I'm tired of sitting here."

"If you'll just hang on," Ronna said, "we should be at Aunt Winifred's sometime this afternoon."

"But we've been riding for days. Why can't we just stop and walk around?"

"We'll stop when we find a roadside park. Just for a minute."

"I hope we don't ever have to do any more riding. I hope Daddy comes and lives with us there, and we don't have to go anywhere else."

Kim reached the fruit and tore off three bananas from the hefty bunch. She glanced up to see if the baby was awake, but he was still sleeping, his head lolled against his shoulder, using it for a pillow. His plump little hands hung limply over the bar across the front of the seat. He loved bananas and was old enough now he could handle them without help. But she could get his when he woke up. She passed out an apple and a banana to both Sara and Kevin. For herself she decided on only the apple.

"Do you want something, Mama?"

"No thanks."

Kim gave Kevin another hard look before she straightened up and dropped back into her seat, but his attention had gone to the peeling of the fruit. Kim glanced then at their mother. But the sadness on her face was no more than usual. Kevin should have known not to mention their dad's coming to live with them; he should know better. Dad had been gone now for three months, just coming home for a few hours at a time. He had even taken away all his clothes. And it was he who had sent them to live with Aunt Winifred in the northern California valley, a place none of them had ever seen, a place that was two thousand miles away from home. Away from Daddy. And, Kim thought, the new wife he would be getting when the divorce was final. Their mother didn't know that she knew, but she did.

At first she had thought he ran away because of her. Because she was only his stepdaughter, and when the baby was born the apartment got too small. That was when she began to hear their raised voices through the wall of the bedroom. At night sometimes they woke her, and she had to cover her head not to hear. It scared her so much that sometimes her own sobs drowned out the rest. They had tried to keep quiet. And never, never did they fight in front of the kids. But after Ivan was born there wasn't any room, so she thought. She left and had gone to stay with a friend for a few days while she thought about it, thought about where to go next. She knew that she might go to Aunt Winifred's, because Aunt Winifred had been writing to her mom all these years and saying she'd love to see the children. So she had thought about getting away out there and how she could do it.

But then her dad came and got her and he told her she was part of the family. He hugged her and took her home, and she was so happy because she thought he was going to stay, too. But it was then, after she was back in the apartment, that he suggested they all go live at Aunt Winifred's. She remembered his every word. "It's the only real home I've ever been able to give you. The kids will love it there. It's a great place to live. The summers are long and the winters are mild. You won't have to fight the cold and snow anymore. The house is big enough for four families. The farm, or ranch, as they call it, is half mine since Dad died. I can't get any money out of it. It's Aunt Winifred's home, but you and the kids can have a home there from now on. I'll send you what money I can."

The kids will love it there, he had said. But they wouldn't love it anywhere without him. The apartment would have been better, even though it was crowded, if he had stayed there with them.

But he hadn't wanted it that way, and Kim knew in her heart, finally, that there was another family he loved now. But she hadn't told Kevin, and so sometimes he said things that hurt their mother.

And it hurt Kim, too.

But Kevin didn't know.

Ronna had tried not to let her children see her cry. They knew something was wrong. You don't pack your clothes and ship them ahead of you and then leave an apartment you've lived in the past five years, heading west to a destination two thousand miles away, unless something has gone wrong. Especially when Daddy doesn't go along. But Daniel had left them before and come home again. She had waited, pretending nothing was wrong the other time. For two months she had waited and was beginning to give up hope. Then, unexpectedly, he was home again, as if nothing had happened; and the children were delighted to see him. So was she, of course. She loved Daniel, had loved him at first sight when she met him ten years ago. It was difficult to hold a grudge against someone who was so important in your life.

This time it was only three weeks before he told her he wanted a divorce. He gave her no explanation, but she knew there was another woman. For a man who cared, or seemed to care, so deeply about his children, he could be very distant. It was almost a relief to have it over, at last, to know this was the end. During all their years of marriage, she had dreaded this day, feeling that it was inevitable. Even when Daniel was tight in her arms she had felt he wanted to be somewhere else. It was a hell of a way to live.

She bypassed Reno without stopping, and the highway rose toward the heights of the mountain range that divided California from Nevada. Over the mountains and in the valley was the small town of Childress, their destination. She had long heard of Childress, a town of about one thousand on the Sacramento River, founded around 1850 by Charlie Childress, Daniel's great-great-grandfather; but other than a few snapshots sent to her by Aunt Winifred, she knew nothing about it. Her own childhood had been spent in Chicago, and it was there she had met and married Daniel. He, too, had been born and brought up in the Midwest. Only after they were married and Kevin was born, when the gifts and letters began coming from Aunt Winifred, did Daniel tell her he used to spend his summers on the farm that had been in his father's family for generations. Not from him but from Aunt Winifred had she heard of the delightful summers: long, lazy days from the time he was seven until he was in his teens. Now it had become their haven. A faraway place with open arms.

"Mom, why don't you turn on the radio?" Kevin said. "I wish we had one of those little bitty television sets that you can set on the car dash."

"You would want me to drive off into one of these canyons? Why don't you read one of your books?"

26

Ronna tuned in easy listening music. Kevin had not reached the stage of favoring any kind of music. She knew he wanted only the noise. Kim was looking out her window, down into the depths of an incredibly deep hollow. At her age, Ronna expected an avid interest in whatever music interested the kids these days, but so far, she seemed uninterested.

"Can't you find a story on?" Kevin asked. "Instead of music?"

"No," Ronna said, without trying. "Read a book."

The road curved to the left away from the canyon and straightened. Ronna relaxed, unaware until then of how tense she had become, and speeded, exceeding the limit by five miles an hour. She didn't blame Kevin for getting restless. She, too, would be glad to have the long trip over.

Although it had been Daniel's suggestion that they go live at Childress, she could still see the indifferent shrug of his shoulders. Yet, as it always had been with Daniel, there was sorrow and hurt in his eyes. Yes there was love and caring but with the odd indifference. There was an ambivalence in the man that was puzzling.

Because she had always been a homemaker, with only occasional part-time jobs, she took his advice. There was nothing to leave behind. The apartment was rented, the furniture nothing great. Friends were few, and family was scattered. She felt a need for roots, a need that extended back into her childhood. She needed to feel that she belonged somewhere.

It was almost like returning to Daniel's arms. Forever. Although he had only spent his summers there, she felt that a large part of Daniel was still there, in Childress, on the ranch, in the town.

Childress unfolded beneath its covering of trees like a well-kept park. It had a wide main street that looked to be about six blocks long, with a couple of drug stores, three or four clothing stores, a furniture store, supermarkets at each end, with the usual scattering of service stations, motels, and convenience stores, most of them closer to the major highway that bypassed the town. Adjacent streets branched off from the main street, short and neat and lined with trees, sidewalks, and comfortable homes. Childress was, Ronna could see, as middle class a town as one could find. She could envision Daniel looking like his high school picture, with his handsome Grecian face and smooth olive skin that complemented his pale blond hair, walking along the sidewalk of the main street, stopping for a Coke at the corner drug store. Would he have been with a girl? Of course. He might have borrowed the family car and gone Saturday nights to the drive-in theatre she had seen outside of town.

"This is it, kids," she said.

Kim straightened up and began looking around. Through the rear-view mirror Ronna saw Kevin stir again after an hour of silence. She had talked him into getting interested in something that would keep him occupied, and he had been making paper toys for Ivan to tear up. The baby had awakened as soon as they got out of the mountains and started his day with fussy squirming, so Kevin's creativity had scored two points. Both boys had come on up along the valley without their usual restlessness. Now Kevin straightened up, too. She could see his nearly white hair come in view in the mirror.

"Can I undo my seat belt now, Mom?"

"Yes," she said.

According to the instructions sent to them by Aunt Winifred, they were to drive on through town along Main Street, past the post office and the Speed-Gro convenience store and take the right-hand street where the road branched. One half mile from the store was the private road up to the house.

Ronna's appreciation was bland. She was so tired she was beginning to tremble. Now that she was near the end of her trip, she could give in and be tired. She wished for privacy, for a comfortable room and a hot bath. But of course that wouldn't be possible.

Ivan would be needing attention and a warm bath himself. He hadn't been changed since morning.

She saw an ice cream store suddenly, with small metal tables and chairs arranged beneath the shadow of a tree on a kind of patio. She glanced into the mirror again, saw no car was behind her, and slammed on the brakes impulsively.

"How about ice cream, kids?"

This way, she thought, she could at least change Ivan before his aunt got hold of him and found his disposables on the verge of crumbling in her hands. This way, too, she could comb everybody's hair and wash their faces. Then, they could proceed on out to the house more rested, perhaps, or at least more presentable.

She parked the car at the curb and got out. It felt

29

almost sinfully good to stretch her muscles. Driving the ten-year-old car was not the easiest job in the world. And now she realized how thankful she was it hadn't broken down on them halfway across the country. She patted its hood in gratitude.

She gave Kim money to buy ice cream for herself, Kevin, and Sara.

"I'm going across the street to the service station," she said, "and see if they'll let me use their rest room. I want to clean Ivan up."

She unbuckled the baby, who had begun to fuss again anxiously, stretching his arms out to her, impatiently wanting out of the restraint of his car seat. With him out and on one arm, she pulled the straps of the diaper bag over the other arm. She felt weighted down, but the burden was pleasantly physical. She was almost light-headed as she crossed the street, glad to be out of the car, glad to be home.

Home.

She longed desperately to feel that it was home, this strange place that was oddly quiet, with so few cars on the street, so few people along the sidewalks. She glanced back and saw Kim and Kevin and Sara carry their ice creams out to the tables where they sat, the only customers on the patio.

A man of about Daniel's age—forty-two—sat beyond the glass wall of the service station office, watching her approach. When he saw that she was coming toward him, he got up to stand in the open door. He had a pleasant roundish face and thinning hair. His body, with an ample bulge over his belt, revealed he was well fed and enjoyed his snacks and lunches. Through the window Ronna saw an open bag of potato chips on the desk. Above the door was a plaque with the words: Proprietor, Milton Phillips.

Ronna stopped between the gas pumps and the door to the office. She smiled at the man and shifted Ivan to a more comfortable spot on her hip. She was about to drop both him and the diaper bag. At nine months of age he was a chunk, at least three pounds heavier than Kevin had been at that age.

"Mr. Phillips?"

"Yes." He straightened from his easy slump against the door. When he smiled a dimple appeared in his left cheek. Ronna had a sudden image of him as a small boy and thought he must have been adorable with his round face and dimples.

"I've just arrived in town," she said, "and I would appreciate so much the use of your rest rooms. I'd like to clean up my baby."

"Sure." He reached up on the inside of the door and took down a key on a large ring. He came out toward her with an energetic walk and extended the key ring to her. "Have you come a long way?" He glanced toward her car, with its luggage rack on top filled almost to overflowing.

"Yes. Chicago. It seemed like a long way to us."

"Are you stopping here?"

"Yes, at the Childress place. My husband is Daniel Childress. He used to spend his summers here. Did you know him?"

Milton Phillips turned steady, inward-searching eyes toward the road out of town. "I know the Childresses," he said. "Winifred Childress buys her gas from me, but that's only about once every two or three months or less. She doesn't like the new self-

31

help pumps, and I'm the only one left in town that gives a full service job. She doesn't drive much, though. Goes around to pay her bills once a month. Goes to the supermarket once in awhile."

"She's my husband's aunt." Ronna felt the warmth of possession as she talked of Daniel. At least she still had a right to call him her husband. The divorce was not final.

"Yeah, I remember who you're talking about. He used to play on the summer softball team some. Daniel Childress. My favorite girl had eyes only for him."

"Really?"

"Yeah. He had curly hair, and I thought that was probably the reason all the girls were crazy about him. A bunch of us guys talked about getting permanents, but our folks got wind of it and laid down the law. He stopped coming at all after Charlene disappeared." His laughter, even his smile, ended. His eyes glazed over as though he were remembering something.

Ronna was puzzled. "Charlene?"

He looked at her. "Charlene Childress. She was his cousin. Winifred's daughter."

Ronna felt herself frowning. She had a strange sensation of having stepped through a door that should have never been opened. She had never heard of Charlene Childress before, and although it wasn't too surprising that Daniel never mentioned her, because he had seldom referred to any of his father's family, it was puzzling that Aunt Winifred herself had not mentioned her own daughter. In all the letters that had come from her in the ten years Ronna and Daniel had been married, in all her information about the ranch and the town, it seemed very odd that no mention was ever made of the daughter.

Ronna said, "I thought—Aunt Winifred was—uh—unmarried. I never knew—anyone named Charlene."

"She was unmarried. At least, so far as I know. She never changed her name, anyway, and Charlene went by the Childress name. She was in my grade at school but was a year younger."

"What happened to her?"

He hunched a shoulder. "Nobody knows. She was fifteen the year she disappeared. We all joined in the search for her. She was a beautiful girl, with long red hair the color of a new copper penny. She had fair skin with some freckles on her face, but on her they looked good. I guess she just ran away. She was pretty mature for her age. She grew up early. She and her cousin, Daniel, used to run around together all the time."

Ivan began to squirm, and Ronna had to readjust him. She was about to lose him again, she felt. Milton Phillips looked at the baby, and his mild eyes softened even more.

"Reminds me of my grandbaby," he said. "He's about a year old now. Walking all over the place."

"Oh yeah?" Ronna looked into the face of her son. Like Kevin and Sara, he resembled his father to an amazing degree. She was glad. They were beautiful children. She wished Kim could have been as pretty, but Kim had taken after her natural father's people also, and had a thin, lanky build, a face that was too pointed and features that were even yet somehow not

33

really pretty.

"Is this Dan's son, or—"

"Yes." She motioned back toward the ice cream parlor with a nod of her head. "Those children there are Daniel's, too." No point in explaining that Kimberly was Daniel's stepdaughter.

"He must have settled down later than I did. My kids are twenty and twenty-two. My daughter is the one with the baby."

Ronna moved toward the left of the building where a sign pointed toward the restrooms. "It's been nice talking to you," she said. "My son is getting hard to hold."

A car drove slowly in to park at the pumps, and Milton went toward it. Freed from more conversation, Ronna took the baby into the ladies' restroom and saw with relief it was clean enough to lay him on the floor while she changed him and cleaned him up. She combed his white hair and parted it on one side.

"Now I wish you could stay like this until we meet Aunt Winifred, at least," she said to Ivan's smiles and gurgles. He put a fist in his mouth and slobbers trickled out around it. Ronna used a fresh Wet-One from the diaper bag and wiped his hand after pulling it out of his mouth. She positioned him on her hip again and pulled the strap of the diaper bag over her other shoulder.

Kim was so busy absorbing her new surroundings that her ice cream melted in its dish. Although they had driven through a lot of little towns, she hadn't stopped in one long enough to get the feel of it. This was almost like being with Heidi, except the moun-

34

tains were across the valley, pushing white peaks against a blue sky. Around her the quiet town was summery and shady. A dog came trotting down the sidewalk, and she watched him with a keen sense of amusement and pleasure. He glanced her way with friendly brown eyes. He glanced at Kevin and Sara without missing a beat in his slightly sideways trot, then crossed the street and entered a yard further down the block. He knew where he was going, and although he wore a collar, he wasn't restrained by a leash.

Kim looked over her shoulder. Ronna was coming across the street now, carrying Ivan. He was pointing at a tree and chattering something, but their mother didn't notice.

She sat down at the metal table and fed Ivan a small serving of ice cream, after which she had to wash his hands and face again. She stared off into the distance then, as if she were reluctant to leave the patio of the ice cream parlor. Kim's earlier feelings of pleasure were displaced by a dread she couldn't name.

"Come on," she said to Kevin and Sara. "We can't go looking like this."

They followed her to the car where she borrowed a couple of Wet-Ones from the box on the floor and wiped their chins. She combed their hair, smoothing the platinum blond curls down with her hands. Sara's hair hung in ringlets past her shoulders, and Kim readjusted the small blue barrettes that held it back behind each ear. Kevin's hair, like Ivan's, curled over his head like a cap. Their dad's hair was blond, too, though darker, and lay in waves. Kim would have given almost anything to have hair like theirs; but that was envy, she admonished herself, so she didn't allow the thought to enter her mind very often.

Ronna came to the car and put Ivan into his seat. He kept chattering, but Ronna didn't answer him as she usually did. Kim watched to see that both Sara and Kevin had fastened their seat belts before she closed the door and got into the front seat.

They drove out onto the nearly empty street. A pickup truck, coming from the opposite direction, ambled past. The driver rode with his elbow out the window. He looked at them curiously.

"Read me the directions, please, Kim," Ronna said.

Kim got Aunt Winifred's last letter out of the glove compartment. "Go down Main Street and around the corner to the right where the road forks. That's right here. Then follow the road that branches right. Go one quarter mile, and there's a lane to the right. The lane is an eighth of a mile long, and is a private lane. The mailbox is on the main road, and has Childress Ranch on it."

Kim looked up. She was aware that Kevin had slipped the traces of his seat belt and was scooted forward in his seat, but she didn't say anything. The car was only going about fifteen miles an hour, and there were no others on the road. She didn't blame him for wanting to see.

Around the corner they came upon the division of the street that Aunt Winifred had called a fork. To the right was a narrow blacktop road that was lined on both sides by large, shading trees. Beyond the trunks were green fields, grape vineyards, and orchards, with occasional houses and barns.

When they reached the lane Kevin cried, pointing

out his open window, "There's the mailbox! Why is it so big? Childress Ranch, it says, just like she said."

"Well, sure," Kim said.

Ronna turned the car slowly into the lane. Kim heard her draw a long breath.

At the end of the lane was a large, two or three story house built of gray brick. It was trimmed in white, but the roof was red tile. Beyond the house there looked to be a large collection of other buildings, one of them an enormous barn that had once been painted red but now had sun-bleached walls that were varied pinks and grays and deep reds. It was partly hidden behind the house and the trees in the big yard, but Kim knew what Kevin was referring to when he said, "Hey, look, hey look!" And she also knew he would be there looking it over as soon as he was allowed.

On the front porch of the house, which reached its full length, stood a woman dressed in blue slacks and striped shirt, red and gray-streaked hair cut short and square, as if she did it herself. She stood as still and straight as one of the porch posts, as if she had been waiting for a long, long time.

"There, that must be Aunt Winifred," Ronna said quietly. "How good of her to make us so welcome."

For the first time, Aunt Winifred became real. But the woman Kim saw on the porch in some way didn't fit the image her letters had created. This woman, Kim saw as they drew near, was not the warm and loving person that Aunt Winifred, the letter writer, the gift sender, had seemed to be.

*   *   *

Interstate 70 unfolded in front of Daniel like an unwinding ribbon, on and on, rolling through the Ohio landscape without really touching the state or the people. He had been driving since one o'clock in the morning, and was beginning now, over twelve hours later, to feel as though something huge had gotten hold of him and was shaking him harder and harder. He had made two stops today, one in Indianapolis to see the manager of a branch office, and one other for coffee. At the second stop he had brought a thermos of coffee along, but that was gone now.

The steering wheel was beginning to vibrate under his hand, as if whatever had begun to shake him was shaking the whole car. The air shimmered ahead of him, a pocket of heat. It lay across the road ahead like a sheet of glass. He closed his eyes for one prolonged blink, making plans. He was on his way to Pittsburg, and there he would stop the night, see the guy he had an appointment with, then tomorrow he would be on his way home to Sharon. Tomorrow night they would have bedtime drinks and a long time in bed. He could see her light, red-gold hair spread out on the pillow, the curve of her cheek pale against it.

Red-gold hair. Red hair, rich with sunlight, or some other light that made the hair seem ablaze, fanned out in front of his eyes, covering his face, smothering him. He opened his eyes. The car lurched as he jerked on the wheel. She was standing in the road in front of him, her figure shimmering in the strange, wavy light. Her hair lifted out away from her face, fanning up, long, burning red. The hood of his car propelled onward toward her, even though his foot had found the brake and slammed it to the floor-

38

board. He was going to hit her. He screamed, a strange, croaking sound that blended discordantly with the squeal of the tires on the pavement.

Charlene.

He jerked the car to the right and came to a halt in the grass off the highway. Sick to his stomach, he stumbled out into the warm air.

The highway coiled ahead, rising and falling over the rolling land, disappearing into the distance. Across the median an eighteen-wheeler thundered closer. A couple of cars made dots in its wake.

There was no one else on the highway. No one in the road. He leaned against the fender, weak and trembling.

He'd go back home—no. He'd go on. He couldn't go back there, to Sharon of the red-gold hair. Why had he chosen her? Suddenly he saw the resemblance that he hadn't seen before. Not consciously.

And he knew he would not go back, ever, for he wouldn't be able to explain why he was leaving.

2

The driveway went on past the end of the house, the fat, shading trees continuing beside it on the left like a wall of green. The trees ended at a wood fence that separated the lawn of the back yard from the grounds of many buildings including the big barn. In the fence enclosure of one small building, Kim could see baby pigs playing. Nearby the large mama was stretched out on the ground.

Kevin was breathing on the back of Kim's head. She could tell by the excitement in his attitude that he was seeing the animals, too. He leaned on the seat, and his elbow pulled her hair. She reached back and pushed him away. "Sit *down*, Kevin!"

Ronna brought the car to a stop at the end of a walk. On each side of the brick pathway, there were roses with fat, pink blossoms. The fragrance wafted up to Kim as she opened the door. The woman who had been standing on the porch was now coming along the walk.

"Hello," she said in a strong voice, bending down

and looking through the car at Ronna. "I'm Winifred. You must be Ronna. I've been expecting you for a couple of days now. Do come in."

Aunt Winifred's eyes were small and sharp and dark brown. They were so deeply set they looked like they were peeping out through cracks, and Kim felt her dismay returning. Aunt Winifred's eyes didn't match her voice, somehow. The eyes scarcely touched Kim, though. They overlooked her and settled on the children who were getting out of the back seat. Kim saw Kevin edge back from her. Though her lips were smiling, and a good smell like cupcakes emanated from her, there was that thing about her eyes; and Kim knew that Kevin saw it, too. Did Aunt Winifred really not want them there? Did she not like them after all?

"I would know you anywhere, Kevin," Aunt Winifred said. "You look just like Daniel did when he was your age. By then he was coming here and spending the whole summer, away from his mother and father. His grandparents were still alive then, and they took very good care of him. He was their only grandson, and they thought the sun rose and set in Daniel. I expect your daddy told you all about his summers here."

"No, ma'am," Kevin said, and Kim looked at him in surprise. He had remembered manners she didn't know he had.

"And you must be Sara," Aunt Winifred said, this time holding out her hand and helping Sara out of the car. Her smile faded. She glanced up at Ronna, who was coming around the car with Ivan in her arms. "What a beautiful child your daughter is,"

Aunt Winifred said.

Kim had the strange feeling of being invisible. Nonexistent, perhaps. Aunt Winifred had said *your daughter* as if there were only one. Only one that mattered. Kim felt a sudden and unreasonable envy of Sara, and then immediately hated herself, for the pretty little face that was turned up to Aunt Winifred was as innocent and trusting as Ivan's. Sara couldn't help that she was prettier.

Aunt Winifred walked around the car to the center of the driveway with a long dipping stride. There was nothing gentle or fluid in her walk, nor even very feminine. It was like her haircut. The smell of the cupcakes was incongruous.

"Frank!" she shouted toward the trees. "They're here." She came back to the car, explaining, "Frank is our handyman. He'll carry your things up to the bedrooms. And if there's anything else you'd like done, just call for Frank. He likes being helpful."

Aunt Winifred's fingers combed through Ivan's soft, short curls. He gave her a big two-tooth smile and gurgled a few sounds. Winifred drew her hand away.

"My goodness," she said, "even the baby looks like Daniel, doesn't he?"

Kim saw a figure moving beyond the trees. The man was about Aunt Winifred's age and was carrying a hoe to the fence where he leaned it. He came on through a gate. In the garden where he had been working vegetables grew in rich, green abundance.

Kevin began edging off toward the barns, and Kim grasped his sleeve just in time, pulling him back.

Ronna stood holding the baby and looking down

at him with that face of pride that mothers always wore when someone was paying attention to their baby. Kim could see that her mother thought Aunt Winifred would take Ivan and carry him into the house, perhaps, but she didn't. Instead she began taking down from the luggage rack the suitcases that had been tied there.

"Your other things arrived in good shape," she said. "I've had Frank put them up in the master bedroom. It hasn't been lived in since Mama died. It was hers and Dad's room. You can have it now."

"Thank you," Ronna said. "That's very kind of you."

"Well, it seemed the only practical solution, since you have the baby. The nursery is right next door to the master bedroom. All of the Childress babies have used that nursery, for well over a hundred years."

"I never expected a separate room for Ivan. He's slept in a crib in our bedroom since he was born."

"Then it's time he was getting his own room and learning to be independent. How old is he, nine months?"

"Yes."

"I thought so. A woman alone with no family, such as I, likes to keep close track of the rest of the family. I'm more than happy to share this big house. I rattle around in it like a dried-up nutmeat in a walnut shell. I suppose Daniel will be along soon?"

Ronna said, "Daniel is often on the road in his business. He may not be here for quite a long time. But he thought this would be a better place for the children to live than where we were."

"Oh yes, I'm sure he's right." Winifred pointed

44

toward the other end of the house. "Boys especially need the room and freedom of a ranch. There, Kevin, is our grape vineyard. You can eat all the grapes you want. And the orchards there are ours, too. The river runs back there behind the fields and orchards. Daniel used to swim there. In fact, he learned to swim in that river."

Ronna looked alarmed. She said quickly, "But don't go to the river alone, Kevin. Don't go without an adult."

Frank came around the corner of the house. Not far behind him came a big, fat, yellow cat. It plopped down in a patch of sunshine and stretched its legs, then gazed toward the distant fields as if he didn't care a whit about the new arrivals. Kim, delighted to see the cat, began crooning deep in her throat. She bent down, sat on her heels and rubbed the cat's thick fur. He stretched languorously and answered her with chuckling purrs.

Frank shook Ronna's hand and patted Ivan's cheek. He said hello and shook hands with Kevin and Sara. Kim left the cat and held out her hand to Frank. He had swarthy skin that was wrinkled tightly against the bones of his face. His eyes were as dark brown as Aunt Winifred's, but they had a softness in them like the eyes of a Beagle pup. His hand clasp was firm and cool.

The next time Kevin started drifting off down the driveway Kim let him go. Aunt Winifred had, in a way, given him permission.

Kevin paused for a few minutes to rub the electric

45

fur of the cat and listen to the loud purring. "What's your name, huh, fella, what's your name?" he asked, rubbing gently. The long yellow fur rose up and followed his hand.

The cat rumbled and stretched, rolling onto its back to have its stomach rubbed. In that way, Kevin thought, it was just like pigs. Pigs like to have their stomachs scratched. He knew that from the time his church school had taken a bunch of the kids out to a farm. They had been allowed to play with the pigs, especially, because of their gentleness and playfulness. They were almost like puppies. And that was where he was going now. To see the pigs.

He thought the cat might get up and follow him, but it didn't. It settled down to washing its face as Kevin went on around the corner of the house.

Kevin went down the driveway. The shade from the walnut trees lay cool and spotless over the dark coating of the drive. Behind the house a green and tidy yard was filled with arrangements of shrubs and flowers. There was a small porch at the back of the house where one wood and screen door opened, and farther on near the corner was a large brick patio with chairs and metal tables. French doors there were standing open. He detoured over to the patio and peeked into the room. It was light, with windows all along two sides. There were chairs and sofas upholstered in floral print. On the walls were shelves with books. But there was a door that led back into the house, and it was like looking into a long, dark tunnel. There was something about it that made Kevin draw away, intimidated by the darkness.

He turned toward the buildings of the farm and

began to run, flailing his arms in the air as if he had been released from a prison. He thought of the cramped car and the long trip and hoped he'd never have to ride that far again. Maybe, when they went home to see his dad they could fly. Now that would be fun. To sit up there so high and look out upon the clouds.

He squatted at the edge of the pig pen and looked between the boards. The mama pig looked huge, and one of her eyes gazed out at him from under long, white eyelashes. She grunted. Still she didn't move from her lazy position on the ground, but that didn't mean she wouldn't move in a hurry if he tried to climb over the fence. The baby pigs were scuffling and playing and paying him no attention. Kevin looked around for something long enough to reach the pig and test out the mama's friendliness. The area around was as neat as the lawn. There was no stray stick. He got up and began to circle the pig pen enclosure. At the rear he found the fence ended at the side of a low building. The pig's house, he guessed. And growing right behind the house was a low-limbed tree that stretched out over the sloping roof of the shed. He began to climb. Maybe, he told himself, he'd find a stick on top of the house with which he could reach the mama pig and scratch her stomach. Then, if she showed herself to be a friendly soul, he could try to crawl into the pen and pet the baby pigs. They were so cute with their little tubelike bodies and short legs with the tiny hooves that made them look like they were wearing high heels. They had cute noses, too, as round as quarters.

He reached the top of the shed with no trouble, but

there was no stick, no fallen dead limb. He climbed to the edge of the pig house and looked over the edge. The mama pig had closed her eyes again, but she was grunting softly. The little ones were still playing.

Kevin turned over and looked into the top of the leafy tree. He could almost see the sky in a few spots. And he could see a bird in the top of the tree. It eyed him but didn't fly away. It turned its head and looked at him from the other eye. Kevin laughed.

He then heard a sound that caused cold waves to ripple over his skin. It sounded like a groan, deep and sorrowful, and it came from somewhere over toward the barn. He sat up and listened. The barn was almost hidden beyond the thick foliage of the tree that hovered over him, and he slid down the roof on his belly until he could see under it.

The roof of the tall barn reached up in a sharp inverted V, the eaves sticking out a couple of feet or more beyond the wall. On the wall beneath the eaves was a faded emblem, a circle with a cross inside. But immediately beneath the eaves were three large birds, and as Kevin watched them mill about on a kind of small ledge that looked as if it had been built especially for them, he heard the groan again. Now he knew what it was, because he had heard it before in the parks of Chicago during the quiet part of the day.

Pigeons.

The noises they made could really be scary sometimes, he reminded himself. But the barn looked even more interesting from this close range than it had from up the drive. On the ground floor were a lot of doors, most of them small like a door to a house, but the center ones were large, as if they had been built for the tractors and farm wagons to come and go. All of the doors were shut though, and there was nothing in the barn lot but a few scraggly weeds.

He climbed down from the pig shed, crossed the lane to the barn fence, and climbed over, counting boards as he went. Five boards, nailed horizontally between heavy wood posts. He liked this fence. It was big and sturdy.

The first door of the barn that he tried to open did not yield.

It clung to the wall as if someone very strong inside were holding it.

Kevin backed away, an unaccustomed fear almost sending him running. But curiosity held him. Maybe, he told himself, his feet set for running should he need to get away, maybe it was a horse or a cow leaning against it from the inside. If a guy was careful, neither one was dangerous. And he really wasn't afraid. Hadn't he seen horses and cows before? He had even ridden horses at that one park, where all the little ponies went around in a circle. And that was a long time ago when he was even smaller than Sara.

He straightened, moved stealthily closer to the barn, put his ear against the rough, faded red wood and listened. Something throbbed, sounding like an engine far away. Something else creaked, as if the boards of the barn floor were supporting a heavy weight that moved a little bit at a time; something that slipped across it quietly; something with eyes perhaps that could see through the wood.

The hair on Kevin's arms stood straight up like stiff little wires. The back of his neck tickled as the hair there stiffened and rose. He jerked his head away from the barn.

He listened. Above him the pigeons cooed. From the pig pen he heard a fine-voiced squeal from one of the baby pigs. The sounds helped bring his hair back to normal. The sunshine was warm and bright on this side of the barn, and from inside now there was silence. He had to look inside. He just had to.

He squared his shoulders and strolled casually along the breadth of the barn, passing the big double doors in the center, passing a smaller door farther on. He came to the corner of the barn and peered around. The length of the barn seemed to go on forever, and Kevin saw more doors scattered along the way, with tiny windows set high in the wall between the doors; and farther down toward the other end was an open area, where there was nothing but posts. He almost leaped in his excitement. There was a way into the barn without opening a door.

He began to run. The dirt was soft and black, with weeds growing now and then. He jumped over them, just to prove that he could. To his left, he saw when he stopped, just beyond the fence, a dark green alfalfa field stretching all the way down to the line of trees by the river. At the edge of the alfalfa field the vineyards started. A few spots between the trees gave him glimpses of the river. As he considered choices he was torn between going down to look at the river and going into the barn. His mother's orders came back to him and nudged, raising a sense of guilt, as if he had already gone to the river. He shrugged and went on to look into the open shed of the barn.

He saw a tractor with big metal wheels, an old tractor whose original red color was faded like the barn, so that they matched. He ran to it and climbed up to the metal seat. He could barely reach the pedals, and the steering wheel was welded with age so that it wouldn't turn an inch. He made engine noises and pretended the wheel turned. He felt as though he were sitting almost up to the roof. He looked up. Like the roof of the pig shed, it sloped, and the rafters were within reach above. Clusters of webs, new and old, were sewn into every crack. A spider looked at him from the depths of one crack. Kevin slid down. He spent several minutes looking the tractor over, finding hidden treasures in an old tool box with a lid that was built into the hood. In there were wrenches, all rusted, nails, bolts, screws, and things he couldn't name. All of it rusted. Some of it rusted together so hard it couldn't be pried apart.

He finally left the tractor, but it had already become a friend, a good place to play. He'd be back, that was for sure.

Along the back of the shed, against the wall of the inner barn, were strange things built of wood that looked like torture chambers of some kind. Wood bars went across the top, holding together movable parts that would clasp an animal at the neck. Then Kevin saw what it was, for stretched the whole length was a feed box. He knew it was a feed box because there were still scraps of hay in it.

And corn. And, he saw as he moved the hay around with his hands, even some other kinds of grain. In some places the grain had wedged into the cracks of the bottom of the feed box and started to grow. Pale green little shoots were bending toward the sunlight, but it was no use. The light was beyond the edge of the roof, twenty feet away. There were others that had tried to grow in other years, and they now lay like dried up little threads on the bottom of the box.

Kevin looked for a way to enter the rest of the barn, and he found to his left a partial door that came up only halfway. It was standing slightly open. An invitation to enter. It was as if something had seen him coming and made sure he would know he was welcome to enter.

Kevin hesitated, and the hair on his arms began to stiffen again. *Don't go in there,* a part of his mind said. But it was the part that Kevin ignored most of the time because it always had to do with things that were fun to do.

He crossed the soft, silent soil of the shed floor and pushed open farther the half door. Its hinges squealed as if they were as rusted as the tractor. Kevin jerked his hand back. But he didn't run, though the voice in his head was shouting, *run, run, run.*

Silence came down again now that the door stood still. There was plenty of room to enter. Kevin edged near, stuck his head in and looked around. It was an empty room except for a tow sack of something in the corner. There were pegs on the wall that held a lot of empty tow sacks. This roof sloped also, like the roof of the wings of the barn on both sides. They both were low and sloping, while the center rose up toward the sky like a huge bird just beginning to take flight. There was a lot of barn to explore. And this was only the first room. It had a wood floor, Kevin saw, and leading out of this room into the center portion of the barn was another door, a full-length wood door that stood wide open. Beyond was darkness, but the longer Kevin stared, the less dark it became. Finally, he stepped into the room and crossed it, his footsteps sounding hollow on the rough boards of the floor. He looked through into the mysterious middle of the big barn. Another room here, he found, but much, much bigger, and the ceiling above was only the floor of a second floor room. He saw cracks there, with bits of hay sticking down through. There were heavy wood pillars spaced at intervals holding up the loft floor. And there were doors, and more doors, and things sitting around on the floor and hanging on pegs on the walls. Kevin entered the twilight world of the old barn.

Kim stood in the center of the bedroom Aunt Winifred had said she could have and looked around. It was pretty, with sheer blue ruffled curtains and matching blue satin bedspread, and a closet so big that her clothes looked lost in it, but she didn't feel the way she had always dreamed she would if she could ever have a room like this all to herself. For one thing, it was very quiet here. She couldn't hear Ivan's gurgles, nor Sara's private little conversations she gave to and from her dolls. She couldn't hear movement of any kind. It seemed to her that Aunt Winifred had put them in oddly separated places in the big second story of the house. Mama's room was at the front, around the balcony that surrounded the big hole above the entry hall. And Ivan's room was right next to hers. From the door of her own room Kim could see the doors to Ivan's and Mama's rooms, but she couldn't see Sara's door, which was along the hall into the back of the house which Aunt Winifred had called the west wing. And she couldn't see Kevin's door, which was also in the west wing at the far back of the house. His windows looked out toward the river. He would like that, she thought.

And so she should like hers, she scolded herself. Stop this whining inside and be appreciative. Here's a real room, all for yourself.

She looked for something to do, but all her things were put away.

She went to the window and looked out. She could see part of the yard, and beyond the trees she could see the greens of orchards and vineyards, and farther on parts of the town. Hers was the only room on the north side of the house that was occupied. All the rest of the rooms were empty, she guessed, because their doors were closed.

She went out into the hall and to the balcony. A white railing went all around it on three sides, punctuated here and there by white columns. On the fourth side the wide stairways came up, branched from one even wider stairway that rose from the hall below.

The house was so quiet.

What was there to do?

She saw that the doors to Ivan's and Mama's rooms were open, and even though Mama had said she was going to take a nap, Kim went to see if one of them might still be awake. Her footsteps were almost totally silent on the thick cream-and-blue patterned carpet.

She came to Ivan's door first and went in. The

54

blinds had been closed, sheltering the crib from the light. Kim tiptoed into the quiet room and looked down into the crib, feeling disappointed that she wasn't to have Ivan's company for quite awhile. He was out of this world, spread-eagled on his back, as soundly asleep as he could get.

Kim sighed. The door between the nursery and the master bedroom was open, but the other room was quiet and dim also. Kim turned to leave, to go back to her own room, perhaps, or to Sara's to see what she was doing. She hardly ever sought out Sara for company, though. Sara was—well, contented by herself.

And Kevin, he was still outside somewhere.

"Kim?" Ronna's voice said softly.

Kim hurried to the door and looked into the large, heavily furnished room that Aunt Winifred had given Ronna. Her mother was lying on the high bed. She sat up, leaning on an elbow. Her hair looked mussed, as if she had been turning a lot instead of sleeping.

"Kim, would you mind going down and seeing if Aunt Winifred needs help? I'm bushed or I'd go. Since you're up wandering around, I thought you might offer to help. She's probably trying to cook dinner for us. You can help her out."

"Sure," Kim said. She was glad to be reminded that there was more than this silent second story with all its halls, its balconies, and its closed doors. She didn't know where the kitchen was, but maybe Aunt Winifred wouldn't mind if she tried to find it.

In the lower hall she passed more closed doors, these all of dark, polished wood that added to the gloom and the darkness. The house was so quiet that Kim felt she should walk as silently as possible. She thought of the contrast of this house to the noisy, busy apartment building, and there seemed to be something lurking and dangerous here, something imprinted, or waiting, as if something terrible had happened, or was waiting to happen. It was so different here in the house than it was outside, too. There the birds sang and the grass grew and the air was bright with sun and wind and the fragrance of roses and other blossoms. In here, in the house, where shades and draperies were closed, where the silence reigned, there was something—*something* wrong. Kim could feel the danger in her bones.

She hurried through the house in search of the kitchen.

She opened wrong doors twice. The first time she looked in upon a dim dining room, a somber and silent room where it looked as if no family had ever gathered, at least not for a very, very long time. She closed the door and discovered another door beyond which the narrowing hallway continued. She opened another door and saw an office, with a roll-top desk and drawers built into the wall. It was all dark wood. The window was heavily shaded. She withdrew hurriedly. Then she stood in the hall clasping her hands and listening. There were two more doors, but one of them was too close to the other to be anything but a closet. She chose the third door and looked into a large kitchen, at last.

It, too, was darker than she had expected, the walls covered with walnut cabinets. Over the sink was one uncurtained window, and working at the sink was

Aunt Winifred.

Kim walked into the room and looked around. At one end were double windows covered by venetian blinds whose slats were nearly closed. A round table with chairs sat in front of the windows. At the opposite end of the room was an open door through which most of the light came. In the room beyond the door Kim saw a room warm with light and windows, with fat, fluffy furniture covered in bright, floral material. The tables were white wicker. The room drew her like a butterfly to a flower. She stood in the doorway and stared. Windows took up the two outside walls, and although there were blinds, they were rolled high. The tables were covered with magazines, books, a small sewing basket, and interesting and varied knickknacks. It was a room that looked like it belonged in another house.

"This is a pretty room," Kim said.

Winifred's head jerked. She looked over her shoulder at Kim as if she hadn't known she was no longer alone. "Yes," she said abruptly.

"Is it your room?"

"It is now," Winifred answered. She was scrubbing potatoes under a slow running stream of water. She added, "It was my mother's favorite room."

Kim came over and looked into the double sink. It was a very old sink and looked as though it were made of zinc. It fit well with the rest of the dreary kitchen. Kim saw potatoes in the sink, as well as carrots, tomatoes, lettuce, and peppers, and some other small vegetables she didn't recognize. There was the faint smell now of something cooking in the oven. A roast, maybe.

"I came down to see if I could help you," Kim said.

"Thank you. I don't need help." Winifred looked up and out the window. Her hands kept scrubbing a baking potato.

Kim squirmed uncomfortably. Mama said help Aunt Winifred, but Aunt Winifred didn't want help. She didn't know what was expected of her now. She looked around.

"Maybe I could set the table."

"No, not yet. It'll be another hour and a half."

"I—uh—I'm used to helping. Mama says I'm good at making salads."

"That's nice."

"I—uh—even make the dressing."

This time Aunt Winifred only grunted, and Kim supposed she made her own dressing, or perhaps already had bottled kinds from the grocery store. Kim glanced again at the bright room and would have liked to go in there and curl up on the soft cushions on the long sofa with some of the magazines.

"This is a nice house," she said, trying desperately to make conversation. "And it's so big."

"Yes."

"Have—uh—have you always lived here?"

"Yes, I have." Winifred glanced up and out the window again. Then, as if giving in to the nagging presence of her girl, she said, "My father's grandfather built this house."

"All by himself?"

"No, of course not. He had workers. It was his plan though, and he was the founder of the town. He used to own quite a lot of land around here, but it's been sold off now. There are only twenty acres left, which

58

is enough. His name was Charlie Benjamin Childress. He named his son Benjamin Charlie."

"Then that means that Charlie Benjamin was my great-great-grandfather, doesn't it?"

Winifred glanced a frown at Kim. "What? No. Certainly not. You aren't a Childress."

A knife in Kim's heart couldn't have hurt more. She felt the blood drain away from her face. "But—yes, Aunt Winifred, I am."

"You most certainly aren't. You were already born before your mother married Daniel."

"But—but—" Kim's eyes were burning, but she couldn't cry, she wouldn't! She *wouldn't*. "My name—" She tried to swallow the growing knot in her throat. "My name—on my report card—"

"What was your daddy's name, anyway? I don't think I was ever told."

"I don't know. Daniel's my daddy. I never had another one."

"Nonsense. Surely you remember him. You were five years old when your mother married Daniel."

"But—I don't—I didn't. Anyway, my name is Childress. It's always Childress. I was adopted by my dad."

"You're imagining things, child. I don't know what your name is, but it isn't Childress. Why should Daniel adopt you? You're his stepdaughter, but your legal name is whatever your mother's first husband's was. If she was married. Otherwise, it's whatever your mother's maiden name was."

Kim backed away. She could feel the wall of rejection between her and Aunt Winifred, and she didn't know how to break through it. She had naturally accepted Aunt Winifred as her own aunt, had always thought of Aunt Winifred as her very own, and she had been glad that she had an aunt on her daddy's side. But now—but now—

She would go upstairs, she decided, and ask her mother about the adoption. Hadn't Daniel always called her his number one daughter? When he was loving and tender, he did.

Kim slipped quietly from the room, making as little noise as possible. She glanced back one time at Aunt Winifred, but she was stationed in front of the sink, working with the vegetables, occasionally raising her head and looking out the window into the back yard, toward the barn and other, smaller buildings of the farm. It was like she had forgotten that Kim had even been there.

Kim went upstairs heavily, the burden of hurt weighing her down, slowing her steps, bowing her head. She was relieved to see that her mother's door was open. Ronna was turned now facing the wall, and she lay very still. She might be asleep, Kim saw, and hesitated. Then, as though Ronna realized instinctively that someone had come into the room, she turned suddenly so that she could see the door. There was a faint look of alarm on her face that faded instantly when she saw Kim.

"Kim, darling. What is it?" She sat up and held out her hand. "You look so downcast."

With her mother's concern reaching out to her, Kim's eyes began to burn with tears again. She blinked rapidly, a trick she had learned long ago that would delay the weeping at least until she could be alone. At school it had been necessary when she had run into the bully of the crowd, the pretty but cruel leader of a group of girls of which Kim floated uncertainly on the edge. There were a couple of the less important girls that Francine had picked on, and Kim seemed to be her main choice. Kim had hoped that here, in her new home, she would be more accepted. But even her Aunt Winifred had pushed her away.

Still, she had too much pride to cry, even in front of her mother.

She put her hand in Ronna's and allowed herself to be pulled to sit on the high, antique bed. The mattress was surprisingly soft. Ronna put her arm around Kim's shoulders.

"Tell me."

"Mama. I am adopted, aren't I? My real name is Childress, isn't it?"

Ronna hesitated. Kim heard her draw a long breath. "What brought that up?"

"Aunt Winifred—said my name isn't Childress. But I was adopted, wasn't I?" Ronna kept hesitating. A faint frown had made bumps between her eyebrows. She stared off across the room. Kim reminded her, "On my school records it's Childress, Mama."

"Yes, I know," Ronna said softly. "But as far as legal adoption goes, we just didn't think it was necessary. But Daniel certainly wants you to use his name. He loves you as much as he does any of the children."

Kim slumped and let her head hang. But the threat of tears, at least, was gone. She suddenly just felt very

61

tired. Ronna's arm squeezed her shoulders.

"Did you offer to help Aunt Winifred with the dinner?"

"Yes. She didn't want me to help."

"Well, I'll go down in a little while. Ivan should be waking up soon. You go back down and tell Aunt Winifred that I'm coming down in just a few minutes. I can't sleep anyway. It isn't fair that she should have to cook for my brood. I wonder how many years it's been since she had to cook for a family like this?"

"I don't know." Kim added, not knowing if she really should, "I don't think she really likes us very well, Mama. Maybe she doesn't want us here after all."

"Oh, Kim! After all the letters she wrote urging us to come live with her? However, we might be a little overwhelming. So do be nice, dear. Of course, I know you will. But you have to forgive some people for their—well, narrow-mindedness. Especially those who are family-proud. And Aunt Winifred seems to be very proud of the fact that her ancestor built this place and started this town. Let her tell you about it. You should be able to make friends with her by encouraging her to talk about her heritage. Forget the other, it's immaterial. Your name is Childress on all your records, and it will stay that way. Now go, and smile!"

Kim went back downstairs. She lingered along the lower halls, paying more attention to the framed photographs that hung on the dark walnut paneling. Some were of men and women who wore their hair in old-fashioned styles. There were three enlarged prints of a group of men in work clothes standing around a building half finished. She could see the river behind the building. Was it a mill? She had heard that the first Childress had built a mill here, and it had been the only one for a hundred miles. But the sense of pride she would have felt an hour ago was gone now.

She still felt a little tired. But more than that she felt smothered by the dimness of hall, the dark monotone of the wood, and the silence. There was no one here running down other halls, there were no doors slamming, no children calling to one another. She felt a sudden, painful homesickness for the noisy, crowded apartment building where she had lived through all her memory.

Kim went on into the kitchen. Aunt Winifred was still at the sink, but she was leaning forward over it, stiffly, her neck angled as if something out the window had captured her attention. She heard Kim's approach and drew back from the sink. Her face, when she turned it toward Kim, was set in a kind of fury, something more than anger. Her small, nearly black eyes snapped fire.

"Your brother," she said, "is down at the barn. I don't remember giving him permission to go into the barn. You go right away and bring him out." The muscles in her face relaxed a bit, and she added, "He could get hurt in there. The barn has been closed for many years, and there are nails and rusty baling wire that has come loose from old bales of hay. He is not to play in the barn."

"Yes ma'am," Kim said, glad of the chance to get out of the house, to have something definite to do, even if Kevin wouldn't like it. At the back door she remembered, and said, "Mama said for me to tell you that she'd be down to help with dinner just as soon as Ivan is awake. I expect she'll wake him up, because she doesn't like for him to sleep too long. If his afternoon naps are too long then he doesn't go to sleep when he's put to bed at night. Bedtime for Sara and Ivan is usually seven o'clock. Kevin gets to stay up until eight or nine if he's quiet. And I—"

"Yes, yes. Hurry on to the barn and get your brother. Then after this I don't want any of you going there."

"Yes ma'am."

Kim went out the back door, closing it carefully behind her, although the air outside seemed much nicer than the cool, slightly stuffy air that Aunt Winifred seemed to like.

There was a small porch at the back, with a roof and steps down to a cement walk that curved to the left toward the driveway. On each side of the porch were trellises, and growing thickly on them were vines that had fragrant yellow flowers.

Where the walk angled to the left Kim paused and glanced back toward the kitchen window where Aunt Winifred would surely be watching, but the porch protected her from the window and the face she knew was there. Instead of crossing the lawn and going straight on back to the grounds of the buildings, Kim chose to follow the walk and go down the drive. Aunt Winifred would probably not want her to walk on the grass.

The paved part of the driveway ended at a long four-car garage. The rest of it went on, a dirt track now. Behind the long garage was parked a pickup. Across a fence to her left she saw the handyman, Frank, at work in a big garden. He was bent over, his back to her. On the pickup hood lay the cat she had petted earlier.

Kim reached for him, naturally and easily, smiling and cooing. "Hello, Mister Kitty Cat," she said softly. "Come with me."

He lay in her arms as if he had lain there all his life. He was a fat, heavy cat, and he felt good against her diaphragm. He gazed up at her with his placid yellow eyes and began to purr loudly.

Kim walked along the fences until she found a gate. From there she crossed a bare yard of another building to the fence that surrounded the barn. She found another gate and, seeing no animals in the barn lot, she left it open behind her.

She remembered Aunt Winifred and looked toward the house, but only a portion of the house was in view: the corner with the beautiful sun room and the second floor wing that stretched north. The kitchen, with the small window, was hidden from her. Aunt Winifred's view of the barn, where she must have caught a glimpse of Kevin, was of the north section. Kim went toward it, walking near the wall, looking up at the sloping roof of the low section. Below the roofline was a row of small windows, but she could see they were very dirty, and some of them appeared totally coated with spiderwebs. The central part of the barn, rising high above the sloping roof, looked massive from her close view. She began to dread her mission.

At the corner of the barn she looked again toward

the house, and sure enough, there was Aunt Winifred's face beyond the window. But even during her first glance, the face turned toward the room behind her and a moment later withdrew. Kim guessed that her mother had entered the kitchen. She felt relieved, knowing that Aunt Winifred would be busy now and not watching her out the window.

On the north side of the barn she found a small door and tried to open it, but it seemed to be locked from inside, or the dirt on the ground had piled up around it and held it fast. She went on. The yellow cat had begun to switch his tail rhythmically. He had turned his head away from her and was looking at the barn.

Kim came to another door in the central section of the barn. It was raised away from the ground, and there was a worn stone step. Unlike the first door she had tried, which had a wooden handle, this door had a knob. She turned it, and the door squeaked reluctantly inward. The cat tensed abruptly in her arms and almost leaped away before she could adjust her hold on him.

She paused to soothe him, holding him comfortably in one arm, using her free hand to caress his head. He relaxed somewhat, but his tail continued to switch, slowly, back and forth.

Kim stepped across the threshold and stopped. She was in a medium-sized room that had scraps of hay and feed scattered across the wooden floor and items of leather, old and musty smelling, hanging on the wood pegs on the walls. She recognized some of the items from visits to farms in Illinois and from books she had read. There were large, circular things called neck yokes hanging on large pegs that she remembered were used on horses back when the horses were hitched to plows and other machinery. There were harnesses, and saddles, and against the wall was a ladder that went up through a hole into the loft above.

She stood still, listening, and it seemed she heard a subtle movement. Kevin, hiding from her? Shifting his position? He would. He would do something like that, all right. He would love all the hiding places that must be here in this barn.

"Kevin?" she called softly, half afraid to hear her own voice in this dusty, hollow place. Her voice came back to her, faintly, as if thrown by the walls mockingly. But Kevin didn't answer.

Kim drew a deep breath. The cat had grown very still in her arms, its face turned away toward the wall beyond. Kim went to the ladder against the wall and looked up. In the murky dimness far above she could see the peak of the barn roof. Spiderwebs dangled, catching sunlight from some source. The loft appeared to be lighter than this lower area.

Holding the cat firmly, using her right hand to grasp the rungs of the ladder, she slowly climbed. When her head was above the floor of the loft she stopped. The length of the unpartitioned barn loft seemed enormous. There were still large stacks of baled hay, one near the center, but off to one side, and another at the far end by the big, closed double doors. If Kevin were up here, he was behind one of the stacks of hay. There was nowhere else to hide, no inner walls, no separate rooms like down below.

"Kevin," she called softly, reluctant to hear her

voice in this quiet place. Pigeons cried their strange, groaning coos from the outer peaks of the barn, and the cat had grown tense again and had grasped her wrist with the claws of one paw. It was hurting, but not enough to release him.

"Kevin!" She was louder this time, and a bit angrier, the anger mixed with an uneasiness that was turning to fear. She felt if she could get her hands on him she'd shake him until his teeth fell out. "Kevin?" she said louder.

But that was too much. Not even Kevin was that ornery. He would have answered by now if he had been here in the loft. Kim gave the large, warm area one more thorough look. The bits of sunlight that touched the webs came from cracks in the walls at each end, and a few in the immense ceiling. Most of it seemed to seep in around the big double doors at each end of the loft. There was just enough to make interesting patterns in the webs and on the floor, not really enough to overcome the gloom.

She backed down the ladder, feeling secure again only when her feet touched the floor. With her hand free again, she slipped her fingers between the cat's paw and her wrist and loosened the sharp little barbs. He had relaxed a bit and was easier to hold, though his tail still twitched and his ears had flattened. He seemed angry, yet not at her. At something else that kept his head turned and his attention elsewhere toward the central part of the barn. Perhaps he was hearing sounds she couldn't hear, or Kevin tiptoeing away. She opened her mouth to yell, to scream Kevin's name, to tell him that he had to come on out of the barn; but at that instant the cat's claws raked her wrist again, and she gasped instead. He arched up in her arms, yet he didn't try to jump down. This time she would have let him go. Instead, he was alert and staring off toward the center of the barn. His tail had grown still. His ears were high and listening.

Kim pressed her lips together and went toward the closed door at the other end of the room. The door opened easily, with only a soft complaint, and she entered a long room that was almost like a hall. In the ceiling above, on the left side, were holes, about four feet by three, spaced evenly apart, which obviously had been used to push hay down from above. There were feeding stanchions beneath and a low wall over which Kim could see into the wing of the barn. Now the holes were crisscrossed with webs, and bits of old hay hung among them. To her right were more doors. She began to walk softly, paying close attention to the cat.

He ignored the first door she came to and, after pausing, so did she. At the second door, however, his claws dug deeper into her arm, and he pushed himself up. Kim waited, listening, and she heard what she thought the cat might be hearing. It was not footsteps, nor the scuttle of mice in the walls. It was a sound almost like a vibration, like that caused when heavy steps occur somewhere else in a house, and ripples of subtle movement are felt. The cat was staring at the door as if he could look through it. So it was somewhere in here, Kim thought, that Kevin could be found. Perhaps he hadn't heard her after all, for the boards of the walls were heavy and thick.

She opened the door.

The cat screamed and tore out of her arms. It dropped to the floor, its back arched, its fur stiff. It faced the open door, hissing. Then, with stiff legs, it backed away. With a final cry it was gone, running toward the open doors left behind in their progress into the interior of the barn.

3

Kim stood transfixed in the doorway. The room was small, square, and quite dark, the only light coming through the cracks from the loft overhead and through the doors she had left open behind.

It was enough to see the weird markings on the walls and floor. Drawn in red paint as dark as old blood there was on the floor a large circle with a complicated but star-shaped emblem inside it. Small, indecipherable figures were drawn into each point and in the circle center. On the wall opposite the door was a face with sharp, pointed horns, and although the eyes were drawn unsymmetrically, as if they had been done by a child or an unartistic person, there was a strange piercing in the red pupils that seemed to look into Kim, making her heart pound in alarm. One eye was larger, rounder than the other, but they stared at her with an intensity they would not have had if they had been symmetrical. The slash of a mouth turned up in evil anticipation. The chin was a sharp point. Encircling the head the drawing on the

71

floor was repeated in miniature, like stars surrounding a god.

A devil.

There was no doubting the message the room contained.

Against the wall beneath the red face was a heavy, low, wooden bench that was splintered and hacked at one end where a dark stain, or many dark stains, made trails down the side and legs. Leaning against the wall was a double-edged ax. Its blades were dark and rusted.

On the floor, propped in sitting positions, lined against opposite walls, was a collection of dolls, their once beautiful clothes darkened with dust. They sat as though they had once been an audience for the horrors that were embedded in the dying wood of the walls and were paralyzed in time by what they had witnessed.

There was a coldness here in the air, a dank mustiness, that went beyond the dust, the dark, and the absorbed impressions. Like nightmares lost before they were remembered, fragments of horrors too deadly to be grasped, the room's memories beat at Kim. She began to back away, her throat constricting, afraid now she would not be able to get away; she backed out into the long, wide hall that ran most of the length of the barn, and then she was free from the pull of the room, and she turned and ran.

She burst out into the sunlight, so weak she had to lean against the barn wall, her heart beating fast, much too fast. It slowed finally so that she could get her breath.

She looked up at the horizon, at the sharp white of

the snow-capped peaks against the blue sky. She saw the green of the nearby trees and the neat rows of the grape vineyard. Birds flew around a birdhouse in the back lawn of the house. She could see the kitchen window that was over the sink, but there was no face looking through it.

The bright, sunny day was an unreal contrast to what she had seen in the barn.

Who had worshipped Satan there?

Whose dolls were those?

Was that why Aunt Winifred didn't want anyone to go into the barn? Was that why there were no animals in the barn anymore?

Where had the cat gone? It knew. It hadn't wanted to go into the barn. Animals knew things that people didn't.

Had something terrible happened to Kevin?

She had a feeling suddenly, a dark, terror-trapped feeling, as if she were suspended over a bottomless pit that led to the bowels of hell, that she would never see Kevin alive anymore; that in some way the old evils in the barn had reached him and made him fall, perhaps, from the loft, to lie broken on the ground; or made something fall on him, pinning his wiry little body hopelessly. There were so many things left hanging in the barn that could break away from the pegs or the rafters and fall, crushing whatever was beneath.

She hurried toward the other end of the far corner, the part that faced the river, her pace growing faster with each step until she was running. In a voice nearly breathless again she began to cry out, "Kevin. Kevin. Kevin."

At the corner of the barn suddenly something loomed up in front of her, and she fell back, both hands covering the aborted scream in her throat. It was a stranger with a wide grin on his face—no, it was Kevin. Taller than she remembered. No, not taller after all.

He had jumped at her from the corner of the barn. Grinning.

"Hey," he cried with delight. "Did I scare you?"

She was so glad to see him she didn't follow her instincts and sock him on the side of the head. She grasped his arms instead, her fingers biting into his slender sinews.

"Are you all right, Kevin?"

"Yeah, sure." He twisted his arms out of her grasp. "Hey, come and look at all the stuff I've found. There's a whole shed full of machinery here, all rusted and stuff. But I'll bet you I could get it to running. And Kim, you ought to see the inside of that big old barn. It's full of little rooms, just like a house, and there's a great big room with all kinds of junk in it, bales of hay, sacks of feed, leather harness on the walls. I even found a barrel of old rotted apples. And mice! And mice had made nests behind the barrels out of string that hung on nails from the walls and had fallen, and they had eaten holes in the sacks of grain and—come and see, Kim."

He pulled at her arm now, urging her onward toward the rear of the barn and the open shed in its center. She could see part of a rusted tractor and another piece of machinery that might have been a big multi-disk plow of some kind. She resisted his pull and attempted to interrupt his flow of words, but he was too excited to listen.

"And, and, Kim? There were baby mice in the nests! Did you ever see a baby mouse? They're tiny and pink and don't have any eyes or hair yet. Come and see. I counted seven in one nest and eight in another. The mothers ran when they saw me, but they came back. They wouldn't leave their babies. I guess the cat doesn't go in there very often or he'd catch them, wouldn't he?"

"No. Yes."

"And, and, Kim, there's ladders up to the loft, and from the other end of the loft you can see through the crack in the doors away out over the tops of everything. It's like being in the Sears Building, only maybe not so high. And Kim—"

"*Stop*," she said. "Stop pulling on me, Kevin. Look, you're not supposed to go into the barn anymore. You're not supposed to go in there at all."

His face changed, and her heart changed with it. She hated to be the bearer of bad news, except in this case it might save his life. He hadn't yet found the—the *room*, but he would, eventually, inevitably, if he were allowed to roam the barn.

"But why?" he cried. "It's a neat place, Kim. And there aren't any animals in there anymore."

"I know. But Aunt Winifred sent me to find you. She said no one is allowed to go into the barn."

"But—but—*why?*"

He was almost crying, his face screwed up, his eyes watching her wistfully. He had found a barn full of treasures. He thought. Kim almost told him about the room, but she was afraid it would scare him, make him have nightmares. She put her arm across

75

his shoulder comfortingly and turned him back toward the house.

"Because Aunt Winifred said so. It's her barn. We have to do what she says."

He walked slowly beside her with his head down. After a thoughtful moment he said, "It's Dad's barn too, isn't it?"

"Well, yes. But Dad isn't here to give you permission, and you have to listen to Aunt Winifred. And she says to stay out of the barn." She added, with emphasis, "You can't play in the barn, Kevin."

On their way back to the house Kim saw the cat sitting on the back walk. The tip of his tail was switching nervously, his hair was wiry and standing out, and his ears lay flat against his head. Kim walked around him. Kevin didn't seem to notice the cat at all.

Their mother was in the kitchen. She was setting the round table with blue and white dinnerware. The tablecloth beneath it hung down all around in folds. It was blue and white checked. It was the only color in the kitchen. The appliances were white, and the cabinets dark walnut, like the paneling on the small amount of wall space that was not covered by cabinets. Aunt Winifred was at the stove stirring something in a low pan. Kim thought that it was brown gravy. The smell of the food was more nauseating than anything else. She was trembling slightly now, and everywhere she looked the sight she had seen in the barn was superimposed. All her surroundings, the dark house, even the bright sun room, had changed. The evil in the small room in the barn permeated this, too.

"Kim," Ronna said, "go up, please, and see about

the baby and Sara. You might have to wake Ivan. He's slept long enough. Get them ready to come down for dinner."

Kim saw that an old-fashioned high chair had been brought in and was standing in one dim corner of the kitchen not far from the table. The sunlight that streaked in through the venetian blinds only emphasized the gloom elsewhere.

Kim left the kitchen and went into the long hall. When she closed the kitchen door she left behind the small sounds of dinner preparation.

She climbed the stairs to the second floor and took the right branch where the stairway divided. She went around the balcony and down the narrower hall at the rear. Although there were other closed doors, indicating several unused bedrooms, Aunt Winifred had put both Sara and Kevin at the rear of the house. Kim wondered why. She could think of no reason. She came to Sara's bedroom. It was near the inner end of the hall, the first door on the right. Her window overlooked the orchards and the rooftops of the town.

Sara's door stood open, and before Kim saw her little sister, she heard her. She was chatting in an animated way for her dolls. A squeaky voice said, "But I don't want it. It's not good." And a deeper voice answered, "You have to eat it. I made it for you. I don't have time to bake cookies every day. I have to work at my job. Look at your baby brother. He's eating his."

Where, Kim wondered, did Sara learn to mimic a mother who worked away from home? Then she remembered. Of course. Sara's best friend in the apartment building had been Janie, whose mother

77

worked, whose mother was tired when she got home.

Kim stood in the doorway allowing her thoughts to linger with the apartment and all the people who had lived there, too, but this time it seemed further than two thousand miles away. It seemed a century away in time and forever in space. And the bridge between was now impassable.

Sara looked up suddenly, saw Kim and hushed. The light from the window behind her shone through her hair and made it look like a halo over her beautiful, oval face.

"It's time to come downstairs, Sara. Time to eat."

Sara got up. She had propped her dolls around a small, makeshift table created of a silver tray she had found on the dresser. The dolls were of various sizes, the largest a Raggedy Ann doll, the smallest no larger than three inches in length. There were two others, one a Barbie doll, all dressed up in an evening gown, and the other was a baby doll with a round face and curved legs and arms. A distant relative of a Cabbage Patch doll.

Kim thought of the dolls in the room in the barn, and a frightened feeling came over her, a near panic that made her want to turn and run, and keep running.

"Can I bring my baby doll along?" Sara asked.

"No!" Kim snapped and immediately was sorry. A look of perplexity and hurt washed over Sara's face. Kim took her hand and patted it between both her own. She added in a gentler tone, "They should stay here and eat their own dinner, don't you think?"

Sara nodded.

They went out into the hall and into the front of

the second floor where the balcony surrounded the large opening of the stairwell.

"You have to wash up," Kim said, "but we'll use the bathroom in Mom's room. We have to get Ivan out of bed."

They entered the nursery and saw the baby just sitting up, blinking awakening eyes. He pulled himself to a standing position, stiffened his small body, smiled widely, and said something that sounded like, "Hi!"

Kim put her arms around him, lifting him out of the crib. His smile was infectious, and she felt her own face relax.

"Hi, sugar," she said. "Give Kimmy a big kiss."

He opened his mouth widely and slobbered on her face. She laughed. Sara laughed, too, and Kim bent over and held Ivan down to Sara.

"And kiss Sara," she said.

When that was finished they went into the bathroom between the nursery and master bedroom. Sara stood on a child's stool there and washed her hands while Kim changed Ivan's diaper.

They were ready to go downstairs now. Kim hated to leave the colorful nursery. While she was there she had forgotten the horrors of the small room in the center of the barn.

Kevin was quiet through dinner, but no one seemed to notice. Nor did he pay a lot of attention to the others. He was grieving over the loss of the most fantastic plaything he had ever had in all his life, and occasionally an obstinate will to disobey entered his

79

mind. He could, he thought furiously, say he was going one place and go to the barn instead. Who would know? On glancing at Aunt Winifred he decided that *she* would know. Somehow, she would know. She had known this afternoon, hadn't she? And sent Kim to get him.

Across the dinner table he watched the sun set beyond the window. The overhead light had been turned on already, and there was a strange mixture of yellow left behind.

He became aware that Sara was whining about something. She had her elbow on the table, too. Her mouth drooped petulantly as she answered something their mother had said. "But I don't want it," Sara said, and Kevin saw the asparagus was left on her plate. But didn't Mama know that Sara never ate asparagus? Kevin looked at Ronna in surprise. Ronna was looking a little embarrassed. She had her head turned sideways, her eyes pinned on Sara in a straight stare. But when she spoke, her voice was soft. It was the kind of softness that had steel in it.

"Sara, eat your vegetables."

Sara's chin trembled. In a minute the tears would roll. Kevin forgot the barn in watching this little drama. Why was Mama trying to make Sara eat what Sara never ate at home? Then he knew. Aunt Winifred had served it.

"Don't you like asparagus, dear child?" Aunt Winifred asked.

"No."

"Then it's quite all right not to eat it, isn't it, Ronna?"

Ronna relaxed. Her eyes softened as she glanced at

Sara again. "She's tired," she said, as if in apology to Aunt Winifred. "We're all tired. I think I should get them to bed early tonight."

"Of course, you go right ahead. I can do the dishes."

"Oh, no, I'll be back down. Putting Ivan to bed, though, will be hard to do since he had a nap."

"Then why don't you stay down here with him and I'll take the children up to bed?"

Kevin said quickly, "Mom hasn't put me to bed since before I was Sara's age."

Aunt Winifred smiled. "But you don't even know which room is yours, do you? You were out looking around all afternoon. Someone will have to show you your room."

Kevin looked at the eyes around the table. For some reason, all of them were looking at him, all except Ivan's. Had he done something wrong, or was he about to do something wrong?

"Yes, ma'am," he said, to be on the safe side.

"Fine. Come along then."

Aunt Winifred took Sara's hand, and Kevin followed behind them.

They went through a long hall and up a wide, forked stairway, then along a balcony that had a railing on one side and fluted posts, then down another hall that wasn't as wide as the others. At the end of the hall was a pair of doors that sat at angles from each other, and Aunt Winifred opened the one on the right. She flipped a light switch, and Kevin saw a blue room with a bed against the wall, and opposite it a window that looked black, as if night had fallen totally now. He didn't feel a bit sleepy, and it seemed a long time until morning.

"This is your room, Kevin. This was the room your father used when he was a little boy. Your clothes are in the closet. And a bathroom is right down the hall, third door. Good night now. Sara, say good night to your brother."

"Good night, Kevin."

Kevin watched them go out. Aunt Winifred pulled the door shut behind her. He remained standing in the middle of the room, staring at the closed door. No sound of footsteps reached him. It was as if they had stepped through the door and out of the world, leaving him alone in a strange room. He had never had a room all by himself before in his life.

He ran to the door and jerked it open. But they hadn't disappeared into another dimension after all. They were halfway down the hall, the tall woman holding the small hand of Sara. Sara's bright hair caught the light from above as if it were alive. They were talking. He could hear Aunt Winifred's questioning and Sara's answering, but he couldn't hear what they were saying. They turned suddenly to the left and went into a room. Sara's room? Kevin didn't feel so isolated.

He went back into his own room, leaving the door open. He went to the window and pressed his face against the glass. The dying light of day gave him a muted view of the barn roof and beyond, a strip of bright, reflecting water.

The river.

He could see the river from his room.

Maybe he could find a fishing pole around somewhere and go fishing.

But no. The river was denied to him also. His mom had said—hadn't she? —that he was not supposed to go to the river.

He sat down on the floor and watched the outside light change until it was gone.

He seemed destined for strange beds in strange rooms, Daniel thought, as he sank onto the motel bed, too tired to rest. He'd done all he was supposed to do today, kept his appointments, talked business over a long dinner, indulged in too many after dinner drinks. But the sale had been made. He should feel relieved. Perhaps he would after a good night's sleep. But he still felt like he was out on that forever highway, being shaken by some kind of monster.

He thought of Sharon with longing. She had filled an emptiness. Or perhaps she had seemed for awhile to point him toward a better future.

He thought of Ronna and the kids, and felt a deep heartbreak that was unbearable. To think of them was to torture himself. He had to stop thinking of the ones he loved most, for that brought to mind his inability to be the husband and father he should be. He had to keep moving. New faces, new places, those were his placebos, his drugs.

The bed was hard, as if there were no springs, and the pillow felt as if it were encased in plastic. He turned onto his stomach and buried his face in it nevertheless, but the blackness he searched for was disturbed by flecks of light that danced tormentingly behind his closed eyelids.

He began to breathe deeply, deliberately courting

the oblivion of sleep. No sheep, he thought, just long, slow breaths. One, two, three . . . twelve . . . twenty . . . His body relaxed and he slept.

The night stilled around him. Traffic on the streets and highway ceased. And in the deep of night he began to be aware. A voice was calling, calling. It reached out at him from the past, from faraway, another land, another dimension.

Daniel—Daniel.

Only a dream, he told himself as he struggled against it. He turned onto his back and found a more comfortable position.

Daniel—I'm waiting.

He began to struggle violently, but there was a cold, dark weight swirling around him, dragging him down, back, back into the darkness, the total blackness. Then, with sudden clarity, he realized what it was. Water. It pulled at him with a current that was strong and insistent, pulling him back beneath the tree, in the hole beneath the tree. He tried to swim and couldn't. He could see. Though the water was black, he saw it. The red hair turned pale from long years in the water undulated in the blackness like millions of live worms. The current swept him forward until the hair touched his face, until faintly, he saw *her,* the face within inches of his own. The flesh of her face had been nibbled away by water, by the mouths of tiny fish, and her lips were almost gone, but still he saw them move, pronouncing his name. *Daniel—I'm so glad you—came.* And her eyes, intact and blazing at him, providing the light that enabled him to see, were laughing. The laughter rolled at him through the black, cold water,

84

silent. His answering cry of terror was as silent as the laughter.

I've been—waiting so long—Daniel.

A hard jolt woke him, and he found himself on the floor, entangled in a sheet and blanket, half in and half out of the nightmare. Deeply relieved that it was only a nightmare he got up and opened the drapes on the window in the front of the motel room, allowing the blessed entry of light from the neon signs.

An anger possessed him, and he felt like hitting or kicking something. Why in the goddamned hell had he started having these dreams, these nightmares? For now he considered the experience on the highway a sort of nightmare, too. He had dozed off for a second and dreamed.

But why?

Why now?

Charlene had been dead for twenty-some years. He didn't even want to remember how long. He refused to think of her, just as he had deliberately kept her out of his mind all these years.

But he couldn't spend the rest of the night in this stifling motel room.

He began to get ready to move on.

4

Kevin walked out along the driveway. The morning sun angled in beneath the trees, throwing long shadows to the west, but it was climbing and warming, and he had a whole day ahead of him. No one had said that he couldn't go down the lane.

The cat had followed behind him for a ways, but then it quit and leaped up to sit on a fence post in the sun. It was still sitting there when he looked back from the end of the lane, but it had its eye on something down in the alfalfa field, and suddenly it leaped and pounced, and pounced again, looking so comical that Kevin laughed out loud.

Kevin looked up and down the blacktop road. In both directions it curved, going out of sight around fences, trees, shrubs. There were no cars in sight. It wasn't far to town, Kevin remembered, and dug into his pockets to see if he had any money. But where would it have come from? He hadn't gotten an allowance on a steady basis since Dad left home. Of course he could walk to town anyway, if he wanted. No one had said he couldn't.

He started down the road toward town, whistling an aimless tune. He walked in the middle of the road where once there had been a white line. It was now a smudgy gray. He tried to stay on it and found himself swaying off like a drunk man. He glanced up and stopped abruptly. There had been a movement among the shrubbery on the right, another fifty feet or so down the road.

Kevin stood still, watching.

The bushes wiggled again, as if a strong wind were playing with a couple of the green branches.

Something was in the small tree. And whatever it was dropped down. Kevin heard the thud even through the distance. He almost turned back. He set his feet to run.

A boy stepped out into the road and stared toward Kevin. He had red hair that grew wild like thatch on an eighteenth century Irish roof.

Kevin stared back at him, making a fast appraisal. The boy was a little taller and maybe a little older. He looked skinny but strong.

"Hi," the red-haired boy said abruptly. There was no smile yet.

"Hi," Kevin answered after a bit. He didn't smile either.

They stood awhile, looking at each other.

The red-haired boy said, "I never saw you around here before."

"I just moved here," Kevin said. Then he added, in case he wanted to challenge his right to the neighborhood, "That's my place there." He jerked his thumb back toward the Childress ranch. The other boy's eyes flicked away from him toward the house, the barn, the fields of Childress Ranch.

"Oh yeah?"

"Yeah."

They stared at each other again for awhile. Kevin let his eyes slide to the right. Beyond the trees and bushes along the fence he saw the edge of a roofline.

"That your house?" he asked.

"Yeah."

"You always lived there?"

"Sure."

Kevin drew a long breath, but he didn't move until the other boy moved first. They took a few steps nearer to each other.

"My name's Carl, what's yours?"

Kevin could see his freckles now. He had a slew of them on his nose, but his cheeks were pink.

"Kevin."

"I'm ten," Carl said. "How old are you?"

"I'll be ten," Kevin said. "My next birthday."

"Oh yeah?"

"Yeah."

They moved closer. Carl's eyes drifted off toward the ranch house. "I didn't know any kids lived in that big house," he said. "That's the biggest house around here."

"I've got two sisters and a baby brother," Kevin said. "We moved here yesterday from Chicago."

Carl smiled. It was a wide grin and showed a couple of big teeth growing down to fill in the hole in the center of his upper gums. They looked four times as big as his other teeth. But all in all the smile was friendly, and Kevin relaxed.

"Hey, that's great," Carl said. "There aren't many kids around here sometimes. Butch, who lives down that way with his mother, goes when school is out and lives with his dad, so he's gone now. And there's two girls that live in that house on the other side of mine, but they're no fun. They're in high school anyway, now. Hey, I bet you can have a lot of fun in that barn."

"No."

"Why not?"

"I'm not allowed to go in there."

"Why not?"

Carl's face looked serious and puzzled.

Kevin shrugged. "I don't know. There aren't any animals in there, so that's not why."

Carl frowned. "Why aren't there any animals?"

"I don't know."

"Who said you can't play in there?"

"My Aunt Winifred."

"Oh. Well, what are you going to do now?"

Kevin shrugged. "I don't know. I was just fooling around."

"Want to go down to the river?" Carl's face took on a sly expression.

Kevin hesitated. He hated to admit that he wasn't allowed to do anything, and his mother had only said not to go to the river alone, hadn't she? If he went with Carl, he wouldn't be alone.

Carl took a step closer and lowered his voice. "We could bend over and go between the rows in the vineyard, and no one would ever see us. Come on, I'll show you."

In Kevin's mind the whole thing took on the

aspect of a great adventure. He had never gone through a grape vineyard before, much less bending over so no one would see him. The answering look on his face was enough for Carl; he jerked his thumb for Kevin to follow.

The grape vineyard edged the alfalfa field, running all the way from the road down to the river. Just beyond it toward town was the English walnut orchard. Carl ran up the road to the first trees of the orchard, where he crawled under the barbed wire fence. Kevin followed, wriggling through on his belly to avoid what looked like dangerous barbs. He didn't want his shirt torn, a telltale sign for his mother to question.

Carl was already running down the first row of the orchard when Kevin got under the wire. He pushed himself up with the heels of his hands, muddying them from a recent irrigation. Without thinking he rubbed the mud off onto the sides of his jeans as he followed in Carl's path, running to catch up, running faster than he had since the day he had to outrun a street gang in Chicago.

About one-third of the way down the row Carl suddenly jogged to the left and squatted beside the grapes. When Kevin caught up Carl was nonchalantly examining a bunch of grapes that were still green.

"Thought I might find me a ripe one," he said, "but I guess not. Don't tell your aunt, but when the grapes are ripe I sneak in here and get me some."

Kevin wiped a few beads of perspiration off his brow. It was cool, damp, and shady beneath the grapes, and there was a moist, earthy, green smell. It would be a neat place to while away time when the grapes were ripe, he thought.

"She said I could eat grapes," Kevin said.

Carl got up, his body bent over. "We have to go like this, or your hired man will see us, or somebody else. We'll zigzag across the vineyard. Follow me."

Kevin followed. When Carl raised his head for a peep over the grapes, so did Kevin, and saw no one. When Carl ducked from one row to another, Kevin followed along, going under the smooth wire that held up the grapevines. When Carl ran, Kevin ran.

They came suddenly to the treeline along the river-bank. The vineyard ended. Grass grew untended, thigh high. They waded into it. Kevin could hear the sounds of the river, and a huge excitement invaded him. He pushed aside a drooping willow limb and saw the damp, slippery bank just a few feet beyond. The dingy water rolled against the bank. Out in the middle there were places where the water swirled, then it smoothed out again in its steady, aggressive flow southward. Far over on the other side another line of trees drooped over the full banks.

"Well," said Carl, "we can't go swimming here."

"Huh?" Kevin replied in surprise. Were they actually going to get into the river?

Carl turned downstream and ducked under a willow branch. "Follow me," he said. "I know where there's a cove."

They followed the bank until it curved inward to the left. They were surrounded now by the trunks of tall trees, flaky trunks that turned white up in the branches. Kevin looked up.

"Hey, these would be neat trees to climb."

"Come on," said Carl. "We can go swimming in

here. See, the water's still as can be. Almost like a swimming pool.''

"Did you ever go swimming here?"

Carl hesitated. "Sure," he said. "Once. Almost. But I was by myself. You're not supposed to go swimming by yourself. That's in case you get a cramp in your leg, then you get paralyzed all over and you sink like a stone. You have to have someone to pull you out. If you get paralyzed, don't worry, I'll pull you out." Carl paused in stripping off his clothes and stood with one leg still in his jeans. "You can swim, can't you? This here water's deep here."

"Sure I can swim. I took Red Cross lessons from the time I was a baby." Kevin looked over the edge of the bank into the murky water. "How can you tell it's deep?"

"I put a stick down in it one time and it didn't touch bottom." He finished getting out of his clothes and stood naked, white and slim on the edge of the bank. "We'll just swim around on top. Here's a root that we can use to pull ourselves out on the bank again. Are you ready?"

"Yeah, almost."

Kevin hurried out of his clothes. Carl had reached down to test the water with one foot and said nothing. He sat down on the bank and pushed himself into the water, like an otter down a mud slide. He sank to his chin, then came up again, his hands grasping a root that barely stuck out of the water.

"Come on in," he said.

Kevin sat down on the slide and let himself go. The shock of the cold water almost made him cry out, but

93

he caught it with a gasp just in time. Carl hadn't said a word about the water's being cold. Kevin reached down with a foot and felt for the bottom, but there was none. He put his hand beside Carl's on the root. They treaded water and looked at each other.

"This is neat," Kevin said, and his teeth chattered involuntarily.

"Let's swim out to there and back," Carl said, indicating a vague point out toward the current.

"All right."

"Follow me."

They swam out, not quite as far as Kevin had feared, and back again to the root. The water seemed to be fighting Kevin, and he had to struggle to stay master of it. He was glad to have the root for support again.

"Want to do it again?" Carl asked a bit breathlessly. His lips were beginning to look a little bluish.

"Sure," Kevin chattered. He clamped his teeth together.

They swam out and back, again and again. Then once more they rested at the root.

"The water's getting warmer now, don't you think?" Carl asked, his first indication that it was at all cold. "Can you swim underwater?"

"Sure."

"Then why don't we see how far down the bottom is? Why don't we look at the roots of this tree?"

"Sure."

Carl's eyes bugged at Kevin as he took in a deep breath. He pressed his blue lips tightly together and went out of sight with a blip. Kevin waited, looking at the surface of the water where Carl had disappeared. Carl's fingers slipped away from the root, then groped for it again. His head bobbed up. His eyes blinked widely, his lashes flipping water droplets.

"Hey, it's really neat. Come on down."

Carl disappeared again. Kevin drew in a lungful of air, closed his eyes and eased himself down. He could feel darkness, depth beyond reasoning, and growing fear. He almost gasped. Then something brushed against him, something smooth and fishy. He opened his eyes abruptly and saw that it was only Carl's leg. No fish, just Carl. And it wasn't as dark here as he had imagined. Nor as deep. He could see the bottom, vaguely, a few rounded stones, whitish sand, and farther back the inward curve of the bank where it was patterned by the emerging roots of the tree. Carl was swimming farther under the roots into the deeper dark, almost purposely. Kevin couldn't figure it out. Why was he going back in there?

Then Kevin saw something that at first appeared to be a loosened section of the tree roots. A slender part of it was moving in the water and as he drew nearer, still following Carl, he saw a hand with long, segmented fingers, a greenish hand, moving in the still waters beneath the tree.

Carl turned back abruptly, pushing him. Suddenly Carl had reversed his swim and his white face was coming at Kevin. His hands pushed Kevin down and he swam on over, going back toward the root at the bank. Kevin rolled over, reversed his direction as Carl had, and followed. When his head came above water, he saw Carl's wide eyes staring and heard Carl heaving for breath.

Kevin, too, was breathless. "What—what—" *Was that?* he tried to say, but Carl understood.

"Did you see—what—that was?" Carl whispered, still reaching for a satisfying breath of air.

"It looked like a hand," Kevin said. "A green hand."

"It was a whole skeleton! It's somebody— *some-body!* They've been there for a long, long time."

"You mean it's just stuck there, under the tree?"

"Maybe somebody drowned and his body washed down here under the tree and got caught in the roots!"

"We better go tell somebody!"

"Yeah. Yeah. But hey, let's see if we can get it out first. Want to go down again and look?"

Kevin didn't really. He'd rather pull out onto the bank now and put his clothes on, even though the water no longer felt so cold. His teeth were chattering again, but this time from the knowledge that they weren't alone in the water. A skeleton beneath the tree? He didn't know if he could swim down and look at it again.

But he heard his voice saying, "Sure."

"Follow me," Carl said and was gone again, dimpling the water.

Kevin sucked in a deep breath and pushed himself down. Carl's white feet were swaying through the water ahead of him, going in beneath the tree, fading into the darkness there.

Kevin swam hard, pulling himself down and back into the murkiness. He caught glimpses of white and knew it was Carl, and felt safer. He followed. He caught up with Carl beneath the roots, in a twilight world of cold water, snaky roots and the other—thing.

It hung in a U shape beneath the tree, scarcely distinguishable from the mud of the nearby bank. The left arm swung out, moving slowly up and down with the current, the bones greenish like the hand, stringy moss hanging down like aberrant green hair. The face of the skull was turned away, and Kevin was glad. If it had been looking at him—well, Carl would know he was a coward after all. The skull still had long hair in spots—or maybe it was more of the moss, stringing away into the water, green and slimy. The legs of the skeleton were either gone or out of sight in the darkness beneath the tree.

Carl grasped Kevin's wrist suddenly and gave him a jerk. Kevin looked at the thing Carl was touching and saw it was a rusted chain. It was surrounding the middle of the skeleton. Carl's hand slid away from Kevin and went to the chain. He moved in beneath the tree and stood down, Kevin saw, among the stones and sand of the bottom. Kevin dropped his feet to the ground and felt better for having something solid beneath him. He saw that Carl was trying to get the chain free.

He had to breathe. His chest was hurting. More than anything in the world he wanted out of the water.

He left Carl fiddling with the chain and swam for the surface. When he reached the root he pulled himself up, sliding belly first into the grass on the bank. He lay weak and panting, and then he began to watch the water for Carl.

Chills radiated over Kevin's body, but they weren't

caused by the air. The air was warm and soft and summery, but the chills kept moving, in waves, up from the soles of his feet to the back of his neck where they made the hair stand out. He hugged himself with his arms. The water back in the small cove beneath the tree looked black now, and dangerous, as if whatever lived there were poisoning it.

"Carl, come on. Come on," he whispered to himself, his eyes burning with the intensity of his stare. How long could Carl hold his breath?

Wasn't he going to come out?

Kevin sat down on the bank, his legs in the water. He grasped the root, ready to swim down and see about Carl. Then suddenly Carl's head bobbed up. Kevin almost cried out in his surprise.

"Hey," he said happily, "I thought you weren't coming back."

Carl pulled himself out of the water and began putting his clothes on. "There's a padlock on that chain. I couldn't get it loose. Do you know w-what?" It was Carl's teeth that were chattering now, and the skin between his freckles was pale. Excitement widened his eyes and made him stammer. "D-do you know w-what? Som-somebody murdered her."

"How do you know that?" Kevin screeched, his voice failing high.

"She wouldn't have padlocked h-herself un-un-under there!" Carl grabbed Kevin's arm and almost pinched it off, but he was too excited to notice that Kevin was trying to twist his arm free. "Let's go to your b-barn and get some tools and get the padlock off."

Kevin got his arm free. He rubbed the bruises with

his other hand, and he looked toward the barn. It was sliced by the branches of the trees, faded red strips.

"I'm not supposed to go into the barn. Maybe we oughta go get Frank."

"W-who's Frank?"

"The man that works for Aunt Winifred. I wonder who that is under the tree?"

"I'd rather do it myself. If I had the right tool, I could get it loose myself, then we could bring it out and lay it on the ground—and *then* we could go tell the police. Come on, get dressed, let's go. We don't have to tell anyone that we borrowed some tools out of the barn."

"Well," Kevin said, thinking. "There's a lot of tools in the shed part of the barn, and that's not really in the barn. It's under the roof, that's all, but there aren't any outside walls there."

Carl was almost into all his clothes while Kevin stood talking. Kevin hushed, watching Carl as he pulled on a dirty sneaker, then he began to put his own clothes on.

"You don't have to put on your shirt if you don't want to," Carl said. "'Cause we got to go back in the water. Now, can we get to the barn without anybody seeing us? Follow me."

They paused to peek out from beneath the lacy, low boughs of a willow tree. The grape vineyard ended at the edge of its field to their left. At the barn, the covering of grapevines came only to the fence. Between the fence and barn was a wide, bare barn lot. Carl looked in the other direction. A golden field stretched to another fence on the right, but the grass in it was quite tall.

"We can go through that field, keeping the barn between us and the house," Carl said. "Follow me."

They moved into the field, bending down so that the developing seed pods on the top of the grass waved in front of their eyes. Kevin kept his gaze over Carl's head, looking for signs of movement around the house or barn or any of the other buildings. But from their view the place might have been deserted.

The sun seemed to be baking mercilessly down on Kevin's back. He began to sweat. The tall grass grew smothering and hot. He almost wished he were back at the river. He would have wished it if it weren't for the skeleton chained beneath the tree.

At last they reached the stockade fence that surrounded the wide barn lot. Carl eased slowly up and twisted his head from the left to the right.

"All clear!" he hissed.

They climbed hurriedly over the fence and ran across the lot to the machine shed in the barn. Carl cast a quick glance around at the rusting machinery. He paused only slightly before he ran to the tractor and climbed up. He opened the tool box on the hood and began rummaging around in the rusty tools. Kevin climbed onto the metal seat and watched over his shoulder. Carl picked out a large monkey wrench.

"This oughta do it. A hammer wouldn't be much help down in that water, but this ought to work. All we have to do is put this part on the chain and tighten it like this—" He demonstrated, screwing a section of the wrench to a narrower width. "And twist. I bet it'd come off. It's been in the water so long that it might be real easy to break."

"But—" Kevin closed his mouth. He was thinking

of the next step, of touching the bones of the skeleton, of bringing it out of the water. The sweat on his forehead, upper lip, and back dried immediately, and he shivered. But admitting to Carl that he was afraid—kind of, anyway—to touch the skeleton, was something he'd never do. If Carl could do it, so could he. He could visualize their going to the police, and saying, "We have found somebody in the water that was murdered a long time ago, and we brought her out!

Her?

"Hey," Kevin said as they climbed down from the tractor. "How'd you know it was a her?"

Carl shrugged. He leaned out from the corner of the wall and looked in both directions. "All clear," he said. "Follow me."

They ran bent over across the barn lot and nearly fell over the fence. When they were in the cover of grass again, Kevin asked, "How'd you know?"

Carl didn't answer until they had reached the willow tree again and could stand up. "I don't know," he said. "I was just guessing. There was some long hair. Or something."

"Some guys have long hair."

"I think of it as she."

Carl began to throw off his clothes. Kevin was slower. He looked at the water with a different eye this time. The pool that was cut out of the riverbank and held by the trees looked darker, stiller and deeper, although he knew now it was probably no more than eight feet deep. Like the deep end of a swimming pool, that was all. There's nothing to be afraid of, he assured himself. The skeleton is dead. Skeletons are

101

always dead.

A slither of ice snaked up his spine, as if in warning. But Carl was saying, "Follow me," as he slid into the water, the bulky, rusted monkey wrench in one hand. Kevin responded quickly, before he could chicken out.

The water was a shock of cold, and Kevin clung an added moment to the root while his body adjusted. His teeth were chattering again, against his will. He kept them clamped tightly shut, but still his chin jerked and his teeth clicked together. Carl didn't hear it, though. He was already gone under water. Kevin took a deep breath and dove in.

He touched the bottom and held desperately to a large stone there. Through the murky twilight of the tainted water he could see the arm of the skeleton reaching out, and the long, jointed fingers seemed to be curling and uncurling slowly. The feet of the skeleton were in the deeper darkness beneath the roots. The face was turned away, and only the back of the head was visible. Like the arm, the skull was a dingy, dark, greenish color, hardly visible at all in the water.

Carl was beneath the skeleton, his hair floating strand by strand away from his head. He was working with the chain. He had the monkey wrench tightened on a portion of it—on the padlock, Kevin guessed.

The hand of the skeleton drew Kevin's attention and held it. His stomach tightened as he watched the fingers. They were moving, opening, closing—they were moving, not caused by the currents in the water, but on their own—opening, reaching, drawing in. Kevin could see the long fingernails now, like claws.

He was going to cramp. His whole body was tightening, drawing together in rising fear. He opened his mouth as if he could scream at Carl: *Come away, let it alone, don't, don't free it!*

He released the stone and swam upward to reach Carl, to draw him away before he broke the padlock and removed the chain. Before he freed it. But as he rose in the water, Carl pushed back, and Kevin saw the chain was now broken.

Without touching Carl, without reaching out to grab him safely away, Kevin backed up, swimming out of Carl's way as he pulled on the chain.

The skeleton moved, rolling with the chain. Kevin saw the right hand now. It was held inward, against the center of the skeleton, and there was a long-bladed knife clutched in the bony fingers.

Carl had the chain loose. In one hand he held the end of the chain and in the other the wrench. The skeleton turned in the water, and its face came toward them, gaping holes filled with debris and moss that was dark and slimy. The eyes looked at them and the mouth grinned hideously with coated teeth. For a couple of heartbeats Carl drifted in the water between Kevin and the skeleton, and then he turned, and Kevin saw his face.

Horror had replaced every other emotion. Carl's eyes looked at Kevin in wide desperation, and his mouth worked as if he were trying to speak. He dropped both the chain and the wrench and stretched out his arms to swim. Kevin whirled to keep out of his way and swam toward the root on the bank, but he felt the thrashing of the water. It reached his feet like waves, pushing him onward. He turned and looked back, afraid to, yet unable not to.

Carl was struggling in the grasp of the skeleton. It had wrapped itself around him, one arm and the legs dark green against Carl's white body. The head of the skeleton bent over Carl, defying Carl's effort to push it away. The right hand with the knife was rising and beginning to fall, in a slow-motion stabbing movement.

Kevin screamed silently. The water was sucked into his mouth and lungs. He was choking, and he was drowning. He could no longer see. He reached upward, and his fingers touched the root. With both hands grasping the root he hauled himself out of the water, and then he bent over on hands and knees and vomited water and the remains of his breakfast.

When he could breathe again he looked back. The water of the quiet cove was no longer still. It churned and rolled, creating small waves that washed against the grass.

Kevin took a deep breath and dived into the water again. For a half dozen pounding heartbeats he hung suspended in the water and looked for Carl. It was a moment before he saw the pale body, limp, floating. The water was muddier now. Carl's body was floating slowly out toward the fierce currents of the river. There was no time to lose. And he might be too late now. Carl might be dead.

Kevin expected the green fingers of the skeleton to reach out and grab him, and he tried to see beneath the roots of the tree to see where it was, yet he didn't want to see it. He swam as hard as he could toward Carl and grabbed him by one foot. It felt cold in his hand, as if he had grabbed hold of something other than his new friend's foot. But he held on and turned, swimming, toward the bank.

When he reached the root he pulled Carl close, put his arm around Carl's chest and tried to push him out onto the bank. But there was nothing for a foothold, nothing to press back against, and there was growing in him again a terrible fear that the skeleton's fingers would close around his own foot and pull him back beneath the tree to its lair.

Kevin reached up and grasped the root again with both his hands, while Carl's limp bódy began to drift away. He pulled himself out, and then he stretched on his belly and reached for Carl. His fingers touched Carl's wrist, slipped away, then caught his fingers, grasped, clung and pulled. Slowly, Carl moved nearer. Kevin reached down and grasped him under the arms and pulled him up, grunting with the weight.

Then with the limp body of Carl lying on the grass beside him, Kevin gave in to sobs of terror.

Only when Kevin ran into the waist-high grass of the field did he realize he was still naked. He stopped, the grass feeling spiky and sharp against his hips and thighs. The sun was warm without warming him. He stood shivering, his teeth beginning to make a noise again, as he squinted through drying tears toward the barn, the other buildings, trying to see through them to Frank. He had been working in the garden, and it was Frank Kevin wanted. Frank would help. He could carry Carl to the house and bring him back to consciousness.

Dress, Kevin ordered himself.

He turned back reluctantly. His clothes lay in a

heap, tangled with Carl's clothes. The first pair of jeans Kevin tugged on were too big, and he threw them off again and got the other pair. The shirts were easier to distinguish. His was a knit shirt, short sleeved, striped. Carl's was a solid blue sleeveless.

When he was dressed Kevin paused and bent over Carl briefly to see if he had opened his eyes yet, but the boy looked dead. With another series of sobs rising in his throat Kevin turned and ran, into the grassy field, across it, fighting the grass back with his arms.

When he reached the fence that separated the field from stockyards, he climbed the first fence and clung to the top railing. He could see the stooped figure of Frank, still in the garden, where he had hoped he would be.

Kevin screamed, "Help! Please, help!"

Carl became vaguely aware of the dampness and coldness of the ground beneath his body and a terrible burning in his chest, nose, eyes, and throat. He fell into a fit of coughing; the water spewed from his mouth like vomit. He tried to sit up but was too weak to move. He opened his eyes. He saw blurred branches of a tree, white branches, stretching far out high above, and thick clusters of green leaves. Above the roar in his head he began to hear the ripple of water. And suddenly he remembered. The river; the cold dark beneath the roots of the tree and the—

He tried to sit up, but he managed only to rise to his elbow. He could see that his feet were at the edge of the riverbank, and the brown water rippled so closely against them he could feel droplets of cold splashing against his toes.

He cried out deep in his throat and turned over onto his stomach. He reached out toward the field of grass and, catching a trampled sprig, he tried to pull himself away from the danger. His efforts seemed futile. His strength was gone, his arms feeling like rubberbands with useless fingers on the ends.

His hearing sharpened and he heard the river behind him open softly, emitting something from its depths, and he looked over his shoulder and screamed, a sound as weak as his efforts to crawl to safety. It was reaching out of the water, the green-brown hand that was nothing but long, segmented fingers. The hand closed around his ankle and began to pull.

Carl reached both arms for the grass, but it slipped out of his hands as his body was pulled slowly back over the damp grass and mud and into the cold, whispering water. His screams were little more than harsh gasps, scarcely heard even by the birds nesting in the tops of the trees.

5

Kim heard a voice calling desperately for help. It sounded as if it were coming from the barn. Kevin? Kevin's voice, distorted by fear or pain.

Kim stood in the back lawn near the pole that held the birdhouse aloft. She had been watching the dark, purple-winged birds that lived there, the babies fluttering their wings at the edge of the narrow porch, the adult bringing food to stick into their gaping mouths. She had been wondering, too, where Kevin had gone this morning to stay out of sight for so long.

Now she knew.

He had disobeyed and gone into the barn, and something there had hurt him.

She hurried toward the sound of his voice, then as she neared the barn, she realized his voice was calling far to the left of the barn. She crossed behind the garage and ducked under the low limbs of a fig tree. She saw Frank, at first standing upright in his garden, in his straw hat and loose clothing almost identical to the scarecrow, twins in the neat vegetable rows, one staring west and the other staring east; and then the one closer to the fence moved and hurriedly walked, and then broke into an awkward trot.

Kevin came in view then, running across the nearly grassless lot between fences. When he saw that Frank had heard him and was coming, he stopped. His words were nearly unintelligible.

"Help—hurry—Carl drowned—he's down here—hurry, please."

Long before Frank had reached him, Kevin whirled and was crossing the barn lot again, and climbing fences only to drop to the other side and keep running. He was going toward the river.

Carl? Who was Carl?

Kim ran, too, following several yards behind Kevin, but she was unable to catch up. She could hear the sounds of Frank not far behind. The sounds of his thudding steps in the tall grass, the sound of his rasping breath. She thought briefly: *He shouldn't be running like that. He's an old man.*

Kevin disappeared into the foliage along the riverbank. When Kim reached the trees she glanced back, for the sounds of Frank had gradually drifted away. She saw that he was still halfway across the field.

Kim rushed into the cool shade of the trees. She pushed aside the low, lacy limbs of a willow tree and found herself beneath the high branches of a cottonwood. The ground was damp, with only occasional sprigs of grass growing. The large tree leaned slightly over the water, round roots holding up the bank. Kevin was going in circles beneath the tree, looking at the ground, going to the edge of the water and then backing away, and from his throat a soft, mewling cry issued, on and on. Kim glimpsed his face and saw it twisted and puckered, as if he were weeping; and yet there were no tears but only the continued, chilling, moaning cry.

There was a small pile of clothing, Kim saw. A pair of jeans, a shirt, white undershorts, and socks and sneakers. *Carl's?*

Kim caught Kevin by the shoulders and stopped his circling walk. "Kevin! What's wrong?"

The tears came. "Carl," Kevin sobbed. "He's gone."

Frank came through the foliage of the smaller trees, stopped and swept the area with his eyes.

"Whose—clothes?" he gasped, breathless.

"Carl's," Kevin sobbed. "He was here. On the ground. I pulled him out of the water. I left him here. He drowned. I ran for help."

"Who?" Kim cried.

Frank was staring at Kevin. "You mean Carl Wagner? The little boy that lives up the road toward town?"

"Y-yes."

"Maybe he went home," Frank said, but he was looking at the forlorn pile of clothes. "Maybe he got up and went home."

Kevin's tears stopped. Hope lighted his eyes as he looked up at Frank. Then he looked out at the water, and Kim saw the spots of color in his cheeks fade again. He edged away from the bank.

Frank bent over with a breathy little groan and gathered up Carl's clothes. "You say Carl was laying here somewhere when you came running across the field?"

"Yes. He was there." Kevin pointed to a spot near the bank, just a few inches from a root that curled up like an elbow at the edge of the water.

"You boys swimmin' here?" Frank asked.

Kevin hesitated, then said faintly, "Yes sir."

Kim felt sorry for him. She saw his lower lip tremble. Then his chin began to jerk and there was a faint chattering of teeth. She put her arm around his shoulders and squeezed him quickly to let him know she was on his side, even if he had disobeyed their mama and gone to the river to swim. But he didn't seem to notice her at all. He was staring entranced at the water as if his memories terrified him. And Kim thought that it must be terrible to watch someone drown.

"But you rescued him," Kim said. "Didn't you?" That memory, she thought, should make up for whatever bad he remembered.

"I—I pulled him onto the bank, that was all," Kevin said. "I didn't know what to do then."

"You did the right thing," Frank said. "But I expect Carl came to and got up and went home. He was probably scared and just forgot his clothes. Come on back up to the house now, and I'll take these things on down to the boy's house."

When Ronna heard what had happened she sent Kevin to his room for the rest of the day. He was not to come down for lunch or supper. Kim wanted to place herself between the two of them, to speak up in defense of Kevin, to remind her mother that he had, after all, rescued the other boy. If he hadn't, the boy would have drowned. He couldn't have revived and walked home. So couldn't she forgive him for going to the river? But Kim wasn't in the habit of talking back to her mother, even in defense of her brother. And if she had been, the look on Kevin's face would have stopped her. For Kevin looked relieved and more at peace. His facial lines smoothed and no longer looked so pinched and fearful. Kim could see he was glad their mother was sending him to his room.

He went out of the kitchen quietly and toward the stairway at the front of the house.

Kim caught a glimpse then of Aunt Winifred's face just before she turned away to go into the sun room. Her black eyes were snapping, and the corners of her mouth were turned up just slightly. She had enjoyed seeing Kevin scolded and sent to his room. Kim thought of the room in the barn. It was Aunt Winifred's room; after all, it was her barn. And for an instant Kim had glimpsed an evil that brought back to her memory the feeling she had experienced on the threshold of *that room*.

Although she wanted to like and be liked by Aunt Winifred, she could not feel at ease with her. The room—it had to be hers. But it must have been a long time ago, because of the dolls.

In the late afternoon Kim prepared a tray to take up to Kevin, with a fat peanut butter sandwich, a glass of milk in which she had stirred three tablespoons of chocolate syrup, and a stack of cookies she found in the cookie jar on the counter. She had felt increasing concern for Kevin as the day passed. She dreaded having him hear that Carl had not gone home after all. Maybe, she hoped, food would help him, bolster him against the news. She asked permission of no one as she prepared his tray. Only Aunt Winifred was aware of her intentions, and called to her from the sun room, "Who's in there?"

"It's me, Aunt Winifred."

Aunt Winifred came to the doorway, a newspaper in her hand. "What are you doing?"

"I'm taking my brother something to eat."

She thought Aunt Winifred was going to object, but she didn't. After a long minute in which Kim waited, Aunt Winifred said, "Well, put everything back where you found it, and don't leave a mess."

"Yes ma'am. No ma'am, I won't." Then, because she really did want to make friends with Aunt Winifred, to be liked by her, she said, "My brother will be grateful. He hasn't had anything to eat since breakfast. But he's a growing boy, and in nutrition class we were taught that growing children need all the vitamins and minerals and calories—"

Aunt Winifred interrupted, "Yes. Well, take it along." She disappeared back into the sun room.

When Kim reached Kevin's room she found him sitting on the floor in front of the long window in the west wall of his room, and she knew he was watching the river. She knew, too, that he could see the unusual activity of the boats there, and the men along the banks.

"Didn't they find him?" he asked, coming to stand in the middle of his room, his brow furrowed with worries.

Kim arranged the tray on the small table at the side of the bed. She pushed the lamp to the rear of the table and unfolded a napkin she had found in a drawer in the dining room. She hadn't asked Aunt Winifred if she could use it, but she was sure it must be all right. It was a pretty napkin: real cloth, smooth cloth, with a delicate lace trim.

"Be careful with the napkin," she said. "It's a special napkin from the dining room. See? It has lace and everything. I brought you lots of food, don't you care?"

"Kim, didn't they find Carl? Wasn't he at home after all?"

"No," she said, her head bowed.

Frank had gone with Carl's clothes, and a few minutes later, after Kevin had been sent to his room by their angry mother, Frank had come back with the news that the boy was not at home, had not been seen since quite early in the morning. She remembered it all as if it were still happening.

"Frank called the rescue unit right away," she said, "after he found out Carl was not home. His mother hadn't seen him since he ate breakfast. He went out to play and didn't come back."

Kevin had gone back to staring out the window. "What are they doing now?" he asked. "Are they looking for him?"

"Yes. Well, here's a late lunch. I'll bring you some dinner, too."

"I don't want it."

Kim stood at the door for a few minutes, watching him. As she left she said, "Well, drink the milk anyway, Kevin. I put chocolate in it."

115

"Okay."

But he was still at the window with his back to the room when she closed the door between them.

When she reached the stairway she could hear Ivan in the nursery half crying. Working up to a walloping cry, probably, if she knew Ivan. Then he went from crying to cooing, and his voice faded away. The rooms were too large and too distantly separated for her to hear every sound the way she was used to, but she knew their mother had gone to him and taken him out of the crib. He had probably finished his afternoon nap.

On the bottom of the stairs Sara sat. She had arranged three dolls on the steps above her and was conducting a school of some kind. Kim merely stepped around her and the dolls and went on across the foyer to the front door, where she let herself quietly out. She didn't want to pass through the rear of the house and go out the kitchen door, or the door in the big utility room, where she might be seen by Aunt Winifred. And she hoped her mother wouldn't be looking out the upper window when she went around the corner of the house. No one had told her she couldn't go down to the river and watch the search for the missing boy, but she had a feeling she'd be stopped if she were seen.

She crossed the porch to the end instead of going down the front steps, and climbed over the railing there. She dropped down, hidden behind an evergreen shrub. She looked up. The windows were too angled above to afford a view down so closely to the house unless the person there leaned out. And her mother would be in the bathroom now, probably,

116

with Ivan. Cleaning him up, nursing him.

Kim ducked around the corner of the house and hurried down the driveway. She went into the trees between the smaller buildings and over the fences. She went down the edge of the grassy field, by the fence that separated it from another grape vineyard.

The activity at the river was downstream from where it had started. She saw that a small dirt road crossed the grape vineyard here and came to a wide, gravelly, sandy strip at the edge of the river where the water spread thinly, widening. In the mud-packed and sandy parking area by this wider, shallower part of the river several cars and pickups were parked, with small groups of people: men, women, and even children standing around watching the two boats out in the deeper center of the river. Kim joined a group at the edge of the parking lot. In another group standing almost in the edge of the gently lapping water she saw Frank, his hands in his overall pockets, his face like all the others: grim and set and watchful.

The sun was lowering, slanting its rays over the water, touching the tops of the waves with gold and leaving the depths darker than they were earlier when she had come down to watch. Then, the boats had been upstream, just a few yards below the place where Carl's clothes had been found. As now, the boats drifted slowly, pulling between them a long chain that she was horrified to see contained huge grappling hooks. Occasionally it was raised and checked.

Now again the boats stopped, and the line between them grew taut and came in sight above the water. Kim held her breath. Two other boats revved up their

117

engines and moved out along the line to check the debris that was picked up by the massive hooks. One of them looked as though it had caught a bag of clothing, or perhaps a body, in which little was left but the mud-covered, tattered rags. Shouts were exchanged by the men in the boats.

A man in the group where Kim stood said, "Do you suppose that might be him?"

A woman answered, "I heard his clothes were left on the bank. He and another little boy had gone swimming, and the other boy dragged the Wagner kid out when he began to drown, then he ran for help. I figure he didn't pull him out far enough."

Someone scoffed. "More than likely he didn't pull him out at all but just said he did."

Kim almost opened her mouth to object. If Kevin said he had pulled Carl out of the water, then he had pulled him out. But before she could speak up, the shouts from the men on the river had increased excitedly. Only they weren't looking at the rags now. They had been drawn instead to another hook that was just barely visible beneath the water. Even though it was out in the center of the river, Kim could see the white, limp body that was in the grasp of the grappling hooks.

A woman in the group turned away, her hand over her mouth. "Oh God," she mumbled, and started hurrying away toward a pickup parked at the side of the road.

Two men in one boat reached out for the body, and Kim saw water streaming down from red hair. She saw the limp legs and arms. And she saw the long scratches on the white flesh, red marks that looked as if they had been made by a knife slashing repeatedly.

"Oh no," a voice said. "Look what those hooks have done to that child's body."

"Well," another voice said, "how else were they to get him out? The river's too muddy this time of year for divers. And the child's dead. Nobody stays in that river for seven hours without being dead."

Kim turned away, ran past the parked cars and trucks and around the end of the barbed wire fence and into the grape vineyard. She felt sick. She wished she hadn't seen any of it.

Dinner was later that night, and the group at the table was quiet. Neither Ivan nor Kevin was among them. Ivan most usually was put to bed at seven, whether he wanted to go or not. He always fussed for awhile, but then he curled up in his knees and chest position and conked out, one fist in his mouth. Kim visualized him fondly, though she hadn't seen him much today.

Sara ate as quietly as ever, leaning on one elbow, half asleep herself. Ronna noticed the elbow also and touched it gently.

"Off the table, Sara."

They were having fried chicken, Kevin's favorite food other than hamburgers. Kim suspected that their mother had cooked it, especially because Kevin liked it. Maybe she was sorry now that she had sent Kevin to his room for so long, but she didn't want to back out of her own disciplinary action.

"Mama," Kim said, "can I take a tray up to Kevin?"

"Of course. I'll fix it for you."

Ronna got up from the table and took a tray from the cabinet. She began to arrange it, choosing from the platter of chicken Kevin's favorite pieces.

Aunt Winifred leaned over and stroked Sara's hair. "Dear child. I think you should be in bed. You've had a very busy day. Did you tell your mother and sister that you helped me in the flower beds?"

Ronna asked, "Oh, did you, Sara?"

"Yes."

Sara was looking at Aunt Winifred with big, shy eyes. Bashful, hesitant like a half-fearful wild thing.

Aunt Winifred said, "Would you like auntie to take you up to your room again tonight?"

Sara edged back against her chair. There was on her lips a small, uncertain smile. Kim could see her discomfort.

"I'm going up now with Kevin's tray. Sara can come with me." Kim saw that Aunt Winifred was not especially pleased. She added, trying to be diplomatic, "That would save you from having to go all the way up there and back, Aunt Winifred."

"Fine," Aunt Winifred said as she rose from the table and began to clear it.

"Kim," Ronna said as Kim and Sara went out of the kitchen, "See to it that Sara has her bath."

"Okay."

The halls were dark except for a small, dim light low on the wall by the stairway that burned day and night. Kim balanced the tray on one arm and felt for the light switches. She turned the wrong one and a large chandelier came to life like a million diamonds suspended in midair in the big foyer. Sara put her

120

hands over her mouth, the way she always did when she was excited about something. The way she did at birthdays and Christmas.

"Oh. Oooh," she said through her fingers.

They stood admiring it for awhile, then Kim turned it off and flipped another switch. A wall light above the stairway came on. At the top of the stairs was another series of light switches, and Kim lit up every hallway of the upper story. For the first time she could see down the south wing. It was like the others: closed in, almost soundless, thick carpets that would deaden footsteps, small tables and chairs spaced opposite each other halfway along the way. Those bedrooms, she supposed, were empty.

Sara whispered, "Who lives there?"

"No one."

Sara whispered again, "Where does Aunt Winifred live?"

"You mean where is her bedroom? She lives all over the house, you know, Sara. I don't know where her bedroom is."

"All over?"

"Yes. Mostly, I think, she lives downstairs in the sun room."

"The room with all the windows? The bright room?"

"Yes."

Kim looked toward the nursery, but the door was closed. She decided to go around the balcony and check on Ivan. He could be awake and fussing and no one would know. But first, before it got cold, she had to take the tray of food to Kevin.

At Sara's doorway Kim said, "Get your pajamas

121

and towel, Sara. You can go on into the bathroom and wait for me there. If you can turn on the water in the tub yourself, go ahead, but be careful you don't scald yourself. If you can't, that's all right. You can brush your teeth while you're waiting."

She paused at the bathroom to turn on a light, then she went on to Kevin's door. She opened it to find the room dark.

Kevin was sitting on his bed with the bedspread pulled up to his nose. His wide eyes stared at her in fear.

"Oh Kevin," she cried, putting the tray down on the floor. "Why are you in the dark?" She turned on the overhead light, and then she reached for the small bedside lamp.

Kevin jumped out of bed and rushed to the window where he grabbed the pull cord of the blind. He ripped it down to cover the window. He was still dressed just as he had been when she brought up his lunch tray.

"What's the matter with you?" she said, then regretted her harsh question. He'd had a new friend, and now that friend was dead. He'd tried to save him and had failed. It was a terribly traumatic experience, and he had a right to act a little weird.

She picked up the tray. "Look," she said. "Mama made you some fried chicken. And there's some other stuff. Cake, for one thing." But there was no place to put it, she saw. The table was still covered by the lunch tray, and it looked as if he hadn't taken a thing off it except a few bites of a peanut butter sandwich. Then she saw that one or two cookies were gone. But almost immediately she spotted them on the napkin, as if he had started to eat them and decided he wasn't hungry.

"Did they find him?" Kevin asked.

Kim set the tray on the bed so that she could remove the other tray. She put it outside the door in the hallway. Then she carefully arranged the tray and napkins on the bedside table. She didn't want to tell him what she had seen, although she knew he would want to know.

"Did they?" he asked again. "I saw the people leave the river. I could see part of the river and some boats from my window. I think the boats left, too."

"Yes, they found him."

Kevin stared at her with a mixture of pain and fear in his eyes. Terrible, she thought, it was terrible for him.

"Was he—he was dead, wasn't he?"

"Yes, he'd been in the water a long time."

"Was that a-all?"

"All?" Was Kevin going crazy because of it? He looked so strange, as if he wanted to run but couldn't decide in what direction or what good it would do.

"I—I mean—" His eyes dropped away from hers and sought out the shadowy places in the room. "Was he just drowned?"

"Yes, of course," Kim said. "Try not to worry about it, Kevin. You did all you could. It wasn't your fault at all. He was used to the river. I don't think you should feel so responsible. It was a terrible thing that happened."

Kevin began to cry. "He was on the bank! I had him up on the bank!"

"Well, maybe he came to and was so disoriented

that he just got up and fell back in, and—and didn't know what he was doing."

Kevin sunk to his knees and buried his face against the bed. "No," he mumbled, his voice absorbed by the blankets so that Kim could hardly hear. "No, it got out of the water and pulled him back in. It did. It did."

Kim knelt and put her arms around the jerking body of her little brother, her heart aching for him. Get his mind off this, instinct told her. Try to keep him from thinking about this. But she heard her own voice questioning instead:

"*What* did?"

"The sk-skeleton."

"*What?*"

"Skeleton. There was a skeleton in the water. A whole skeleton. It moved. It grabbed Carl."

"Some roots. Some limbs of the trees—"

"No. I saw it. It grabbed Carl and held him."

Roots. Sticks. Debris. In rivers and lakes there was always debris around the edges in some places. "Kevin, don't ever let Mama hear you talking like this, or anyone else, or they'll think you've gone off your rocker. There's no such thing as a skeleton that can grab someone."

"Yes! I saw it!"

"The—" No, she couldn't listen to more of this. And it wasn't good for Kevin to let his imagination go so far. "Perhaps," she said, "there were some sticks in the water. I saw a lot of roots and things. Now, Kevin, dry your tears and forget about this. If Mama knows you're crying about it, she might take you to a doctor."

"I want my daddy," he sobbed.

Kim hesitated, then she lied: "He's coming. One of these days he'll be here to stay with us." She lifted Kevin to the bed and started removing his shoes and sox. Then she unzipped his jeans and pulled them down over his narrow little hips. "Now you get into bed, and you sit there and eat your supper. Tomorrow I'll see if I can find you some books to read. I don't think there's any television in the house except the one down in the sun room, and it's too big to bring up. Besides, Aunt Winifred watches it. So, tonight you eat and sleep. Tomorrow I'll find you some books to read. Good night, Kevin."

She kissed him on the cheek and hugged him once more.

As soon as she was gone, Kevin slipped out of bed and ran to the door where he turned off the overhead light, then he hurried back to the bedside lamp and pushed its on-off button. The room was pitch dark. But the dark comforted him as it never had before in his life. In the dark he couldn't be seen—or could he? If the skeleton could move, if it had the power to drag Carl back into the water and perhaps to stab him to death, could it not also find him in the dark?

The starlight from outdoors made a rectangle on the wall where the window was, and Kevin went to it, and let the blind up a few inches. He sat down on the floor, leaning his arms on the deep windowsill, and looked out toward the river.

Beyond the black trees, beyond the vague outlines of the barn and smaller buildings, he could see the starlight glowing palely on the strip of river. He could see, too, the tall group of cottonwoods where he and Carl had gone into the river, and where they had released the skeleton.

If he strained his eyes, he could make out the willow tree and the field of grass, and if he watched carefully he might see if the skeleton came out of the river. If he watched carefully.

6

Winifred stood on the second floor balcony listening. They were asleep, Ronna and her brood, and Winifred could draw a deep breath and move about her house with freedom, without running into one of them or being disturbed by their noises. She had come upstairs to find all the lights on, even the lights in the wing that was usually kept closed. Had she inadvertently left those doors open? Whatever had happened, they were now closed, pulled away from the wall where they doubled back looking like part of the paneling and pulled together to close off a wing that was not to be disturbed. It was there, at the end of the hall, where Charlene's room was. A large room with windows on two walls, and the other wall opening into a private bath and large, walk-in closets. Charlene's clothes still hung there. The satin sheets on the bed hadn't been changed in all these years. The room was exactly like it was.

Winifred went down the divided stairway, on the north side. She left on behind her only one light, directly above the stairs, a soft light that threw as much shadow as visibility.

In the utility room she took a lantern down from a shelf and set it on the laundry table. She took a book of matches from her pocket, raised the globe on the lantern and struck a match, putting its tiny, yellow flame to the kerosene-soaked wick. The flame caught, rose, and began to flicker wildly. She lowered the globe. The flame settled to a gently flickering blob of light, pale, but sufficient. It would give all the light that Winifred needed.

She turned off the utility room light and let herself out the door. There was a small screened porch here, with honeysuckle vines growing upon it so heavily it was like a green wall. She crossed the porch and closed the screen door quietly behind her. She went down the walk toward the barn, shielding the lantern with her body, in case the boy should be awake and looking out his window. None of the others had rooms facing in this direction, and she wasn't worried about them, except perhaps, for the girl, Kim. She seemed to be unusually snoopy, making herself quite at home, as if she belonged. Winifred's resentment was gall in her throat and mouth. But it wouldn't be long, she assured herself. Within a month they would be gone. The children dead, and Kim and her mother gone. *Gone.* She would be alone again in her house, and Charlene's death would be vindicated at least in part. Only in part. Never, never would the lives of Daniel's three children make up for Charlene's.

Winifred entered into the darkness of the barn cautiously, using a small door that had to be unlatched, with steps up from the soft dirt of the old barnyard. The starlight through the open door was filtered through a large, sticky, gray web that covered the upper third of the doorway. She stooped to avoid contact with it. A long-legged, long-bodied brown spider skittered into the darkness above the door, backing down into the silken hole in the center of its web. The lantern light caught its swift movement, but Winifred moved on, uninterested in the spider.

Winifred paused inside the door, holding the lantern out so that its light splayed faintly over the wide boards of the floor toward the gray walls, the ladders to the loft above, the doors to other sections of the barn.

In the silence were the stored sounds of long ago: the breathing and shuffling of cows in the milk stalls, the movement of horses in the adjoining sheds, the crunch of hay and grain being eaten. The stanchions of the milk room, visible over a low divider, stood as silent and dusty as the floor upon which Winifred walked as she went from the old feed room into the even darker tack room that still held leather harnesses on the walls and bits of old, moldy feed in the covered bins.

She paused, holding the lantern aloft, looking at the covered wooden bins. The hinges were of leather, now cracked and dry, made long ago when the barn was first built. It was here, in one of these large feed bins, where last night she had dreamed she would find Charlene's body. Yet in her dream the girl was alive. She had looked up at her from her cramped position in the bin, hands raised in a silent cry for help.

Winifred moved nearer, and a board beneath her feet gave and groaned. She paused.

As if the sound had awakened something, there was the sound of movement within the feed box against the wall. Like fingers scratching feebly, or perhaps furtively.

The skin on Winifred's body tightened, prickled with goosebumps. She was suddenly afraid, and yet she was breathlessly anxious to lift the lid and see, at last, her daughter.

Charlene. I'm coming, baby. Mommy's coming.

She crossed the dusty, hay-sprinkled floor and placed the lantern on top of a feed bin. She raised the lid of the bin next to it, using both hands to lift the heavy plank. The leather hinges made a faint, stretching sound, as if they would snap from the unaccustomed strain.

Winifred looked into the deep bin and into a pair of small eyes that glared out from the bottom of the bin, the light of the lantern reflected like burning red buttons.

She cried out in dismay, from the depths of a tortured soul, and almost dropped the lid.

Behind the eyes was a furred face, long and narrow of muzzle, snout tapering to a pointed nose, mouth open and fangs dripping as it snarled in surprise up at her. It was crouched to leap. The glowing eyes moved toward her as the animal jumped. The long body of a large brown rat brushed her arm as it leaped out to safety. It ran across the floor with the noise of an animal many times its size and disappeared into a corner and a hole that had been eaten out of the wood.

In the corner of the feed bin another pair of eyes reflected briefly from a hole there, then backed away out of the sight.

The bin was empty now.

Charlene's body was not there after all.

Winifred stood back from the bin, letting the lid fall into place. The sound, like a gun shot, echoed faintly from deeper sections of the barn. Her heart was pounding audibly. She put both hands to her chest and stood slightly stooped until her heart slowed.

After a few moments she picked up the lantern and went on through a door into a large, inner section of the barn. A few blocks of baled hay were piled haphazardly on one side of the room. Toward the center were some old sacks of feed, with their contents spilling out holes mice had made. And at a spot to one side of the room, not far from the sacks of feed, was a trap door, invisible under the debris.

Winifred set the lantern down and bent, using her hands to clear away the dirt, the mouse and rat pills, the scraps of hay that stung her hands like briars. At last she found the edges of the door, buried in the boards of the floor, and the small leather tab that lifted it.

She sat back on her heels and eased the door up. It took all of her strength to lift it. The door hadn't been opened, to her knowledge, since she was a young woman, since the cellar below was used to store apples, potatoes, and other vegetables and fruits the farm produced. No one now living even knew the cellar was here, with its invisible trap door.

She laid the door back onto the floor and picked up

the lantern. She held it down into the blackness of the hole and looked, her eyes following the light that barely illuminated the corners of the walled cellar, the dirt floor, and the huge clusters of spiderwebs that hung down from the roof and spread over the boards of the walls.

The ladder was still there, she saw, still sturdy and strong, secured to the wall directly down from the edge of the door. With a blade of straw she wiped away the cobwebs beneath the door, then turning cautiously, putting her foot down on the top rung, she began to descend.

The musty smell increased, almost stifling her breath. Apples left in a basket in the corner had rotted and then dried into hard little knots. Potatoes in a box had split the staves and spilled out, to become part of the soil. They were visible now only as lumps, like clods of earth.

A mouse scuttled beneath the horizontal boards of the walls, boards that didn't quite meet but had been put up simply to hold the dirt back from falling in and filling up the cellar. Little tunnels had been made into the soil by something other than mice or rats. Moles or gophers, perhaps, or snakes.

As she looked around her eyes began to gleam. Perfect. It was perfect. She would bring Sara here, and she would die here. The child wouldn't scream. She would merely huddle in terror. That, Winifred saw, was the type of child Sara was.

Let Daniel wonder where she was. And wonder, and wonder.

Let him hurt.

Let him search for her. He would never find

her. Never.

Winifred climbed the ladder to the floor above and carefully let the trap door down. She brushed the debris back over it, just in case someone came into the barn unexpectedly. That girl, Kim. With her around, one never knew.

The girl had sharp eyes, Winifred thought, that saw everything.

When she reached the door into the barnyard, Winifred pressed the small lever that lifted the lantern globe and blew out the light. She stood for a moment in the doorway, allowing her eyes to adjust.

Starlight spread a thin film of light over the land, touching the tops of the trees, fences, and grass and leaving total blackness beneath. From the barnyard Winifred looked toward the river. It was hidden in the blackness, but she could hear the murmur of its movement. It was still high from the melting winter snows in the mountains, high and dingy in color, running at the crest of the banks. The boys should have known better than try to go swimming in it now. At least the local boy should have known better. But, put two boys together and what wouldn't they think to do? She was glad it wasn't Kevin who had drowned. An untimely death such as that would have cheated her of her rights.

She turned toward the house and went through a small gate into the area behind the poultry house, where once a variety of fowl had lived: chickens, ducks, geese, peafowl. She sometimes missed their company, the sounds of their voices, happy in the poultry yard and around the barn lot. But—it had been necessary to get rid of them. To get rid of every

133

living thing. And after Charlene's death, she hadn't the heart to replace them.

She returned to the house the way she had exited, leaving the lantern in the utility room on the shelf.

From there she went into an area she seldom used: a dark, close-walled space that held the service stairs. They were steep and narrow, but they came out at a very convenient place: the west wing, where she had put the children. This way she could keep an eye on them. This way she would know things that she couldn't have known if she had given them rooms up front near their mother. Fortunately, Ronna hadn't questioned the locations of her children's bedrooms.

Ronna seemed to be a quiet and trusting soul, like Sara. Ineffectual, even. Namby-pamby. There was no place in this world for people like that.

Winifred turned on no light in the stairway. She simply put out her hands, felt the walls on both sides of the rising stairs, and went up in the dark. The steps made sounds, a squeak of the century-old wood, soft and low, a squeal, louder, a cracking as if the boards were going, the support rotted away. She climbed on, slowly, carefully, through the darkness toward the top where a door opened out into the west wing.

Kevin woke abruptly. He had lain down on top the covers on his bed, fully dressed. He hadn't intended to go to sleep.

He sat up, listening, blinking hard into the darkness of his room.

There was a sound coming from beyond the wall at the head of his bed. Or in the wall. *A mouse, please. A mouse.* But no, too large for a mouse. There was the creak of footsteps, moving slowly, climbing up through his wall, it seemed, bending the boards as it climbed. *Was it coming to get him?*

He slid off his bed and stood, and then found himself so paralyzed with fear that he couldn't move. Silence in the wall now, for a heartbeat, and then came another faint squeak of a board, nearer now, higher in the wall. And suddenly Kevin was moving. He ran into the wall, his hands out, and began feeling for the door. It wasn't there. His door had disappeared and left him in a nightmare of darkness where there was nothing but walls, and with it coming through the walls, climbing, climbing, until now it had reached the level on which Kevin waited helplessly. He could feel the fingers, green with moss and slime, reaching into the wall, coming right through the plaster, closing around his ankle, or his arm.

He found the doorknob, and it was slippery in his hands. He struggled to turn it, and finally it moved, and a faint crack of light appeared as he drew the door inward. The carpeted hall stretched away from him, barely lighted. It was a beautiful, welcome sight, and he started to go out into it when he stopped abruptly.

The door that stood at right angles from his own door was moving. The knob turned, and hinges squeaked faintly. A crack of darkness appeared as the door was pulled inward.

Kevin stepped back into his room and closed his own door until there was only a narrow space left for him to see through. His heart was exploding in his chest, one burst after another. His hands were glued to the doorknob.

The door that led into the darkness opened entirely back, and then a figure stepped into view. But it wasn't the skeleton, after all. It was only Aunt Winifred.

Kevin stood still, holding his breath. His heart settled back to a near-normal beat.

Aunt Winifred didn't pull the door shut behind her but left it wide open, and Kevin could see through the pale spill of light into the dark area that it was a stairway. A narrow stairway that dropped down steeply and was swallowed by the dark.

Aunt Winifred stood for a long moment in the hallway, within Kevin's reach, but she did not look toward his door. She was looking down the hall. Then, as Kevin watched her, puzzlement growing, she began walking on, slowly, as if she were trying to be very, very quiet.

She stopped at a door halfway down the hall and opened it.

Sara's room? Kevin frowned, wondering why Aunt Winifred was going into Sara's room now, in the night, in the cold depths of the night.

Going to check on her to see if she were all right?

Probably. Aunt Winifred liked Sara.

Kevin inched his door shut and groped his way across the room to the window. The night outside was no lighter, and though he strained his eyes, he could not see any movement in the darkness by the river.

He went back to bed, and this time he pulled off his jeans and climbed in beneath the covers.

There was some comfort in knowing that Aunt Winifred was still awake. Now, he could sleep.

He pulled the covers over his head and burrowed into the soft night.

Kim was writing letters. She had written three already, to Janet, Sue, and Misty, three of her best friends, and now, hesitantly, she was starting a letter to Damon; but she wasn't sure she was going to mail it. She'd had a thing for Damon since they were both in kindergarten, and there had been times when she thought he liked her, too, but he never asked her out, like some of the other boys did. She was a one-boy girl, though, and rather than go with someone other than Damon, she didn't go at all.

She looked up from the desk at the wall and allowed herself to revel in the pleasure of her surroundings. She didn't know whose room this was, but she had found it accidentally when she was looking for Sara's room and had opened the wrong door. Then she saw it was closer to the end of the hall, closer to the larger bedrooms and the balcony. But it was such a great little room, with leather chairs and a desk, with stationery on the desk and a pen in a holder, that she couldn't resist it. She had wondered if Aunt Winifred would mind, and then thought to herself she wouldn't touch anything but some of the stationery. And tomorrow she could ask Aunt Winifred if she minded.

The room was so tiny and cozy and elegant, and Kim felt quite at home in it. She ran her hand over the leather pad on the desk, over the smooth wood of the desk, and the small lamp that emitted a pool of soft light, and allowed herself a fantasy. *This is my room, and I'm a beautiful lady writing my letters of invitation to my friends. I'm having a garden party soon, dears, and I want you all to come. We will have thirty different cakes, a hundred different cookies, punch of all colors and flavors, and hot dogs roasted over an open fire—*

A sudden cry in the night broke Kim's reverie. She dropped her pen. It clattered upon the top of the desk and sounded in the sudden silence like a gunshot. She swung the chair away from the desk and stood up.

Sara's room was just next door, and Kim knew it was Sara who had cried. One sound, soft, so soft Kim wouldn't have heard it at all if she hadn't been sitting here at the desk.

She went into the hall and stopped. Sara's door was open, and a long shadow was angled across the door. As Kim watched, the shadow moved. Then Kim heard the murmur of a voice. She went to the doorway and looked in.

Aunt Winifred was bending over Sara. The small table lamp was still burning, just the way she had left it when she said good night to Sara.

As if Aunt Winifred sensed Kim's approach, she straightened abruptly and looked over her shoulder. She smiled.

"I think your little sister was having a nightmare," Aunt Winifred said. "I heard her crying."

Sara was scrunched onto the far side of her bed, looking at both of them with widened, fear-filled eyes.

"She'd probably feel better with you," Aunt Winifred said as she came away from the bed and passed by Kim. "She's more used to you. Good night."

Kim murmured a good night and went to tuck Sara into bed again. After another ritual of arranging dolls and putting them to sleep, Sara settled down, her eyes drooping with sleep again.

When Kim went back to the den next door, she found that Aunt Winifred had shut off the desk lamp, a subtle hint, it seemed to Kim, for her to stay out of the room. She turned the light back on only long enough to collect the letters she had written, then she went to her own room.

But something was bothering her.

It didn't seem true that Aunt Winifred had heard Sara having a nightmare and had gone to her room to comfort her. How could she have heard when Kim, sitting right across the hall, hadn't?

There was something wrong.

7

None of the Childress family went to the funeral of ten-year-old Carl Wagner, but they sent condolences and flowers.

"I'm not sure how they'd feel about us being there," Ronna said, "since we're strangers. And—" She didn't say it, but she felt it might be natural that the parents of Carl would feel resentment toward Kevin, the last person to see Carl alive, the boy who had gone into the river swimming with him. They might feel, as she was sure she would—and did—that if Kevin had not been there, Carl wouldn't have gone alone. And although in her heart she knew that Kevin was not to blame—after all, the other boy was older, and he knew the river and what he was doing while Kevin did not—if she were the mother of the other boy, she would blame Kevin.

So, although Kevin was not confined to his room now, he wasn't encouraged to go very far away from it, and Ronna noticed that he stayed quietly near his room. Kim had roamed the house until she found the library and had taken Kevin a stack of books. Kevin came down for meals now, but he was quiet and sad and did not seem to have much appetite. Ronna wished she could suffer for him, but, of course, that was impossible. All she did was hug him, brush his hair back, kiss his forehead, and then hug him again fiercely when she remembered that it might have been he who drowned. It could so easily have been. The river was big, wide, and wild with melting snows; nothing at all like the swimming pools Kevin was used to.

Ronna spent her days either in the kitchen cooking or cleaning up, or in the laundry room washing and ironing, or up in the master bedroom where she would be close to Ivan. Handling a baby in a large house that hadn't had a baby in it for over half a century was very awkward. Leaving him in the nursery alone made her uneasy, but hauling him around with her, and nowhere to put him except in his stroller, was a problem.

Sometimes she gave him over to Kim to babysit, but she hated to burden the girl with a heavy, wriggly baby too much of the time. She found herself hurting with loneliness for the small apartment and, of course, for Daniel. Coming so far away from him hadn't helped her at all. Nearly every night she had awakened crying, weeping into her pillow, coming out of a dream about Daniel. Hurting dreams. Sad dreams. Dreams in which he kept turning away from her. Dreams edging into nightmares in which someone else was appearing, a woman, a girl, with long, red hair and a strange, very evil look in her eyes when they met Ronna's. A smile that defied interpretation.

She had never dreamed of another woman before, and this one was increasingly disturbing because it was beginning to repeat itself, each time adding a bit more, like a story growing.

She stood now beside the front door looking out through the panel of glass, one of the pair inset on each side, and felt a sudden sense of panic. It welled up from somewhere in her subconscious depths and swelled to a physical burning through her chest and shoulders. She was trapped, as she never had been before. Trapped by her responsibilities.

She suddenly felt like opening the door and running. Alone. Forever.

The children—helpless—needing her.

The voice in her head came, reminding her. But her needs argued. Aunt Winifred would take care of the children. And then perhaps Daniel would return to them. Also, Kim was old enough now to see after the younger ones and—

As if rising to her senses again Ronna began thinking of Kimberly. She had been babysitting for hours now, while Ronna took care of the laundry. It was time to relieve her, allow her to do whatever she did when she was on her own.

The burning, the panic receded, leaving Ronna feeling tired but relieved. On neutral ground again where emotions did not rampage and destroy. Where there was a sense of control over one's own feelings, at least.

She turned back from the door and continued on her way upstairs.

Kim was sitting on the floor with Ivan, both of them surrounded by his toys. The wide, double win-

143

dows were open behind them, and a lively breeze stirred their hair. It was a couple of moments before Kim saw Ronna, and Ronna watched her as she dangled in front of the baby a toy that he reached for and managed to grab, his face all grins and delights; but it was Kim's profile that held Ronna's attention. It was a lovely profile, features maturing perhaps into a kind of beauty that was like a rose opening. Ronna had never looked at Kim before and thought her pretty. But with the wind stirring her long, straight hair and pushing it across her cheek, with the gentle smile on her face, she was pretty after all.

Why should it matter? Ronna wondered. But it did. The world still treated beauty with extra kindness.

Ronna went forward. Kim looked up. Ivan looked up also and instantly began to whimper, his arms reaching. Ronna stooped and picked him up.

"Hungry, eh?" She pushed curls off his forehead. "Thanks, Kimmy. You can go now. Take a couple of dollars out of my purse and walk to town if you want to for a Coke. You can ask Kevin and Sara to go along if you want to, or not. Maybe you'd rather be alone for awhile. Maybe you could meet some other kids your age and get acquainted. Just do whatever you want to for the rest of the day."

"Okay." Kim got up, opened her mother's purse which was on top of a chest of drawers near the door and removed two one dollar bills. She folded them together carefully, rolled them still further into a tube the size of a lipstick, her mind clearly on something else. She stuffed the bills into her jeans' pocket. "Mom, you know those double doors at the corner of the nursery? Where the balcony turns?"

"Ummm? Yes, I think I noticed doors there. Looks like the paneling on the walls. Hard to see."

"It's another hallway. Would it be all right if I went in there? It's a hallway to the south wing."

"Oh yeah? How do you know?"

"When we first came those doors were partly opened, and I could see that it was a hallway. I wondered if I could go in there."

"They're probably just empty rooms. I don't know why you can't. But be sure to close the doors behind you. Aunt Winifred must have shut them."

"Okay."

Ronna took Ivan toward the bathroom that separated master bedroom from the small, bright nursery, and Kim went out into the hall, closing the nursery door behind her.

Kim stood in the hall in the south wing and listened. The wind was making a sound somewhere, a faint, musical whine, double pitched, not unpleasant. Farther away, louder and yet muted by the thickness of the walls, came the moan of a motorboat on the river, and Kim immediately shrugged off the sound, put it out of her mind. It had brought back, for one depressing moment, the sight of the boy's body being brought up from the riverbed, white-skinned, the flesh torn by rocks, perhaps, and boulders, and also by the hooks.

For two nights she had dreamed of the river, of the horrors of a body rising, a nightmare that had ended before she could see who it was. In her dream it had been someone she knew, but she was too afraid to know.

She put it all out of her mind. *Scratch that,* she told herself firmly, and visualized a large double mark crossing out the scene and the thought. The hall was quiet again, the motorboat gone, the wind settled. There were no outside windows here to emit light, and another unpleasant thought entered her mind: *It's like the barn: dark, musty, silent, spooky.*

She shook her head, refusing that thought to dwell also. She wanted to be happy. Every beat of her heart sought happiness above its alternative.

She opened the first door and found a small bedroom furnished only with bed and dresser. The bed was covered only by a sheet. There was nothing here of interest, but at least she now was beginning to learn her new environment. Of course she hadn't looked into any of the rooms in the wing opposite this, because she had noticed that Aunt Winifred had her room in that area.

She opened the door opposite and found an identical bedroom. A couple of spare rooms for guests, nothing else. She didn't bother to cross the thresholds. A third door opened onto a linen closet. It was perhaps six feet square with shelves built around three walls and was far and away the most fascinating place she had found in this closed wing. A vacuum cleaner stood against the wall, with feather dusters hanging on pegs, as well as a couple of small brooms, a large broom, and dust pans. On the shelves were stacks of bed linens and towels. She didn't touch anything. But she could see, under the light she had pulled on by a string that had dangled into her face, that a thin coating of dust lay over it all.

After a few minutes she pulled out the light and closed the door. The wind had risen again, bringing this time a three-note tune that reminded her again of the barn. She paused, within reach of the door at the end of the hall, listening, sensing something in this closed, dim place that was unsettling.

As she tried to do with all unpleasant experiences, she shrugged it off, turned her mind away from it, deliberately, even though she felt a more thoughtful analysis would allow her to understand why this part of the house made her uneasy.

She reached out her hand to the door at the end of the hall.

The shades were drawn over the twin sets of double windows, and the room was filled with shadows, but Kim could see enough to make her gasp softly. This room was like none of the others she had seen. It was large and elegant, with pink satin draperies over cream lace, with both the satin and the lace repeated on the bed. A curved canopy was supported on tall posts, and ruffled satin and lace hung in drooping swags, longer at each post, rising in the centers. There was a deep rose carpet on the floor and several white, fluffy throw rugs. There was a long vanity table with triple mirrors and a glass top covered with bottles of perfume and other odds and ends that made Kim stare: barrettes, ribbons, a locket and rings, bracelets. So many things that made Kim yearn to forget her mother's orders to touch nothing.

She walked slowly into the room and swiveled her head, her arms hanging straight down at her sides. There were shelves against the wall by the door, holding not only books but stuffed animals, from tiny teddy bears to large ones that had to lie down to fit, from little stuffed mice to larger than life-sized cats. Across the wall on the other side was a desk, and above it on the wall many framed photographs. Kim went closer. One of the pictures was vaguely familiar: a little girl about four and a young woman. Kim stared at the woman. Curly red hair, a bit darker than the child's; a happy, laughing face. Then she knew. Aunt Winifred.

A photograph on the desk held the smiling face of a girl about Kim's age, a very pretty girl with dark-fringed eyes and long, red hair. It was the same girl, grown up, Kim saw.

There was scattered stationery on the desk as if someone had recently been writing a letter. Kim bent down, her hands carefully behind her. The pink envelope had a stamped return address and name, and Kim read: Charlene Childress.

It struck her suddenly, as if she had been sleep-walking.

This was *someone's* room. A real person.

She was intruding.

She turned quickly toward the door and stopped, her eye caught by something on the floor that brought fear down around her, like a black cloud surrounding her body.

There was a row of dolls against the wall, arranged as they were in the barn. But these had been mutilated, heads slashed away, tiny fingers torn from hands, bodies cut through the delicate clothing and the cotton stuffing spilling out. The door, pushed back, almost hid them. Almost.

In the deep shadows behind the door the dolls were like miniature people who had been sacrificed to some evil idol.

Kim arranged the plates on the table, slowly, her mind not on her work. Aunt Winifred was finishing up the dinner that Ronna had started. Ronna had gone upstairs again to take care of Ivan, to clean him up and bring him down where the high chair was already set with his food cooling. He was being allowed to eat some of the vegetables from the table: garden peas and soft potatoes.

Sara was in the sun room, and Kim could see Kevin sitting on the step off the small kitchen porch. It was the first time he had been outdoors, that she knew of, since three days ago when he went to the river with the boy who drowned.

Kim drew a long breath. She had been dying to ask Aunt Winifred about Charlene, yet was afraid to. Now suddenly the words were spilling.

"Aunt Winifred, who is Charlene?"

During the three hours since she had found the room, Kim had fantasized all kinds of things surrounding the beautiful girl: she was away at college; she was through college and was a PhD somewhere, an elegant professor maybe. Or she was a model, or she was studying acting. Or maybe she was just away for the summer, a girl not much older than herself, someone who would be back in the fall and with whom she would go to school.

She had forgotten about the dolls. She had put them out of her mind as not belonging to the image she had built around the beautiful Charlene Childress.

"Charlene," Aunt Winifred said dreamily. "That's the first time I've heard her name spoken in years." She was staring at the wall, a steaming casserole held in her mittened hands.

Kim looked at her, stymied.

Then Aunt Winifred said, as though in a kind of trance, "She was my daughter."

Kim caught the past tense immediately. "Was," she repeated, an arrow of sorrow piercing her heart. All her dreams, her imagery, wrong. She thought of the dolls, again, briefly. A dark thought that was akin to the nightmare part of her dreams.

"Yes. Charlene died when she was just your age, a little older, a year or so. She was fifteen the last I saw her. She was my only child, my daughter."

Aunt Winifred began to move again. She set the casserole on the table, on the little wooden holder with the button feet to protect the table cloth and the varnish of the tabletop. Her face had gone back to its former droop of ill humor, for a moment removed by memories.

"Oh. I'm—sorry." The expression was sincere. Kim felt as if she had lost a friend. Her afternoon had been spent weaving dreams about the mysterious Charlene, making her real, bringing her alive. And now with a few words from Aunt Winifred, the woman's own remorse became Kim's, too. She said, without thinking, "You've kept her room and everything just as it was when Charlene lived in it, haven't you?"

Aunt Winifred looked sharply at Kim. "You've gone into Charlene's room?"

"I—I didn't touch anything."

"I had the double doors closed to that wing. Your snooping is going to get you into trouble one of these days, young lady."

Kim felt tears sting her eyes. She frowned and blinked rapidly to keep them from overflowing. "I wasn't sn-snooping. I was just—just looking around. I won't go there again. I closed all the doors just like they were. Mama told me to. I would have anyway."

"Well," Aunt Winifred said, which seemed to Kim an affirmation. She went to the refrigerator and brought the salad back to the table.

"It's a beautiful room," Kim said. "I like the colors."

"Yes. Charlene picked out the colors. The room has been closed now for twenty-six years. Nothing has been touched. I don't want any of you children in there—"

Kim cried softly, interrupting, "*That* long!"

"As I was saying, I don't want any of you children going in there. If I find that you've gone again, I'll have locks put on the door."

"I won't."

Kim placed the flatware carefully, one knife, two forks, one spoon, the way she had been taught in home economics. The water glass precisely at the tip of the knife. Sara wouldn't be using her knife. In her hands a knife became very large and awkward, in constant danger of falling, but Kim didn't want to ruin her arrangement by leaving a knife away from one of the plates. She wondered as she worked exactly what had happened to Charlene. What did she die of? But she didn't ask.

151

She worked in silence, an awkward companion to the woman who had pleaded for so long for them to come live with her, but who now seemed not to like them here. Kim had never seen Aunt Winifred and Ronna sit and visit. Nor had she seen Aunt Winifred look with approval at any of the children except Sara. To Sara the attention she gave was ambivalent, as if she liked her, yet didn't really. Maybe, Kim thought, it was because Sara reminded her a little bit of Charlene, and that pleased Aunt Winifred. But knowing she wasn't Charlene made Aunt Winifred angry and brought on those strange looks that Kim had seen her give the little girl; stares as if she were thinking of something unpleasant.

What did Charlene die of, Kim wondered. It was so long ago, twenty-six years, such a very long time. It seemed like another age, with Charlene like the heroin in a novel set centuries ago. Back when medical science had not advanced very far, and people died young of such illnesses as pneumonia or influenza. Or maybe she died having a baby.

But then she hadn't been married, had she? She was only fifteen.

Of course girls didn't have to be married to get pregnant.

How silly of her to even think otherwise.

The question slipped out almost before she realized it was going to. She bit her tongue too late.

"Aunt Winifred, what did Charlene die of?"

"Charlene was murdered."

"Murdered?"

Murdered? How could it be? Such a young girl living here in such a nice, quiet little town. Of all things this would not have entered Kim's mind, and

152

she felt the horror of it move over her flesh, leaving goose bumps in its wake.

"Yes," Aunt Winifred said dryly. "By your step-father, Daniel Childress."

There must be some mistake. *There must be some mistake.* Her dad wouldn't have done a thing like that. Maybe it was an accident, another drowning in the river, and like Kevin was being blamed for the other boy's death Daniel had been blamed for Charlene's.

Maybe.

It had to be.

Kim pressed her lips tightly shut. She couldn't ask. She'd never ask Aunt Winifred another question about Charlene. She wished now she hadn't gone into the south wing and found the bedroom.

Her feelings erupted savagely, and she realized something she hadn't faced before. She didn't like Aunt Winifred. Worse than that, she hated her.

She finished setting the table hastily, as Aunt Winifred turned on the wagon-wheel lights that hung over the dining table. Kim hadn't noticed that the room was getting dark. The darkness had seemed only an extension of her thoughts, her feelings.

Kevin was still sitting on the edge of the porch step, and Kim went out to sit beside him. She had nothing to say, not aloud. Her lips were pursed tightly and she could feel the wrinkles that were created. Now she knew why Aunt Winifred had wrinkles all around her lips. She had held them pursed all these years against her hatred of Daniel. It must be that way, if she really blamed him for Charlene's death.

Kimberly slid her hands down into her jeans' pockets and felt the roll of dollar bills. She had forgotten all about going to the store, to town for a treat.

"Where'd you get the money?" Kevin asked, as if he couldn't really care less.

"Mom gave it to me."

"For babysitting?"

Kim shrugged. "No, it was just a—well, a gift I guess you could say. She said I could either go alone or take you and Sara and buy something for all of us. Ice cream, maybe. I wish I had," Kim added bitterly.

But Kevin seemed not to notice that she had said anything at all. He was squinting through the growing dark toward the river again, as if he were alone after all.

It began to stir in its water-filled grave, brought to activity by the dying light of the day, the last slants of the sun now gone from the surface of the river. It moved jerkily as if leaping, away from the tree root and toward the bank. A school of minnows became alarmed by its movements and swept away like a silver-lined cloud in the water's depths, their white bellies glistening.

Long, greenish-white, bony fingers reached up, easing out of the water into the twilight, grasped a root and pulled. It slid up, slicing the water silently, and stood in the deep shadows beneath the tree, its face pointed toward the barn across the meadow.

Birds in the treetop skittered away to fly silently through the lowering night, disturbed, frightened.

It waited for the night to fall.

8

Kevin didn't notice when Kim went into the house. He moved only after his mother had called him a second time. By then a fat, orange moon had risen over the orchards and was casting a faint glow around the edges of the house. As the night deepened the light would grow brighter, and he would be able to watch from his window. To watch and to see. He wished he had the courage to go again into the water, to see if it was still there or if he had imagined the whole thing. Maybe Carl had just drowned, pulled down by the roots and limbs that were under water.

After dinner he went out to sit on the terrace steps, the unroofed brick porch by the sun room. No one stopped him. No one questioned why he was sitting out in the dark, in the shadow of the house. For awhile there was light across part of the terrace from the room with all the windows and the sound of a television. Aunt Winifred was in there, and so was Sara. But his mother never stayed downstairs to watch television. Ivan fussed too much. He crawled and pulled things off the tables, and Kevin had noticed that Aunt Winifred looked at him as if she'd like to spank him. But he was only a baby. So only Aunt Winifred and Sara were alone in the room with the windows and the knickknacks and magazines. He could hear Sara's voice once in awhile, saying something to Aunt Winifred and the blunt replies of Aunt Winifred. He realized their presence was a comfort only after they were gone, with the lights out now and a deep darkness spreading across the terrace. Yet in another way he felt safer in the darkness, surrounded by it like a larvae in its cocoon.

The barn was like a great, dark mountain, throwing shadows as black as the trees by the river. Yet in the strange, greenish moon-lighted barnyard, Kevin could see shadows moving as he squinted his eyes desperately to make out their shapes. Shadows that had no form and were gone like will-o'-the-wisps, before his vision could grasp them.

His sharpened hearing caught sounds that were like footsteps in soft, dry dirt, coming through the dark shadows cast by the barn, by the trees, even the fence. *The fence. The posts.* Wouldn't the shadow of the skeleton be like the shadows thrown by the fences and posts? How could he distinguish one from the other? One was stationary. The other was not. But now as he strained to see across the moon-lighted yard, beyond the white shed and the tree there, beyond the birdhouse to the skeletal shadows of the fence, it seemed that it was moving, just off to the left of where he was looking, or the right, and when he looked hard, it stood still again, waiting for him to look away.

Kevin got up silently and walked backward toward the kitchen porch and the open door.

A touch on the back of his legs stopped his heart, his breath. Something pushed against him, moving softly, curling around his calves. He heard a sound then and almost collapsed in relief. The cat. Only the cat. Its purr was beautiful. But so loud. Too loud.

Kevin reached down and put his hand on the cat's head. "Shhh," he said. "Be quiet. I know you're here." His whisper was softer than the purr of the cat.

As if in obedience, the cat suddenly grew quiet. Kevin felt it stiffen beneath his hand. He felt the back arch and the head turn toward the barn. He felt it rise, the hair on its body becoming suddenly as stiff as fine wires.

Its yowl split through the soft sounds of the night, stilling the crickets, the murmur of birds in the birdhouse, leaving in its wake a silence chilling in its terror.

Then the cat was gone away from Kevin, leaping into the darkness and disappearing instantly, leaving him alone and unable to move. He looked up into the moonlight of the yard.

It stood in the shadow thrown by the birdhouse, its huge, black eye sockets staring toward him, the birdhouse shadow creating a second head on its skeletal shoulders. But the head that stared toward him glinted white in the moonlight, the black horror of its stare trailing rivulets of muddy river water down across the protruding cheekbones and into the wide, toothy grin of its mouth like dark blood running.

There was no scream left in Kevin. His voice was a dry, soundless echo of the cat's cry. He stood,

157

returning the stare of the thing from the river.

He had been watching and watching for it, and then in a moment of diversion by the cat, suddenly it was here, in the moonlight, in the yard not ten feet away. Clearly he could see the long, pale fingers of the left hand, and the right, curled around the handle of the knife. He could see the hand begin to rise, so slowly at first that it seemed only part of his imagination. At first in one position, and then abruptly into another, higher, as if it were freed from the laws of nature and could move in its own way and its own time.

The knife was raised now, in a striking position, and the face grinned at him in its horrible, stained purpose. And in slow-motion acceptance of what was happening, Kevin saw it begin to come toward him, a birdlike foot raised to take the first step.

He whirled and ran, fighting his way through the darkness toward the kitchen door, feeling beneath his bare feet the rough brick of the walkway, and feeling it hold him back as if each small rise in the bricks had become mountains for him to cross. The terror he felt was beyond any nightmare he had ever had. All his nightmares combined had not prepared him for the terror of this moment, in knowing that right behind him came the *thing*, the thing that was more horrible even than its purpose, which was to kill him, as it had killed Carl, as it would kill them all if it got into the house.

The darkness that he had felt protected him was no longer a cover. It had seen him, though it stood in the moonlight while he stood in the shadow of the house. It had seen him though it had no eyes, only mud and bits of weed that had settled there. It had seen him. It saw him now. It watched him struggle to reach the door.

Suddenly the screen of the door was against his face and hands, and he fumbled for the metal handle. His fingers shook violently as he grasped it and pulled. Then, like a miracle in a dream, he was inside the house and facing out through the screen, the pitifully thin screen wire that separated him from the *thing*.

It had come onto the porch, as though it had leaped, and now stood where he had stood just a second ago. The arm with the knife was raised high over its head, but worse than that the other arm had reached out, the long, fleshless fingers like claws, ready to grab him and pull him back. Ready to reach into the wire of the screen and tear it away. The face's hideous grin glowed in the shadows, the teeth large and white.

Kevin grabbed the heavy wood kitchen door and slammed it shut, pushing the knob in to set the lock. Above, he had noticed before, was a bolt, and he reached up and shot it home. Then he leaned against the door, his cheek pressed weakly to the wood, and sobbed wearily.

The screen door opened outward. The squeak it made came through the wood of the door and stung Kevin's ear. He held his breath and waited.

Would it be able to come on through the wood of the door?

There was no sound at all except the beat of his heart.

It kept beating, and beating, so loudly it seemed there was no other sound in the whole universe.

How could it keep beating in such terror without exploding?

Could the thing outside hear it?

And know where he was?

And know he was just on the other side of the wood.

Then there was another sound, coming even above the pounding of his heart. A faint, long, drawn-out squeak, as the screen door moved again, and closed.

Kevin waited, listening with all his power.

Silence.

Total silence beyond his own body.

The crickets of the night still had not raised their sounds. They waited as if they knew that something unnatural had risen in their world, something that could not be anticipated, something that moved to a different rhythm. To a god different from their own.

Kevin thought of the doors to the sun room suddenly, the glass doors that had little sections of glass all the way from top to bottom. French doors, Kim had said. Did Aunt Winifred keep them locked? Sometimes they even stood open, but that was in the daytime. Did she lock them at night? He remembered, suddenly, out of his subconscious, the sound of the doors closing, of a lock being set, just before the lights had gone out earlier in the night when Aunt Winifred and Sara had gone upstairs. The doors were locked. Would the thing know it could step through the glass? Or would some faraway memory take it instead to other doors, searching for one that was open?

He ran through the house, his footsteps clubbing across the linoleum of the kitchen floor and down the carpet of the long hall. He came at last to the front door and felt for the lock. It was a small lever beside a square, old-fashioned metal plate. It was down. He tried the knob and found it immovable. So the doors were locked. All the doors that he knew about. Perhaps there was another, somewhere, that he hadn't seen; a door the skeleton might know about. But he had done all he could.

The stairway was faintly lighted, so that the steps could be climbed safely, but Kevin looked for the switch that turned them out. He still felt safer in the dark. His trembling hand found a switch in the on position and flipped it. The light went out. The house now was as black as the nightmare he was struggling through.

He felt his way upward in the dark.

At the top of the stairs he looked back, and through the narrow panels of glass on the front door, he saw light on the front porch. Somewhere a room was lighted, and its light spilled out softly.

But Kevin couldn't go back and look for it. He went on to his room, feeling his way along the hall to the door that sat at a slant at the end, the door on the right. To his left was the door that hid the steep, narrow stairway that went down into the rear of the house, and he shivered when he passed it.

He felt for his door and found it partly open. He stumbled in and pushed the door shut, and then he sat down on the floor, leaned back against the door, and tried to pray.

God—don't—let . . .

*   *   *

Winifred was trying to read. After she had taken Sara up to bed she had come back down to the silence of the library, hoping that the nosy Kim had not decided this night to look through the books again.

At first she had thought that this would be the night. Sara trusted her enough now that she would follow wherever she was led. But the hour was not late enough yet. The tall grandfather clock with its muted tick-tock claimed the hour was still twenty minutes short of eleven. So Winifred waited, thinking of the children, the noisy, grabby baby who had a strong will of his own, one that needed tanning and setting straight. He was really her least favorite of the bunch. It would be easy to slip upstairs during the dark hours of the night and hold a pillow over his face until he stopped struggling. His death then would cast no suspicion on her. Crib deaths were quite common these days, it seemed. One more in the population would not cast any blame on her. Then she could take her time devising ways to kill Kevin.

Yet, she had not tried a sudden death for one reason: It might send Ronna running with her other children, away, back to the home she obviously missed, with a superstitious fear that something terrible would happen to her other children if she stayed.

So the kidnapping of Sara was the best. The loss of the child, with no idea of where she might be, would keep Ronna near, waiting, waiting.

Just as she, Winifred, had waited and waited for Charlene, hoping that maybe her intuitions were wrong after all, that she was not dead, that she would come home.

A sound diverted Winifred's thoughts.

Someone was walking on the porch.

No. Someone was dragging something.

Winifred put her hands on the arms of her chair and pushed herself partly upright from the seat and remained there, suspended between sitting and standing, staring at the window over the porch, the window whose draperies she never pulled closed. No one ever came up on this end of the front porch. Local people, when they came to her house, came to the back door. Only invited guests used the front door, which was thirty feet down the porch. And no one had been a guest in this house since the death of her mother.

The sound on the porch stilled, and Winifred had a creepy feeling that whoever was there was looking at her through the window where only sheer curtains filtered the view.

But then the sound began again, and Winifred knew her feelings had been wrong. The clattering steps were still several feet beyond the window, toward the end of the porch. Whoever it was had come up over the end, over the banister, and was slowly moving, dragging something, toward the light that flowed out from the library window across the porch.

Kevin! Of course. The little bastard had been outside when she turned out the lights in the sun room, sitting there on the step of the patio like a lump of contumacy. He had probably been waiting to pull something on her. So now here he was dragging something across the porch.

She stalked to the window and jerked the cord that

closed the heavy draperies. They swung with the movement and finally fell into place to hang heavily, dark brocade closing out the world. She smiled tightly. Let him try to see through that.

She went to the door then, looking for something with which to wallop him. There was nothing but the umbrellas in the stand in the hall. She chose the longest one, an old-fashioned black umbrella that had belonged to her father. The black silk of its cover had faded in places to a sickly gray. But the metal was sturdy and strong, and she gripped it tightly in her hand. She unlocked and opened the door, and stepped out onto the long front veranda. And then she stopped, staring, blinking toward the far end.

The darkness was overwhelming, and she was blinded. Behind her a faint glow came onto the carpet of the hallway and edged out through the partly open door. But it served only to further blind her.

She had a sense of movement at the end of the porch, a whisper of the thing that had clattered briefly there, something that disappeared into the deep shadows thrown by the house. Beyond the shadows the moonlight lay harshly bright, almost like day, a filtered light that seemed brighter than it was. She stood, unnerved, trembling slightly, anger mixed with fear.

The light of the moon gradually penetrated the area beneath the porch roof. Her eyes adjusted, and there was nothing but the chairs and tables that were spaced at intervals along the way. And yet there seemed to be more. Something that she could not see in the wan light.

She reached back into the entry hall and felt among a row of light switches. The top one turned on hall lights in the lower part of the house, the second one turned on the chandelier. The third was the one she wanted. Three lights, embedded in the ceiling of the porch, came on softly, leaving no area of the porch unlighted.

She stood alone on the porch.

She started to go back into the house when she hesitated, staring. There was something foreign on the polished gray boards of the porch, near the distant end, trailing over the banister and reaching perhaps ten feet onto the porch, something that glistened darkly under the light.

Unaware of the frown etched deeply into her forehead, Winifred went toward the porch end and bent stiffly over the first wet blob she came to. Mud. Thin, watery, with bits of stringy brown grass, and green, glossy moss. She looked, counting, toward the banister. Seven globs, with muddy drops between, and over the banister the revolting moss hanging like threads, catching the light like something slimy and alive.

Winifred backed away.

The child had been to the river in the dark to gather this just to irritate her?

She tried to recapture her anger, but fear kept beating in upon her, a growing fear that made her want to hurry into the safety of her house. And yet that seemed contradictory, for wasn't the boy in the house also?

She should clean off the mud, tonight, hose it off before it stained the floor. But she couldn't see herself going around the corner of the house to the hydrant and the hose that was coiled over it. Tomorrow would do. Frank could remove the stain, perhaps.

She returned to the door, moving quietly, looking occasionally over her shoulder, uneasy as she never had been before in this familiar place.

She reached the entry hall and locked the front door, and when she shoved the umbrella back into its stand, her courage and her anger returned.

Someone had turned out the lights in the upper hall and the stairway. Of course it was the boy, hiding his tracks, hiding from her.

When she reached the upper hall she proceeded on to the rear and jerked open the door to Kevin's room. To her surprise he stood in the middle of the floor, his eyes like frightened glass, wide, staring at her. His small mouth was pinched, as if he were holding his breath. She saw him blink, as if he were going to burst into tears.

"What were you doing on the porch?" she demanded.

His throat worked visibly, but no words came out.

"Mud *stains*, if you didn't know. And tomorrow you'll have the job of cleaning it off."

There. She took a deep breath and pulled the door shut as she moved away from the threshold. That settled who was going to clean the porch. Not Frank but Kevin. Let him know that she was not to be duped.

As she returned down the hall to her own room, she stopped suddenly, remembering something she hadn't thought of before. All of the hall lights had been out when she left the library to see what was on the porch.

How could Kevin have turned out the lights when he was still on the porch?

She shrugged it away as unimportant and went on to the north wing and her room.

Winifred was having trouble sleeping. She turned in the softness of her bed and tossed back the blanket. She settled down and tried to sleep, and found the night too chill without the blanket. She pulled it up again, smoothing it, turning the sheet down over the satin binding.

This was the night she should go and get the child, Sara, and take her into the barn. But she had already made plans to take her Wednesday night, tomorrow night. She still had a few things to take down into the cellar to make it more comfortable for the child. There was no reason to leave her entirely without light, food, water, or bedding. Tomorrow she would take the food down. Or tomorrow evening when the others were settled in and not likely to see her carrying food into the barn. If she got up and did it tonight it might spoil before tomorrow night. But, of course, that wasn't likely, because the air in the cellar was always cold.

She drifted to sleep, lightly, and dreamed of unformed, unclear horrors that were only moving shades of gray and black, shapes that threatened to form yet did not. And into the midst of it came a cry, a scream, a wavering, tortured scream that went on and on and finally brought her upright, and she realized that it was not part of her dream.

Someone was screaming. *Someone . . .*

Not in the house. The sound came mostly through her open bedroom window where the lace curtain fanned in the night breeze. The sound rose and fell, chilling her in the depths of her bones. And then she realized something more as she fell out of bed and stumbled to the window. It was not human. It was one of the pigs. Beneath the scream was a deeper, softer sound: the grunting of the mother sow, a frightened, helpless grunting.

Winifred ran out of the room and into the softly lighted upper hall. The sound here was so muffled it was almost inaudible, yet she heard it, in her mind perhaps; echoes of the torture to which the little pig was being subjected.

Possibilities hurdled through her mind as she ran down the stairs and toward the back of the house. Wild animals down from the mountains. *Of course not.* It had never happened. Someone stealing the pig? It would not continue to cry, to scream, like that.

And then a memory—unwanted, long ago put to rest. When Charlene was nine years old, the scream of an animal, the first, from the—the—

No.

Her mind blocked it out.

She reached the kitchen, jerked open the back door and ran out onto the walk, and stopped, the coldness, the terror in her heart going beyond her nightmares.

The sound was coming from the barn. The scream, pausing at times now, as if the little animal were growing exhausted. The mother sow still in her pen several yards south of the barn was grunting even more desperately in fear and concern.

Winifred backed up slowly and closed the kitchen

door between her and the barn. She went to the telephone on the wall by the inner door and with a shaking hand dialed Frank's number.

He answered after the fourth ring, his voice gruff with sleepiness.

"Frank. Hurry over here. There's something got one of the pigs. Hurry. I'll be waiting in the back yard."

She didn't go out of the kitchen though until she saw the lights of his pickup enter the driveway about ten minutes later. When she hurried down the rear walk she noticed there was only silence from the barn now. Sometime during the ten to twelve minutes since she had retreated into the kitchen to make the call to Frank, the scream had stopped, but she hadn't noticed, for it had continued in her heart, beating to a rhythm of memory that she struggled to keep buried.

Frank was carrying a strong electric torch, and he arched its light over the yard, the small out-buildings, through the trees and to the pig house and pen. The mother pig was still grunting but only sporadically now. Occasionally one of the piglets in the pen squealed, but it was the kind of sound that was made and hastily dropped, as when a mother pig accidentally steps on one of her babies.

"Got here as fast as I could," Frank said, going toward the pig pen. "Cora sounds disturbed."

Winifred trotted to catch up with him. The pigs were his, in a way, brought onto the farm after long persuasions that Winifred had ignored. She had finally given in, thinking it would be no harm, now, to have animals again. Frank loved the pigs, naming not only the huge, ungainly mother a delicate name like Cora, but naming each of the ten pigs also.

He climbed a couple of boards on the fence and shined his flashlight over into the pen. The sow had lain down, grunting more softly, and nine of her pigs were swarming upon her belly to nurse. Winifred caught up while Frank was still leaning over the fence.

"It's Jake," he said, glumly. "Jake is missing."

He swung the light around the area outside the fence.

"The barn, Frank," Winifred said.

They stared at each other, the beam of the light lying on the ground between them. The shadows of the tree danced around them like wild horses cavorting on the desert, playing between the light created by man and the light of the moon. Shadows angled across the harsh planes of Frank's face, displaying no emotion that might be hidden there.

"The barn, you say."

His voice was as flat as his eyes, buried in the darkness and shadows of night.

She nodded.

"Then let's see."

He led the way, following the narrow path of light made by the flashlight, across the area between the pig pen and the fence that surrounded the barn lot. He paused at the fence to unlock a gate, then pushed it far back against the fence and left it. He went on ahead with quick, long strides, in silence. Winifred hurried to keep up, her dread increasing with each step toward the barn.

Frank unlatched a small door on the southern end of the barn. There was a wooden step, then his heavy boots clumped loudly onto the wide boards of the inner barn floor. He paused, held the light for Winifred to step safely up and into the barn. Without speaking he turned and led the way on, through a room and down a passageway. He stopped at a closed door and looked back at Winifred. Their eyes met in silence. He opened the door.

As though reluctant to go into the room, Frank held the beam of the light down where it shined upon the toes of his boots. Dim light splayed out into the room from the beam and seemed to gather with burning strength upon the old red symbols on the floor and on the wall. Winifred could see a small white body spilling darkness on the bench against the wall. As she stared, Frank raised the light to the bench, and Winifred saw the dark streaks were fresh blood.

She followed Frank into the room and stopped to stand in the center of the devil's symbol on the floor, unaware of where she was, seeing only the tiny, mutilated body on the bench.

"Oh God," Frank said in a breaking voice, "it's little Jake." He touched the pink, round snout of the piglet, the only part of its body that appeared to be untouched, then he turned abruptly away and faced Winifred.

"She's come back," he said furiously. "Charlene is back."

"No! Charlene is dead."

"She's back!" He swept the beam behind him again to cover the bench and the body of the pig. "She's back, and up to her old tricks again. *See?* It's thirty years ago, repeating itself. In a day or two she'll be showing up at the house. This is just her way of saying she's come back."

"No! It's not Charlene, it's one of Daniel's children doing this."

Frank brought the light back again, its beam lying on the floor between them.

He was persistent, adamant, his dislike of Charlene brought back and disclosed not only in his words but in his eyes. This was the one thing about Frank that Winifred had never liked: his disapproval and dislike of her little girl. She remembered the day he had first brought her into the barn to show her what Charlene's playhouse looked like. On that day the mother cat had been the sacrifice, and he had insisted that it was Charlene's doing. They had fought then, Winifred and Frank, verbally. She had fired him, but of course he did not work for her then; he worked for her father, and his employment was assured. Later, when she could have fired him, when she alone was in authority, she hadn't bothered. The quarrel about Charlene was long in the past.

"It's the kind of thing she did," he was saying. "It's her, I know it is. She's not satisfied with a clean, sure cut across the throat. She's got to torture, too."

Winifred wrung her hands together and began to pace the floor, back and forth, back and forth, never going any nearer to the sacrificial bench. Her voice raised hysterically.

"I told you not to bring animals here! I told you. Now you're going to have to take them away, all of them, as soon as it's light in the morning. You'll have to get a man with a truck and load them and get them out of here. I don't want any animals here, and I

172

didn't want them here when you brought them. If you can't listen to my instructions, then you'll just have to find employment elsewhere."

"You're right. They've got to be moved. And to make sure the rest of them are safe, I'm going to sleep in my pickup the rest of the night."

"I just know it's that awful boy. Or that half sister of his. One of them got mud on the porch, too, and it has to be cleaned off, and mud stains. Mud stains. Somebody is playing a terrible joke on me, and it's got to be one of those kids."

As she neared Frank on her return walk past him, he reached out and touched her arm lightly.

"Better get out of here, Miss Winifred. There's no use staying here. I'll clean this up at daybreak."

As though he had pushed her, Winifred pivoted toward the door. She went down the passageway ahead of him, in the long shadow thrown by her own body. She was still rubbing her hands, her elbows, her upper arms nervously.

"It has to be Daniel's kids. It has to be. Wasn't he with her sometimes? Years ago. When they played in the barn? He was there. He knew about it."

"And he told on her because he didn't like what she was doing. You ought to remember that, too."

As if she hadn't heard, Winifred said, "Daniel must have told Kim or Kevin about what they used to do. It was Daniel that was responsible, not Charlene. Charlene is dead. She was murdered by Daniel."

She went over the bulky threshold in the barn door and down the step, stumbling. Frank caught her arm to steady her.

"Miss Winifred, why don't you take a sleeping pill

173

and go on back to bed? I'll keep an eye on things from my pickup. Arguing and fussing ain't going to change nothing. Go on back to bed."

"You've got to get those animals off the place."

"Yes, I'll do that."

He stood by the gate and watched her go toward the house, and even with the pale light of the moon he could see that she looked stooped and old suddenly, as if she had leaped forward in time to the near end of her days.

A terrible anxiety was growing in Daniel. Too much coffee, he had told himself, searching for a reason. He had cut back, but still the anxiety was there. He couldn't sleep. He got out of bed and searched for a cigarette. The room was strange, he reminded himself. Even worse than usual. No motel this time; it was a rented room, moved into because it was the first place he found. He had come back to town knowing that he couldn't go to Sharon's apartment, even for his clothes. He had called her, however, and talked just long enough to let her know it was over for him, and it had nothing to do with her as a person. He had ended that with a sigh that should have been one of relief. After all, one more string cut.

But the anxiety plagued him and was growing. He was afraid to sleep even though he hadn't had any more nightmares.

Kevin.

Kevin was on his mind, his beautiful little face that had mostly been all smiles looking serious and sad.

Suddenly Daniel knew what was causing his anxiety. He was sorry he had sent Ronna and the kids so far away. He wished they were still here, within an hour's drive, so he could go over and spend the day with them.

He found a cigarette and stood at the window smoking it. Whatever view there might have been was blocked by a brick wall. But it didn't matter. Daniel stared at it, seeing Kevin's face in the slanted spots of light from a street lamp.

Behind Kevin then something was forming. A pale, ghostly figure was taking shape, taller than Kevin, and seeming to hover threateningly over him. The figure became more distinct, and long hair flowed out from the head, catching the light of the street lamp, turning red.

Daniel jerked away from the window. He was going crazy. What was wrong with him? Seeing things in a brick wall. A trick of the changing light, of course, he saw when he glanced back. Somewhere down the street a neon light was slowly blinking on and off, green, yellow, red. The images were gone, nothing more than lines in the brick and the changing lights.

But Daniel drew the blind and turned on the light in the room. He sat on the bed and smoked the cigarette.

He could fly west and be with Ronna and the kids in a few hours.

He needed them. All of them. He hadn't held Ivan much at all, he remembered. A few times. He hardly knew his own baby son. And the girls, Kim and Sara, good kids, both of them. Had he ever taken Kevin and the girls to a ball game? He'd started to once—twice. The disappointment on their faces came back now to haunt him.

He needed to be with them. He needed Ronna's arms around him again. And the kids to climb onto his lap, all of them at once. His arms ached to enclose the four of them.

He could probably get a plane out in an hour and be there before noon.

But no.

He could never return to Childress.

9

Kim opened her bedroom door and looked out. The passageway around the balcony, which Aunt Winifred had called a mezzanine, was dimly lighted by a wall lamp on the far side. The white columns spaced along the banister threw long, dark shadows across the carpet toward her, and the shadows of the low banister looked like the teeth of a monster. But otherwise the area was empty.

A few minutes ago she had struggled awake on the remnants of a dream, vaguely aware that somewhere, someone was screaming in terror or pain. Yet though she listened with all her might, she heard nothing.

There was a quality in the emptiness and silence of the mezzanine that was like her memory of the scream, and it made her draw her thin robe closer around her body.

Walking slowly and soundlessly she went to her mother's door. It was closed. She hesitated, then went on to the nursery door. It, too, was closed. After a moment she opened it. The room was softly lighted by a small lamp on the chest of drawers, and she could see Ivan in his crib, sleeping soundly, facedown, humped up over his bent knees in his usual position.

Kim went to the door that separated the nursery from the master bedroom and looked in without crossing the threshold. Moonlight fell softly through the curtains, and from its glow she could see her mother. She, too, was soundly asleep, on her back, snoring daintily. There was nothing wrong here.

Kim went back around the mezzanine and into the west hallway and looked in upon Sara. The little girl was twisted in her blanket, with most of it around her upper body. Kim closed the door softly.

Kevin, too, was asleep, his head buried in his blanket. But as Kim stood in the darkness of his room, she saw a light flash briefly against the windowpane. She pushed aside the curtains and looked out.

There was the barn, moonlight glowing on its roof. And the other buildings, dwarfed beside the barn, shadowed by trees here and there through the area. Then she saw the light again, far over to the left, near a pickup parked in the open. She recognized Frank's old red pickup, and after a silent search, she saw Frank. He was leaning over the pig pen, his feet on the second board of the six foot fence. Through the branches of a tree she could see the light shining from his hand. But as she watched, he turned the light off, and a few minutes later he walked through the strip of moonlight to his pickup and got into it. She waited for the truck to start, but it didn't.

Kim let the curtains drop back into place and

started to leave Kevin's room.

A sound in the wall stopped her. A board squeaked, then another, higher, closer. A door opened with a faint, rusty twinge. Kim stepped out into the hall and was face to face with Aunt Winifred. The look on her face was frightening. Her narrow eyes looked black in the glare she pinned upon Kimberly, black and mean and heartless, and something more that Kim could not define. She pointed a long finger that missed Kim's chest by a fraction of an inch.

"You don't fool me at all, girl. I know what you're up to, you and your brother. You can snigger behind your hands tonight, but you'll be crying tomorrow."

She went on down the hall while Kim watched her, stunned, puzzled.

Long after Aunt Winifred and all sounds of her had disappeared into the north wing, Kim went back to her room. But the night was coming to an end, and she chose a pair of shorts and a blouse from among her clothes and bathed and dressed. Then she went downstairs and out onto the terrace where she listened to the singing birds and watched the sun rise.

Frank's pickup left and returned after awhile. Another truck pulled in behind him and Kim, standing well out of the way, watched the two men usher the large mother sow and all her pigs into a kind of ramp that led up into the back of the larger truck. She could hear the voices of the men interspersed between the complaining grunts of the pigs, but she couldn't understand their words. She stood behind a tree as both trucks pulled out, and she felt unaccountably lonesome, as if the pigs had added something to the place that she had not recognized before.

Kevin didn't come out. Nor did he come down for breakfast. Instead of sending Kim up to see what was wrong, Ronna went, telling Kim to keep an eye on Ivan. He sat well back from the table in his high chair where, nevertheless, he kept reaching for things he couldn't have. Aunt Winifred was tight lipped and noncommunicative, but Kim was feeling sad and lonely and not inclined to talk to anyone anyway.

After several minutes Ronna came back and said that Kevin had a slight fever. She poured a glass of orange juice and took it back upstairs, and Kim was left with Sara and Ivan and Aunt Winifred. Ivan was beginning to fuss, leaning over his dish of oatmeal and reaching toward Sara's hair now. Aunt Winifred walked back and forth across the kitchen, carrying things, wiping things, seeming to Kim to move angrily and unnecessarily, darting occasional glances at the baby, at Kim herself. Kim tried to avoid her eyes. Once she almost forgot and started to ask if the pigs had been sold and why, but she remembered in time, before she said anything. She wondered, but she wouldn't ask.

Ronna came back finally and took the baby out of the high chair. "Help your Aunt Winifred clean up the kitchen, Kim, please. I'll take Ivan up and give him his bath."

"I don't need any help," Winifred said. "Go on out, but stay out of the barn!"

Kim hadn't been in the barn since that first day, and she wondered at the savagery of Aunt Winifred's command. She was glad, though, to be able to get out on her own. She still had the two dollars, she remembered, upstairs in her jeans. Instead of going out, as Aunt Winifred had ordered, she went toward the hallway.

"Where are you going?"

Kim stopped. "I have to go upstairs to get something."

"What?"

"Mama gave me some money yesterday and told me I could go to town. I thought I'd go up and get it."

"Oh. All right. Go on. You might as well go out the front door. It's all right if you leave the door unlocked."

Kim looked at Sara. The little girl was just sliding off her chair, and Kim thought about asking her if she'd like to go along to town, but at that moment Aunt Winifred bent over Sara, her expression changed, smoothing away wrinkles of displeasure and almost smiling. She brushed the curly bangs off Sara's forehead. The little girl's eyes looked up at her trustingly. Kim was glad Aunt Winifred was not mad at Sara.

"Would you like to come out to the sun room and have a cup of sweet tea with Auntie Winifred?"

Sara smiled bashfully and nodded. Kim turned away and closed behind her the door that separated the kitchen from the silent, dim central hall. She paused there in the near darkness, thinking of the hidden stairway that went up somewhere in the rear of the house and came out the door right beside Kevin's. Someday she'd look for it. Wherever it was, it must be a shortcut to the second floor. Up from the laundry room, perhaps, to make the work easier for the laundress.

Kim got her money and went out the front door of the house and down the wide steps. The air was cool this morning and breezy. The tall, brown grass at the roadside waved, and the leaves of the trees rustled as she walked along beneath them.

She reached the blacktop road and looked in both directions. There were bends and turns and orchard after orchard of English walnuts, cutting her view. The long, cool, recently irrigated rows beneath the trees stretched on into green oblivion, stopping at fences sometimes or irrigation ditches around which the grass was green. Kim turned left toward town, putting aside the desire to climb over the fence and walk beneath the walnut trees.

She passed a few houses, buried in the orchards. She wondered which house had belonged to the boy who had drowned.

The day passed slowly, even with the trip to town. She ate ice cream at the parlor where they had stopped the first day, and even though there were a couple of girls there about her age, she didn't speak and neither did they. After the ice cream she looked through the stores, but it only made her want things she couldn't have: a new dress, a new blouse, jewelry, so she finished her circle of town by looking only through the windows.

When she left town she bought herself a Coke and then intended to spend the rest on candy for Kevin and Sara, but found herself with too little money. She sipped her Coke guiltily and contemplated prices of things. Two dollars just didn't buy much. Maybe her mother hadn't intended for her to treat the others, but she felt terrible for not having bought their treat first.

She had been selfish, she told herself. She should have gotten only one thing for herself, which would have left money enough to buy candy for them.

She went home in a blue funk, her head hanging, her steps slow and dragging. It was the selling of the pigs, she decided. They had been kind of sweet, grunting whenever she went out to look at them. Turning onto their backs to be scratched whenever she reached between the boards.

And now they were gone, and it didn't seem fair.

Kevin had liked the pigs, too, although he hadn't spent as much time with them as she had. Not since the drowning.

So many things were going wrong since they had gotten here. When were they going to go right?

Even with the blanket wrapped around him, Kevin shivered. His glazed eyes stared out from the bed and saw the walls of his room move unsteadily, back and forth, forward and back. He watched the door of the closet as it moved, opening. Although he got out of bed frequently and saw to it the door was shut, when he watched it from the bed it seemed to open again, leaving just a slit of darkness at its edge, through which the skeleton stared at him.

Yet he knew better. The skeleton was not in his closet. It had gone back to the water, to the river, and was now sunk deep in the cold, dark place beneath the tree roots. During the day it would stay out of sight, in the dark hole in the river, because dead things don't walk in the sunlight. That was a rule. Somehow, it had become a rule of life and death, that dead things rise only after the sun goes down.

But what if that rule had been broken? For after all, wasn't the rule based only on stories and movies? And this was real life, and the thing from the river was real, and it might have found a way into the house after all.

It might now be hiding in the closet, looking at him from the crack in the door that wouldn't stay closed.

Shaking so hard his teeth clicked in broken rhythm, he threw back his blanket and ran across the room to the door again, and found it shut. With his small remaining courage gathering in his throat to nauseate him, he opened the closet door and pushed aside his few clothes. The back of the closet wall was painted white, like the sides and the ceiling. A bulb hanging from the ceiling had a string that he pulled, and the light dispelled almost all the shadows. There were no cracks in the wall, except one in the corner, so narrow he couldn't have gotten his finger in it. There was no way for the skeleton to get into the closet. Nevertheless, he slammed the door shut firmly, leaving the light on so that the crack wouldn't show darkness if the door opened again. Then, for extra security, he brought out the one chair in the room and tilted it beneath the doorknob.

He ran back to bed, feeling the hands reaching for him.

And stared at the window, the most vulnerable part of his room.

The heavy chain hung down from the tree root,

oscillating slowly, pushed by the current of the river. It made a faint sound, a discordant, metallic rustle, that moved out from it in waves. Schools of fish gave it wide berth, scooting away in their small clouds of coordinated movement. The vibration of the chain's movement touched the skeleton that hovered in the dark mud beneath the bank, and it lunged out and began to hack, violently at the root over which the chain hung. The chain slithered down, like a metallic snake, loosened forever from the root, and coiled on the gravel bottom of the river. The skeleton struck at it with the knife and found it immobile.

For a long while the skeleton hovered over the chain, striking at it intermittently, and then it moved on and with the left hand pulled itself out of the water. It stood in the shadows beneath the trees, concealed by the foliage, unmoving, patient. Time had no meaning.

Winifred waited for the day to end. From the sun room she watched the rays of sunlight grow slanted across the windows and lose most of their brightness, then abruptly, it seemed, the light was gone and darkness lay beneath the trees and over the lawn. She made no suggestion of television to anyone, hoping they would go quickly up to their rooms and leave her with her planning. She still had things to gather, although most of them were in a basket in the utility room, ready to be taken down to the barn. She did not invite Sara to stay with her this evening. She wanted the child taken upstairs by her mother or by Kim.

Fortunately, because of Kevin's fever, Ronna had

spent most of her day and all of her evening upstairs. Winifred had asked about him only once, at dinner-time.

"Does he need to see a doctor?"

"No, I don't think so. He just has a very slight fever. Less than one hundred degrees. He seems listless and melancholy. I think it may be a delayed reaction to the drowning of the other boy. I've read that stress will cause physical illness sometimes. I'm hoping he'll get over it soon. He's so young to have so many problems. I told him it wasn't his fault."

Winifred said nothing more. She hadn't expected a speech about the matter and wanted to hear no more about it. Her only concern was that he live long enough for her to get her way with him.

Sitting in the declining light of the sun room, she tried to anticipate the reactions of the family when Sara was discovered missing. Since she would be taken from her room, they might suspect her. But she would say, of course, that the last she had seen of the child was when she went upstairs with Kim to be put to bed.

They would call the police. That was part of it. The police had been called when Charlene disappeared, too. And the police would take notes and walk around the yard and house, and perhaps even the barn. Once again there would be questions about the strange room in the barn, especially now, with the fresh blood on the bench. But she would simply tell them, as before, that it was nothing but a very old play room. A child's play room. And then, if they noticed the freshness of the blood, she would tell them to ask Kevin and Kim about it; the brother and

186

sister team whose arrival here had brought such mischief. On the other hand Frank had said he would clean up the mess. The fresh blood would be washed away, leaving only stains. The dampness in the floor might be questioned. She would have to see to it that Frank did not talk too much. He knew nothing. He was a prejudiced old man who still hated Charlene after all these years.

Later, when Kevin, too, disappeared—well, those details had to be worked out later.

The guests in Winifred's house seemed to be asleep. The house, settling here softly with a faint groan and there rustling gently with movement, seemed also to be asleep, twisting and turning slightly into the most comfortable position for the long night.

The moon had not yet risen, but it would, throwing its pale, white light down to reveal Winifred to anyone upstairs who might be looking out a back window. It was time to go now, to hurry before the moon rose. She knew her way around in the blackest of night. She had been practicing for a long time.

She went upstairs and into Sara's room. The girl lay on her back, her profile outlined by a nightlight on the far side of the bed. Her lips were slightly parted, and for a moment Winifred stood staring, shocked by the resemblance to Charlene. She had noticed the family resemblance before, but not so much as now. Of course it was one childish face resembling another, which might be expected. After Charlene matured into a young lady she began to take on a lot of the characteristics of her father: the slightly slanted eyes, the high cheekbones, the

187

full lips.

The father. Her love for Charlene had helped to put him out of Winifred's mind, but still he returned at times, hauntingly. He had come into her life, a young soldier, and gone out again within two months. He had left her an address, but he never answered her letters. After a few months she had stopped writing. She never told him she was pregnant. In those days out of wedlock pregnancy was a terrible sin, and even though he was the one who had gotten her that way, she hadn't wanted him to know she was—*that way*. That kind of girl. What a laugh.

She remembered his name: Johnny Clowski. But she had forgotten exactly where he said he was from. Somewhere in the East. Detroit. Philadelphia. Somewhere. It didn't matter anymore. He had given her the most beautiful gift that one human can give another. And for that she would always remember him.

Winifred bent over the narrow bed.

"Sara," she whispered.

The large eyes opened, looking very dark and very surprised in the muted light. To stop her from speaking out loud Winifred slipped her hand over the small mouth.

"Shhh. Sara, come with me."

Sara put her hand in Winifred's and slid out of bed obediently. Fuzzy house slippers sat in the shadow of the bed, and Winifred looked at them. If a kidnapper picked the child up and carried her out, the house slippers would be left at the side of the bed. But if something happened to make the child get up and walk out, the house slippers would probably be worn.

Winifred bent and helped Sara slip her feet into the slippers.

The little girl came quietly and without question at Winifred's side. Partly, it was her personality. She was a quiet little thing, easily led, easily befriended. And partly, Winifred felt with satisfaction, it was the days and hours she had spent making sure that Sara trusted her. The trust was important, at this point.

They went through the softly lighted hallway and onto the mezzanine. Winifred halted, listening, but there seemed to be no movement from the other bedrooms. This was the most dangerous area, the place where Ronna might just be up for a few minutes and just happen to look out. Or Kim. That girl who seemed always to be in the wrong place at the wrong time, minding everybody's business but her own. Winifred had considered taking Sara down the back stairs, but she was afraid the darkness, steepness and strangeness of that old stairway might frighten her and make her stubborn and reluctant to go farther, for Winifred had an idea that Sara would react with a stubbornness if she were pushed too far. Charlene certainly had. It was a trait that had always stymied Winifred and led to tantrums on Charlene's part. And, of course, acquiescence on Winifred's.

Winifred tugged at Sara's hand and hurried her on down the wide, carpeted stairs. She drew a long breath of relief when they reached the hallway on the first floor.

When they went out the kitchen door onto the small porch and the strip of walkway, Sara spoke up.

"Where are we going, Aunt Winifred?"

Winifred felt a lagging for the first time, a reluctance to go into the darkness outside, although she had gone through the darkness of the lower hall and the kitchen without a whimper.

"It's just a little ways farther," Winifred said. "There's something I've got to show you. A surprise."

After a few moments, after several hesitant steps down the path toward the barn, Sara asked, "What is it?"

"It's something special. Do you remember seeing our big old cat?"

"Yes?" An eagerness had crept into her voice, as if she knew what Aunt Winifred was going to say. Her steps quickened. They passed from the solid cement walk onto the grass and went on past the hen house.

"Well," Aunt Winifred said softly, "it's had kittens. I thought you might like to see them before anyone else does."

Sara hurried beside her, keeping up when Winifred began walking faster.

Winifred unlatched the gate in the barn lot fence and left it open. Sara spoke in a loud whisper.

"Are they in the barn?"

"Yes."

They crossed the barn lot to the small door that led into the central area of the barn. Winifred unlatched it and helped Sara up the steps. She felt the small girl press closer against her, felt her fingers tighten on her own.

Winifred untangled her fingers from the desperate grasp of the child. "Here now, let go of me. I'll light the lantern."

Sara stood still beside her while Winifred took the

lantern down from the peg where she had left it. The light it gave out when she touched a match to the wick and lowered the globe was dingy and pale. It seemed to bring out the black knotholes in the walls and floors and emphasize the cracks that looked through into total darknesses beyond. Small feet skittered away from the light, shapes moved and disappeared behind old feed sacks still slumped with their dwindling loads of ground feed.

Winifred felt Sara's hand groping for hers again. She clasped it within her palm, a warm, soft little thing that fluttered nervously.

Winifred started forward but stopped suddenly as a different, louder sound came from deep in the center of the barn. Sara jerked back, and Winifred tightened her hand to hold her from running away. She listened, hard, but the sound was not repeated. She wondered what it could be. Would rats be so noisy? It had sounded more like a door closing. Or something large jumping from one level to another.

Winifred waited, listening, but all she heard now was silence. The mice had fled. The rats were hiding. Even the pigeons up high under the eaves were quiet, not rustling and murmuring as they usually did.

"I'd rather wait until tomorrow," Sara whispered.

"It's all right," Winifred answered, adjusting her hand to hold Sara's even more firmly. "It was only the cat jumping down. It's heard us coming, no doubt."

They crossed the feed room and went into the long hall that separated feed stanchions from the interior. Winifred carried the lantern in her right hand and pulled Sara along with her left. They passed by the closed door of the horrible play room. Winifred couldn't remember shutting it after she and Frank were in it last night, but perhaps Frank had. She hurried her steps to get away from it, but she slipped into a tiptoe walk, as if to keep the room from hearing them. Sara's steps were soft and sliding, her fuzzy slippers making almost no sound.

They came at last to the large central room, and once again there were skittering sounds and a few squeaks as mice, surprised, hurried into hiding. Sara was lagging again, pulling back.

"Where are they?" she asked in her loud whisper.

"Shh. Here."

Winifred had to drop Sara's hand in order to open the cellar door. She set the lantern down and then had a second thought.

"Would you like to hold the lantern for me, Sara?"

The little girl nodded.

The lantern was almost too large. With its wire handle in Sara's hand, the bottom bumped against the floor. But it seemed to give the child courage. She watched intently as Winifred moved the sack of feed from the trapdoor and while she bent and slipped her fingers into the hole of the door. It was nearly invisible in the wood floor, the hole looking like a hundred other knotholes scattered around the room in both floor and walk. Sara stared half in fear, half in eagerness into the large dark square that was revealed in the floor when the door was laid back.

"Now, see the ladder going down?"

Sara nodded, staring into the darkness below.

"Can you go down without help?"

Sara shook her head.

"But that is where the kittens are." Winifred hesitated, watching her. "Shall I go down first?"

"Y-yes," Sara whispered.

"All right, I'll go down the ladder and reach up for you. You have to follow me, or you'll be left up here in the darkness."

Sara glanced behind her and took a step nearer the hole in the floor.

Winifred turned around and put her left foot on the second rung of the perpendicular ladder. Already the smells of the cellar were wafting up, musty, dank, and fetid. There was the stink of mouse beds and rat droppings. There also was the lingering smell of vegetables and fruits long decayed. As she descended something much larger than a mouse ran, scrambling into the wall where boards, separated by six inches of dirt wall, held back the earth from falling in.

Winifred looked up after she was three-fourths of the way down the ladder. Sara's face, lighted by the flickering flare of the lantern, looked down at her from the surrounding darkness above. She looked as though she would start screaming any moment, and Winifred paused. Also, she had the lantern tilted dangerously to one side, so that the flame was about to flicker out. Winifred reached up.

"Here! Hand me the lantern. You're going to have us in darkness in a minute."

Sara gingerly edged the lantern over the drop into the cellar, and Winifred snatched it away and righted it. She went on down the ladder quickly and set the lantern on the dirt floor. When she looked up again Sara had turned around and was coming down the ladder, her hands gripping the rungs so tightly and desperately her knuckles looked white in the twilight at the top of the ladder. Winifred reached up for her and helped her descend.

"I don't see any kittens," Sara whispered.

Winifred set the lantern on the old plank table that stood against one wall. Yesterday she had brought down a plastic container with crackers and apples and a small hunk of cheese. There was a jar of water, too, and another lantern filled with kerosene and waiting. Winifred took a packet of matches from her pocket and lighted the extra lantern. Its light, added to the other, seemed to more than double the brightness in the cellar. The boards in the walls had holes dug into the dirt between them, small exits and entrances made by unseen animals or rodents. An ant hill took up one corner of the room, and in the light the small ants looked aglow with fire. They scurried out of the light and unusual activity, going up their slender trails to the top of the ground above, or scrambling excitedly into the interior of the hill. A trail of them angled inward, going behind the boards, following tiny roads in the earth.

There was an old rickety chair in the corner, brought down ages ago by someone who wanted to sit while they worked with the fruit and the vegetables. Winifred pointed at it.

"You can sit there, Sara, while I go up and get the kitties. You must be very quiet or the bad things will come out of the wall and get you."

Sara obediently went to the chair and climbed onto its crooked wooden seat. She grasped its leaning arm as she pulled her feet onto the chair. Her eyes were taking in the room in fear, looking at the spaces of earth between the boards, looking at the barrels against the far wall that once had held fresh potatoes and fragrant apples.

Winifred took the lantern she had brought down. She paused, looking at Sara, but the little girl was engrossed in her surroundings, staring in silence from one thing to another.

Later, when she was alone, she might start screaming. Sometimes those quiet little children surprised one.

"Sara," she said, "there are no kittens. I'm going to be gone a long time, and if I hear you make a sound I'm coming back to kill you. Do you understand what kill means? I will kill you when I come back if you speak one word."

Winifred returned the frightened stare of the little girl. Sara had forgotten the kittens, forgotten even her surroundings.

She would find the water when she grew thirsty, and she would find the food. All she had to do was take the lid off the plastic container. Winifred had no more to say to her. She began to climb the ladder. She didn't look back into the cellar when she reached the floor above. She set the lantern aside and let the trap-door down into place. As she dragged the heavy feed sack back to cover the door she heard Sara sob, but her voice sounded faint and faraway.

Sara scrambled off the chair and ran to the ladder, looking up. The door was closed, the hole into the cellar stopped up so that now it looked part of the ceiling. She began to scream.

"Aunt Winifred! Aunt Winifred don't leave me here! *Aunt Winifred!*" Desperation, growing, made her voice shrill and penetrating, high-pitched, quavering.

She climbed the ladder and pushed up on the ceiling where the door was, but it was as immovable as the rest of the ceiling. She pounded it with one small, soft fist as she screamed for Aunt Winifred. She clung to the top rung of the ladder with her left hand, gripping so hard her knuckles turned white and knobby. Spiderwebs hanging in long threads from the ceiling vibrated from the unaccustomed sound and drifted into her hair and face. She jerked back and almost fell. With both hands then she clutched the top rung while she pushed in against the cliff-straight ladder with her trembling body.

Footsteps came across the floor above so hard and fast they shook the ceiling and the ladder attached to it. Tap, tap, faster and faster, closer, stopping almost over Sara's head. Sara stopped screaming but continued to sob, unable to control that. The fear had settled so deeply into her heart that her small body convulsed with each breath she drew. She stared upward, her eyes blurred by tears that rolled freely down her cheeks, and she tried to stop sobbing, so that Aunt Winifred wouldn't be mad at her.

Something above was being moved, dragged away from the trapdoor. Then the door opened, and Aunt Winifred's face looked down at her from the darkness, a ghostly white face with dark hair hanging forward and her eyes black like holes into faraway space. There was a terrible look in the eyes, a

196

look that stunned Sara into drawing farther away, going down one rung of the ladder.

"Stop that screaming, Sara. I could hear you halfway across the barn. I told you I'd kill you, and I'm coming back to do that the next time I come, if you scream again."

"Aunt Winifred!" The sound, the cry, escaped from Sara almost involuntarily, so great was her terror of the cellar. "Don't leave me here!"

A hand reached down suddenly and slapped Sara full in the face. Sara fell backward, her left hand dragging away from the rung and catching a long splinter of wood in the palm. She hardly noticed the sting of entry. From the ground she stared up at her aunt's face and saw in the eyes, hidden in the face, those deep, dark holes, the blazing with their strange light, something that frightened her even more than the cellar. She sensed a difference, something showing now in her aunt's eyes that made her something to be feared above all else. It was true, she felt, that Aunt Winifred was going to kill her. The instinct for survival brought her up from the ground to stand staring up at Aunt Winifred, a white face suspended in the square of black. A long finger pointed at Sara.

"I had a little girl once, and your daddy killed her. So, I'm going to kill you. Now you get on that chair and you stay there. If you scream one more time, that will be the last time."

Sara's sobbing had stopped, closing into her chest in terror.

The trapdoor slammed shut. Sara listened hard and heard the dragging sound again, and finally, Aunt Winifred's footsteps going away across the floor above and fading into the creaking sounds of the barn.

Sara went back to the chair and huddled there, her feet drawn up.

She began to pick at the splinter in her palm.

With each breath she drew her body shuddered, but the only sound in the cellar was her soft, long intakes of air.

Tomorrow, Winifred thought, her anger ebbing, when she could get away from the searchers who were most surely coming to look for the little girl, she would bring her fresh water and more food. She would replenish the oil in the lantern. Sara was sufficiently frightened now, she felt, to remain silent if anyone went through the barn. She would try to guide them through so that the central portion was missed. A glance in from the door should be enough to satisfy them that no one was there.

Winifred went back down the long passageway quickly, but when she came opposite to the playroom she paused, while every cell in her body urged her to run, *run*. The door stood open now, and the light from her lantern reached into the darkness and brought the sacrificial bench into view.

Winifred's heart pounded nervously.

Someone had been in the room while she was down in the cellar. Perhaps they had been there when she and Sara walked past, when the door was closed.

Winifred hurried on, almost running. The next time she came to the barn, she promised herself, she would go to the far end and enter a door there. She would not pass by this way again.

She was glad to get out into the barn lot. The moon had risen and was shining through the trees beyond the tall roof of the house.

Winifred levered the globe on the lantern up and blew out the light. She went on toward the house, pausing to latch the gate behind her.

She went into the sun room to rest, feeling as if she had worked hard all day long. It was the strain, she told herself, and now the relief at finally beginning the annihilation of Daniel's family.

She would have to kill Sara eventually but how, exactly? Let her starve to death? No, not that. She would have to destroy her, but not yet. She had food and water and light and air, and she would survive while the countryside searched for her. The method of killing could be figured out later.

Sitting back in her favorite chair, the recliner with the handy little pockets down beneath each arm, pockets that had interested Sara immensely, Winifred thought of the child with nothing but the hard wood chair. There was no place for her to lie down unless she used the plank table, which was certainly long enough. She could make her bed there, but she had no blanket.

The nights would get cold.

Cold never left the cellar, and neither did night.

Winifred pushed her chair up and sat thinking. There were plenty of old blankets in the utility room, stuffed into the shelves after they had been washed and dried. What harm would it do to take one or two of them down to the child?

With a groan for the aching of her bones, Winifred

pushed herself out of the chair.

In the utility room she lighted the lantern again and took down from a shelf in the cabinet two blankets, one of them wool, the other cotton flannel. The flannel blanket would make a suitable mattress, and the wool blanket would keep out the chill. Winifred tucked the blankets under her left arm, and in her right hand she carried the lantern.

Once again she crossed the lawn of the back yard, passed beneath the shadows of a tree, then turned to the left behind the hen house, going this time to the far end of the barn and a door there that would lead her to the central room without going past the playroom.

To her left was a hedge, planted along the north side of the driveway for twenty or so feet. It shadowed the path along which she had to walk, and she hesitated, even though she carried a lantern in her hand. She had a vague feeling that something had moved there, settling back into the shadows, watching her. Those kids again, of course. They had been in the playroom, closing the door, opening it. And now they were here, watching her from the hedge. They would know what she had done. They might even have brought Sara up from the cellar already. There was no way the child could get out of there by herself, but the two older children working together would be able to lift the heavy lid. Then if she must, she would kill them all, tonight, even Kimberly, and put their bodies into the cellar to rot with Sara.

"That's enough!" she said aloud, furiously, her voice quaking with the strength of her emotions.

The distant end of the hedge rustled.

"Come out of there this moment!"

Moonlight glinted on something that flashed briefly above and beyond the hedge. Winifred took several quick steps forward and then she stopped, her gasp audible in the night. She dropped the blankets, though her other hand held the lantern in a death grip. She stared with bulging eyes at the apparition that stood partly in the moonlight at the end of the hedge.

It was a human figure, and yet it was fleshless, its bones glowing almost supernaturally, a dull, nearly invisible gray in the dark. It faced toward her, the eye holes in its skull dark with mud, the teeth still intact and grinning hideously. It was standing, as if something held its bones together, some tendon that had not deteriorated, a sinew still holding. Its right arm was raised over its head, and Winifred saw, but scarcely recognized in her paralyzing fear, that its long, bony, palmless hand held a butcher knife with a sharp, pointed blade, a blade that tapered to a needle point. And somewhere, suddenly, from the depths of her memory, that knife loomed, and in a second's fleeting thought she remembered the morning she had missed that old knife: two days before Charlene's disappearance. It was a special knife, with a point that she had used many times to slaughter food for the table: chicken, ducks, rabbits. One prick with the point of that knife and the creature was dead.

She had missed the knife, and then she had forgotten it.

And now she knew.

She wasn't aware that she was struggling to make

201

words in her throat. "My God. My God. Charlene—
Charlene?"

Frank was right. Charlene had come home, risen
from her grave, and the terror in Winifred's heart
mixed with horror, and she stared, unable to move,
her mind groping for answers. The barn—it had
something to do with the room in the barn, with the
devil's face painted on the wall and all the symbols.
They had meant more than a child's silly scribblings.

It took a step toward her, and Winifred stumbled
backward. The lantern fell from her hand and rolled.
Its flare waved drunkenly and went out, and
Winifred was standing in the deep shadows thrown
by the trees and hen house. With a last effort she
turned to run, to try to escape, though her heart urged
her to stay, to be with her daughter however she
could. As though the earth loomed up in agreement
with her heart, she stumbled over a clump of grass
and fell, catching herself on the heels of her hands.
Before she could push herself upright, she felt the
point of the knife rip into the flesh on her back. The
pain drove her down.

She thought of Sara, alone in the terrible cellar,
with no blanket to keep her warm. She sobbed,
strangling on the blood in her throat. She hadn't
meant to hurt the child, not really.

Not really.

But now the little girl was doomed to die a horrible
death because no one would ever find her.

10

The house was alive around Kevin. His walls creaked and moved, seeming to come closer in the darkness of his room where only a filtered moonlight came in at the curtained window. He had awakened from a bad dream that he couldn't totally remember, a dream in which he had groaned in agony, trying to escape the rubbery arm of the skeleton as it reached longer and longer toward him, so that no matter how hard he ran or how far, the arm was right there, ready to grab him from behind. But now that he was awake, shivering in his bed, he still heard the groan. It came from beyond him. He heard it clearly.

He thought he did.

Yet he wasn't sure.

A soft wind moved around the corners of the house, and there was a high-pitched, far away sigh that was weirdly musical. So it was the wind, after all. And yet—

He heard it again, and now that he was wide awake, there was no doubt in his mind. His ears were sharply attuned to all that was beyond him. He was only a small seed in the surroundings, a small, pulsating seed hidden in its pod; but he was aware of the world beyond. He heard its every movement, with its sighing and sobbing and moaning.

There was a cry then, a word that sounded like "*Help.*" And it came from beyond the wall. It was not the house crying, nor the wind.

Forgetting for a moment the danger to himself, Kevin slid out of bed and ran through the ghostly shadows of his room to the window. He parted the curtains. The moonlight seemed almost as bright as day, falling in patches among the trees and shrubs and down into the back yard in a great glob of pale, white light. He saw the looming roof of the barn, still and sharply outlined by the moonlight. He saw the black trees down at the river and the dark rows of grapevines in the vineyard, and beyond that, the thick, dark trees of the orchards. Then he looked again into the back yard, toward the hen house and the tree behind it and the hedge along the driveway. He could see part of the roof of the pig's house, and the fig tree there, the tree that leaned so closely over the roof, so that he had been able to climb up with no problem and lie on the sloping lift of the pig house roof and look down and watch the little pigs at play. He smiled, remembering. They played almost like kittens, or puppies, rooting one another with their flat, pink little noses, rooting the ground, digging it up in little furrows. They played in the trough of water, like children in a swimming pool. They loved their life, and now they were gone. Kevin didn't know where. Or why.

Kevin's eyes swept the area visible from his windows, searching every spot of moonlight for the figure of his nightmares. It seemed a nightmare, now, his encounter with the thing from the river. Sometimes he had trouble separating nightmares from reality. He wasn't sure, just now, if what he had thought happened really had. He hoped it hadn't, that it had all been one long, horrible nightmare, and he would wake up from it soon. He would wake up and find himself back home, in the crowded apartment with his mama and brother and sisters there, within reach; where they weren't separated by long halls and empty rooms, and walls that creaked and moved in the darkness, and skeletons that came up out of the dark waters of the river.

Someone was sobbing. A far, faraway sound. Yet it was real. It was not a dream, nor a nightmare, nor one of his bad thoughts.

He unlatched the window and eased it up, and put his face against the screen. He caught a glimpse of movement below, down at the edge of the black shadows thrown by the tree behind the empty hen house. Something on the ground, something reaching, a hand, a real hand, reaching, pale and white and distant. It lay in the moonlight like a skinned and suffering animal, too weak to move farther away from its tormentor.

The groan wafted up faintly, followed by tired, almost soundless sobbing, and words that sounded like, "Oh help, oh help."

Kevin turned away from the window, letting the curtains fall into place, closing out the glow from the moonlight on the slanting roofline below and the sound that had awakened him.

He ran through the shadows of his room and flung open his door. The hallway was faintly lighted from the wall lamp near the front, and Kevin ran faster and faster, feeling the thick carpet on his bare feet, hearing nothing but the roar of rushing blood in his ears and the echoes of the cry beyond the window.

He burst into Kim's room. The door cracked back against the wall and then almost closed itself again.

"Kim. Kim!"

He leaped upon the lump in the middle of the bed and felt her warm body wriggle and sit up. Her face was a pale oval in the near dark.

"Kevin?"

He was tugging at her arm and feeling her pull back, trying to loosen his grasp.

"Kim, hurry, come with me to my room. There's something outside groaning."

"*What?* What is it?"

"Come, please. Hurry."

She reached over with her free hand and turned on the lamp beside her bed. After she saw his face she hesitated no longer. She threw back her cover and followed him, allowing him to drag her along, both his hands clasping hers.

"I heard it," he was whispering in loud hisses as he pulled her down the hall toward his room. "I thought it was my dream, but it wasn't. I looked out my window, and I saw a hand on the grass, reaching toward the house. There's someone there, groaning and asking for help.

Kim frowned and made no comment.

"I'll show you," he said. "Hurry."

206

They parted the curtains at his window and put their heads together against the screen. Kevin's voice was quieter, almost inaudible.

"See, down there. It's still down there. The hand."

Kim searched the back yard carefully and saw nothing. Wind sighed in the trees, and the leaves moved, making dark shadows dance at the edge of the moon-lighted areas. The birdhouse seemed to sway slightly in the wind, its shadow across the lawn long and spidery. Her frown deepened. Kevin was still pointing, his blunt little finger pressed against the screen, but she couldn't follow its aim precisely. She looked and looked and saw nothing.

"There!" he cried impatiently, sensing her doubts. "See it there, just at the edge of the dark by the hen house. *See?*"

Her eyes moved nearer the hen house and the dark shadows, the black area shrouded by tree and building and hedge beyond, and then she saw it. Something paler than the grass, something alien, not belonging where it was.

"What is it?" she whispered.

"It's a hand," he sobbed in frustration. "Can't you see it? Can't you see it move?"

It wasn't moving, whatever it was. She thought of the fever Kevin had had, and thought he must be feverish again. And yet, something was there, on the grass, whatever it was. And suddenly it seemed to her there was a sound, too, a sound different from the ones made by the wind and the night.

"Hear it!" Kevin demanded. "It's moaning again."

Kim moved back from the window. "I'll go see what it is."

To her surprise he grabbed her and held her from leaving. "No, no, don't go down. It will get you, too." He was weeping. She could hear it in his voice, though his tears were hidden by the darkness.

Kim put her hands on his cheeks and felt the wetness under her thumbs. She wiped the tears away.

"Kevin, if someone is hurt, we have to help, don't we?"

He nodded.

"I have to go down and see what it is."

"It might be the skeleton."

"Oh Kevin," she said softly, scolding.

"It might be just doing that to make you think it's someone. It might be a trick. I don't want you to go down, Kim."

"Then what do you want me to do? Call the police?"

"I don't know. I don't know."

"Do you want to come with me? I know where the switch to the back yard light is. It will flood the whole yard, and we'll be able to see."

Kevin drew a breath on a sob and released his hold on her. He got to his feet. "All right."

Kim held his hand as they went down to the utility room. The lower hall was like going deeper and deeper into a tunnel where light was left behind at the entrance. The kitchen was lighter, the moonlight reflecting in at the windows.

At the outer door by the utility room, Kim flipped a switch, and twin lights on the walk on each side of the porch steps came on. Another switch turned on a floodlight attached to a pole in the back yard.

When they went out onto the terrace they could see

208

her, body outlined by the light on the pole.

She was lying facedown, and the back of her dress was ripped, slashed and darkened with blood. One arm reached toward the house, the other dragged beside her body. One side of her face was lying on the grass, her face turned away.

"Aunt Winifred," Kim cried, hardly aware that she had spoken at all. She began to run.

Kim kneeled on the grass beside the body, peering into the twisted features of Aunt Winifred's face. The eyes were closed, the mouth open. Blood ran out the lower corner of the mouth, making a small black puddle beneath her chin in the shadows of the grass. Kim started to touch the bloody shoulder but drew her hand back.

"Aunt Winifred! Aunt Winifred."

The eyes fluttered and opened, and the woman made an effort to rise up, her mouth working as if to speak. After a few fruitless tries a gurgling sound came from her throat.

"S-Sa . . ." Her head fell back to the ground. Another effort to rise failed. But her eyes looked up beseechingly at Kim, and her voice came more clearly. "Sara . . . Sa . . . Sara."

Abruptly her head fell and her eyes remained half open, staring. There was a sudden gush of blood from her mouth, and then she was very still. Kim knew without having ever seen a dying creature before that Aunt Winifred had died. She drew back instinctively, sitting on her heels, staring down at the still face and the staring eyes, at the pool of blood beneath the chin. The blood had stopped running now.

"She died," Kim said in a growing horror. She pushed away, backward, and stumbled to her feet. She glanced up and saw Kevin standing several feet away. She added, "She's dead now."

"Was she stabbed?" Kevin asked.

"I don't know." Kim looked at the body and saw the long slashes on the back, slashes that had opened the clothing and bared the pale body, slashes that had opened the skin and the flesh from shoulders to hips. She saw holes in the body: short, dark places that had been made by the blade of a knife going straight in. A lot of them, like periods placed erratically on a page.

"Yes, I think so."

Kevin was backing toward the house now, the lighted porch. "Kim, let's go."

She saw his eyes searching all the areas beyond her, the lighted areas and the black, unlighted areas, as if he were terrified of what might be hiding there. She, too, thought of their vulnerability. They were alone with a murderer. Her mind brought up the image of a faceless man, tall and looming, the bloody knife in his hand.

She grabbed Kevin by the shoulder and hurried him toward the house, pushing him along. Together they ran, going into the kitchen door they had left standing open. She had visions now of the man having gone into the house to wait for them around some shadowed corner.

Her fingers dug into Kevin's shoulder as she held him back from entering the hall.

"Where's the door to the back stairs?" she whispered.

"I don't know." Kevin twisted away from her and

locked the kitchen door.

Kim pulled him into the utility room and opened a door to the right of the washer and dryer, but it was only a large walk-in closet with an arrangement of cleaning aids from sponges to brooms and vacuum cleaners.

Near the corner, almost hidden behind a stand that held old coats, sweaters, and hats, was another door. Kim opened it gingerly and saw a flight of dark, steep, narrow steps going up.

"Here it is," she whispered. "Here. Let me find a light."

She ran her hand along the wall just inside the door and felt the sticky, fine substance of a spiderweb. It entangled her fingers, and she shook her hand vigorously, shuddering, but the web clung. She had to use the other hand to clear away the web.

"There's no light," she said. But more optimistically, she added, "There's got to be."

Kevin ducked under her arm and looked up into the dark, rising tunnel of the stairs. Walls enclosed it on both sides. There was nothing but the steps and the walls and the darkness. He backed out into the lighted utility room.

"Let's go the other way," he said.

"No! The murderer might have come into the house, and he might be waiting for us in the sun room or the hall."

Kevin shook his head. "No, it's not in here. I don't think it knows how to come into the house yet."

But Kim wasn't listening to him. She got him by the arm again and pulled him with her into the narrow stairwell. "Come on," she said. "I'll go first.

You stay right behind me. I'll hold your hand if you want. The light from the utility room will show us the way."

But by the time they had gone halfway up the stairs the faint light from the utility room was left behind. Kim was almost afraid to touch the wall for support, afraid she would put her hand into another spider-web. Yet Aunt Winifred had climbed these stairs a lot, and she must have touched the stair wall all the time, to help her along, to keep her from falling. Kim reached out and found a rail set about three inches from the wall. It felt smooth and polished, as if hands had rubbed its length many times.

They came at last to the upper hall and the soft light and thick carpets. The stairwell door creaked as they opened and closed it, just as a step now and then had given under their feet, creaking ominously.

By silent, mutual agreement they began to run, hand in hand, down the hall and around the balcony toward their mother's room.

Ronna was rising up in bed, staring toward them as they flung the door open, as if she had been awakened by their running in the hall. She reached for a lamp at the side of her bed and turned it on. Her hair was mussed, and her eyes blinking, widening. She started to question them, but Kim interrupted.

"Mama! Aunt Winifred's been murdered. She's dying. I think already dead."

Ronna's mouth moved as if to answer, but she said nothing. Her mouth closed again.

"We have to call the police, Mama," Kim cried softly, touching her, urging her to follow. "The murderer might be here right now in the house."

"Where is your Aunt Winifred?" Ronna asked, sounding calm and doubtful.

"She's outside. Kevin heard someone groaning, and we went out to see what it was."

Ronna began to search for her house slippers. "You shouldn't have done that," she said. "You should have come for me."

They went down the divided stairway in the front and along the wide hall. There was no one hiding, Kim saw, as they passed each corner. Her mother walked without hesitation as if the thought of the murderer had not really penetrated her mind. She was hurrying to Aunt Winifred.

The back yard was still brightly lighted, and the body visible from the porch. Ronna hesitated only briefly, staring at the still form of Aunt Winifred several yards away, her feet still in the shadows thrown by the tree. Then she went down and across the yard, quickly, and bent over. She straightened and stepped back.

"Oh my God. You're right."

Aunt Winifred's eyes stared steadily across the grass, her face in the full light of the floodlight on the pole. They were like glass beads now, Kim saw. Flat, black, glass beads.

Ronna grasped Kim and shoved her toward the house much as Kim had shoved Kevin earlier. Kevin, they saw, was still on the terrace, his head swiveling slowly as he stared all around, into the shadows of the trees and the buildings.

Kim remembered suddenly what he had said about the murderer not knowing the way into the house yet, but it seemed a crazy thing to say and she dismissed it.

Ronna used the kitchen phone to call the police. She had to search for the phone book first, and Kim located it in the little drawer of the table beneath the phone. Then she fumbled as she turned the pages and almost dropped it. Only in that way was Kim able to see how nervous her mother had become. She made the call with a steady voice. When she hung up the phone she turned to look at the children.

Kim remembered something else. "Sara!" she cried, "Mama, Aunt Winifred was trying to say something about Sara when she died."

Ronna stared at Kim for a long moment, as if her information were sinking in very, very slowly. Her face seemed to grow even whiter. Then suddenly she whirled and slammed through the door into the hall. Kim and Kevin followed, running, but neither of them caught up with Ronna before she looked into Sara's room.

"Sara!" she cried out. "Sara!"

Ronna made a quick circle of Sara's room before she came back out into the hall.

"Hurry," she ordered. "Look for her. See if she's anywhere in the house. Find her! We've got to find Sara."

11

The sun had risen and was well overhead now, but it looked bleak, dimmed, not quite right. Ronna sat in the kitchen while Ivan scooted around on the floor at her feet, pulling himself up by holding the table leg, the chair leg, or his mother's knee. She sat as if deflated, her body drooping. The police were still wandering around. An ambulance had come and taken away the body after long hours of leaving it there in the sun while pictures were taken and the area around it closely examined.

Kevin sat in a corner of the kitchen, his back pressed into the angle made by two walls, his arms around bent knees. He hadn't said anything since an outburst hours ago, before the police had arrived when, after they had looked the house over, they had come at last to the kitchen, Ronna carrying an awakened, weepy Ivan. The memory of Kevin's words still raised goose bumps on Kim's arms.

"It was the skeleton that did it! It killed Carl down in the river, and it killed Aunt Winifred and carried

Sara away. She's in the river where its home is. I saw it! I helped Carl turn it loose. It was chained under a big tree at the edge of the river, and when we took the chain off it began to move. It had a knife in its hand. It can walk and move around, at night. It comes out only at night.''

She didn't believe him any more than her mother had, but nevertheless she was glad the day had come, and the sunshine. Though it was a weak sunshine, not carrying the warmth it usually did, as if there were a partial eclipse, it was more than welcome and made her feel different, as if the things of the night weren't really real. As if Sara weren't gone and Aunt Winifred dead. Though she knew these things were real, perhaps that was the reason the sun seemed to have lost some of its brightness.

Their mother had scolded Kevin for his wild imagination. She had seemed really angry, so much that Kevin had backed away in tears. Kim still was hurting for him. Didn't her mother remember how it felt to be a little kid? It was easier to explain the bad things by thinking up ghosts or monsters when you didn't want to think that people, big people, old people, the very ones you had to depend on, were the real reasons for all the bad things.

At the moment Kim, herself, was feeling younger and more vulnerable. She almost envied Ivan, who was concerned only with getting away from their mother's control and trying out his little legs on his own.

Kim heard another car come into the driveway. She went into the sun room and watched from a window. It was an unmarked car, but she sensed these men getting out of it were more policemen. They talked for a few minutes to men in uniforms, then they talked to Frank briefly. He led them toward the barn, through the gate and into a door at the end of the barn.

In the silence of Sara's world came the sound of footsteps in the distance, on the board floor of the barn. Her hopes rose and then fell, and she cowered in fear against the back of the chair. Aunt Winifred was coming back now to kill her. She had said she would, and Sara's fear of the cellar was transferred to a greater fear of Aunt Winifred.

All her tears had been shed, in the lost hours, the long, long time that she had been sitting in the chair, her bare legs drawn up away from the mice that ran squeaking across the floor, from the other, much larger animal that came out of a hole and looked toward her with its beady little eyes, its black nose twitching. When it had run again, back into its hole, she had thought to herself that it was afraid, too, of her; and her tears had fallen for the rodent also.

The footsteps moved and stopped, and others moved and stopped with them like echoes. In her mind she saw only Aunt Winifred, coming through the barn, going into other rooms, perhaps, before she came here, to the cellar again, to kill her.

Sara pressed against the back of the chair, her hands gripping the wooden bars, her cheek pressed against the solid part that held the bars upright. The chair leaned, tipping back suddenly, almost falling. Sara leaned instinctively the other way, righting it. One of its legs was loose and almost broken. Sara looked at the dirt floor beneath the chair as if it were made of quicksand. Terror clogged her throat. She dared not move. She dared not make a sound.

The boards above her thundered hollowly as the footsteps came nearer. She covered her face with her hands and bent almost double on the chair, her eyes tightly closed. To shut out the sound of the footsteps she moved the heels of her hands to press hard against her ears, and so there was just the thundering in her head and the darkness in her eyes.

After a long time she moved her hands, looking up in surprise. Aunt Winifred had not come down into the cellar after all. The barn was quiet again, the footsteps gone.

Kim stood behind her mother and listened to the policemen. Ivan was still trying to get away, crying when Ronna automatically pulled him back. Her face was tight and pale, and Kim could see a nerve twitching in her cheek. She nodded her head occasionally as the policeman spoke and sometimes answered with a murmured word or two.

"We have to assume that whoever murdered Winifred Childress also took the child. We found a lantern and two blankets not far from where your aunt died. Do you know what they were doing there?"

"No."

"We have searched the barn and the house the best we could. I think we're wasting our time here."

Ronna drew a long breath.

"Your—uh—husband is not here?"

"No."

"Has he been notified?"

"No, not yet."

"Is there a possibility that he could have taken the little girl? I mean, were you divorced? Sometimes a parent will kidnap his own child, as I'm sure you know."

"Oh, no, Daniel would never do that. And he certainly wouldn't—wouldn't—do the other."

"Where can he be reached?"

Ronna got up and turned to Kim. "Watch Ivan, Kim." To the policemen she said, "I'll go get the addresses. He's on the road a lot, so he's hard to reach at home. At his apartment."

Kim let Ivan crawl away. He got down on all fours and was on his way to the sun room when he noticed that his mother was leaving the kitchen and going in the other direction. He sat up and began to howl. The policeman had started to say something to Kim, but he waited until she had picked up the baby. With Ivan half crying on her shoulder and reaching toward the door that hid his mother from him, Kim tried to give her attention to the officer.

"You're the young lady who found the body? Who first went to her—your aunt."

He seemed a bit flustered, as if he weren't used to questioning anyone who was only fourteen years old.

"My brother and I found her."

"Could you tell us about it, please?"

She described as quickly and briefly as she could the circumstances of last night. One of the men was sitting at the table, a tape recorder nearby, wrinkling the tablecloth, and a pen and open pad under his hand. He looked up.

"She *spoke* to you?"

"She only said the one thing. Sara."

"Like she was trying to tell you something?"

"Yes, sir."

Ronna came back into the room and gave to the officer a sheet of notepaper with names, addresses, and phone numbers. "These are the only places I know where to reach him. His office would probably be the quickest. I was going to call his office." She added, almost to herself, "I *will* call his office, first."

The man with the tape recorder turned toward Kevin and asked, "Can you add anything to your sister's statement, son?"

Kim watched him, her breath held, wondering if he would come out with the skeleton bunk again. She was only half aware when her mother took the squirmy Ivan off her hands.

Kevin stood up, though he stayed pressed into the corner. "I just heard the groaning, that's all, and I went to get Kim, my sister."

"Did you hear any sounds other than the groans?"

"No, sir. Well—I thought I heard someone say, *help me*. I looked out the window and I saw a hand in the moonlight. Then I went after Kim, and we went down."

"So you heard nothing at all before that?"

"No."

The policeman was quiet, making notes in the book. The other man wandered over to a window and looked out. A police car started and moved out slowly along the drive, very slowly as if the driver were still searching every hiding place along the drive, every

220

clump of brown grass, every tree trunk that might conceal someone.

Just when Kim thought the questions were over, and Kevin would not tell his fears about that *thing*, he spoke up:

"Sir," he said, in a stronger, more determined voice, "have you looked in the river?"

"In the river?"

"For Sara. Maybe she's been drowned, too."

The man at the window turned and looked at Kevin. The other man asked softly, "Oh, yes, you're the little boy that was with the one that drowned last week, aren't you?"

"Yes, sir, but—"

Say no more, Kim thought vigorously as she moved nearer him, trying to stare her silent command into his eyes. *Say no more, or they'll take you away and put you in a psychiatric hospital, and you'll be gone, like Sara is gone.*

Kevin glanced at Kim and said no more. She leaned against the wall beside him, her arm touching his shoulder reassuringly.

The men were preparing to leave. The tape recorder was shut off, the notebook folded and tucked into a pocket. The pen went in beside it, clipped to the pocket edge, then the coat was pressed down into place, and all of it was hidden now: the notebook and pencil and the shoulder holster with the black-handled gun.

"We'll certainly keep you informed, Mrs. Childress. And if anything comes up, if the kids remember anything, of course you'll let us know?"

"Yes."

Ronna hung back near the wall phone, and when Kim followed the men outside Ronna had already put Ivan onto the floor again and was beginning to dial. Kim looked back at Kevin, inviting him silently to join her in going outside, but he went instead toward the hall and out of sight. He was going up to his room again. Kim respected his need to be alone and went on out to the yard by herself.

Frank's truck was in the back driveway, near the buildings, where he always parked it. He was leaning against a fender and stuffing tobacco into a pipe, as he watched the policemen get into their car and move away.

Kim had never seen Frank smoke before, and she wondered if he were like her dad, lighting up when he was nervous and otherwise trying like mad to quit. But her dad smoked cigarettes, not a pipe. She didn't suppose there was much of a difference, though.

She went toward him. She had a terrible yearning to talk to someone, to *do* something about Sara, instead of just waiting, waiting.

"What are they going to do now?" she asked.

"Well, I guess they'll have her watched for all over the country. Nowadays with these computer things, it's easy enough to send and get information in a hurry. They'll be checking the state here, and especially this end of it, for anything suspicious or unusual. The police will be looking for a little girl now, everywhere, parking lots, shopping centers, camping places. Don't you worry, they'll find her."

But he didn't look as if he believed his own words. He puffed on his pipe and frowned off toward the south, overlooking his garden as if he didn't work there anymore.

"Are you—are you going to keep working here now that Aunt Winifred is dead?"

"I wouldn't know what else to do."

Kim looked at the garden with its neat rows, its lush, green growth. The ground was still dark and damp where he had flooded it a couple of days ago from the irrigation ditch that ran along the east end. Tomatoes were beginning to ripen, and the garden pea pods were fat and full. He had already brought a basket of vegetables to the kitchen: new potatoes, garden peas, radishes, onions, lettuce, and more. There had been a big salad that night and creamed peas and potatoes. Sara had helped Aunt Winifred with the shelling of the peas. Kim had seen her standing at Aunt Winifred's knees and shelling into the large plastic bowl Aunt Winifred held in her lap. She shelled one to Aunt Winifred's dozen.

"Aunt Winifred liked Sara a lot," Kim said, mostly to herself, feeling a double piercing of pain: the loss of Sara and the lack of Aunt Winifred's love. She had come here prepared to love the aunt, and had grown to hate her instead. Now she was sorry that she had hated her. It only made her feel sad and guilty now.

"Reminded her, I expect, of her own little girl," Frank said.

"Aunt Winifred tried to protect Sara, I think," Kim said. "When Kevin and I got to her, there on the yard grass, she was still alive. And she tried to tell me something about Sara."

"Is that a fact!" Frank said, looking at Kim for the first time, removing the pipe from his mouth. "What did she say?"

"She just said, 'Sara.' She tried a couple of times before she said it. Who do you think killed her and kidnapped Sara, Uncle Frank?"

He puffed on his pipe a few more times. The smoke fogged up around his face. He was looking east again, staring at the green depths of the English walnut orchard across the highway. "I got my thoughts on it," he finally said. "But I ain't said nothing yet to the police, because I ain't thought it out too much. But I've got reason to believe that the daughter, Charlene, is back again."

Kim gasped. "But—but I thought she was dead!"

"Never was no proof of that."

"Aunt Winifred told me she was murdered, a long time ago." She hesitated, then in a lowered voice, hating to give it credence by putting it in words, she added, "She said—she said my daddy murdered her."

Frank snorted. "I shouldn't say anything bad about Miss Winifred. She was mostly good to me, all the years I've worked here, and I started when I was just a lad, thirteen years old, and she was a little girl about eight. I watched Winifred grow up and I watched that daughter of hern, too. That daughter, that Charlene. Winifred spoiled her. The grandparents spoiled her, Mr. and Mrs. Childress. But there was more than that to her. It was like she was born bad, that kid. That little boy, Daniel, used to follow her around like a puppy dog. And a few other kids from the town. They followed her and got to doing things that made all of them sick but her, that kid, that girl. They ran away. I saw Daniel sitting out on the grass, pale as a sheet, and sick to his stomach, at what that Charlene was doing. Huh! If somebody murdered her, she deserved it. But nobody did. She probably ran off with some feller."

Kim stared at Frank, hearing only part of his tumbled words, his emotional, angry words. But in her heart she felt a bit better. She hadn't for one moment believed that her daddy had killed anyone, but she had pushed it to the back of her mind where it had set up its own little network of worry and wonder.

"Why did Aunt Winifred think Daddy killed her?"

"She had to blame someone, I reckon, and Daniel was someone that was around every summer, one of Charlene's followers. They were cousins. As close, almost, as brother and sister. I suppose Winifred had to blame somebody. But there's no evidence that Charlene was done away with. She just up and left, that's what everyone thought, even the police. And now, I think maybe she's come back."

"And killed her own mother?" Kim cried in horror. "Why would she do that?"

"Charlene didn't think the way you do, young lady. There's no way you'd ever understand a person like Charlene. She's just mean, that's all. She was spawned by the devil if you ask me."

Kim thought of the dark, silent room in the barn with the occult emblems on the floor and walls. Just thinking of it chilled her, gave her the pure old creeps. She pulled her arms in against her ribs and tried to pull her very skin tighter over her bones. She thought of the bench with the old, dark stains of blood.

"Sara," she said. "What would she want with Sara?"

Frank removed his pipe from his mouth. "Hah, yeah, what?" He hesitated, and added, "I'm going to be staying around here for awhile. I'll be sleeping in my truck bed if I sleep at all. I'll go home late today, just long enough to get me a few quilts and a piller. I'll be keeping my eyes open a good part of the time."

Kim felt a bit better just knowing he would be there, as if nothing more could happen so long as Frank was keeping watch.

Something at the house drew her, a silent beckoning that caused her to turn and look at the large rear wall, the low jutting wing of the kitchen and sun room area, the roof that sloped up from it to join the tall main section. Her eyes went immediately to Kevin's bedroom window.

His face was pressed there, surrounded by the curtains he had pushed aside, as startling as a hidden face in the background of a painting. He was staring straight ahead, it seemed, not at her but beyond. At first she thought he was looking at the barn, but then she saw he was looking even beyond that. The river. It was the river that held him enthralled in a kind of terror, with the fear written so clearly on his face that he seemed a stranger now, a child who had gone mad from the fantasies in his own mind.

The sounds of the barn had settled again. The footsteps weren't coming back. Sara had to move. She had to go to the bathroom, again. The other times she'd had to go, she'd held it at first, until she couldn't hold it any longer. Then she'd gone right there in the chair and tried to clean it off with her

226

hands. She wept in disgust, her empty stomach aching and feeling sick. Her panties and pajamas had dried now, and this time she dared get off the chair. The mice scattered when she moved and disappeared into the holes in the dirt walls. Only the big rat stayed looking out his tunnel at her, nose twitching, eyes beady and black in the flickering yellow light of the lamp.

Sara hurried and climbed back on her chair. She stared at the rat and drew a long sigh of relief when it pulled back and disappeared.

She began to notice the table and the things on it. There was a plastic container near the lamp, and shadows within it looked like they might be cookies or something. There was another container just behind it, a jar, maybe. Water? Sara yearned toward it, but her hands continued to cling to the chair, afraid of leaving it, afraid to cross the floor between the chair and the table.

12

They weren't going to search the river after all. Kevin had been watching them all morning from his window. He had seen all the police cars come and the men milling around like insects, big, clothed, black beetles that were like characters from books for little kids, characters who wore clothes and carried things like sticks, cameras, and other things he couldn't identify because of the distance and the curtains he looked through to keep from being seen by them. He had seen them stand around and look down at Aunt Winifred on the ground, and he had seen them put a rope fence around a big area, as if they were making a room around her. They hadn't even changed her position. She looked so uncomfortable, sprawled face down, with one arm stretched out and the other bent, with one leg pulled up as if she were trying to get up. They should have straightened her out, made her more comfortable on the grass, but they didn't.

He should have done it himself, he thought, when he was down there with Kim. Before she died. He should have helped her stretch out and be comfortable on the grass.

He should have talked to her, found out about Sara.

But of course he didn't have to do that, because he knew about Sara. He knew where Sara was. And all day, after the policemen left, he had watched the river for signs of a search down there, but there was none.

They had stayed a long time, the policemen had. They had taken pictures, from every angle, pointing the cameras at Aunt Winifred in her awkward position, with her dress torn from her back with the blood dried and turning black. It was a bad, bad thing to do.

Aunt Winifred hadn't been a very nice person most of the time, but still it was a bad thing to do to her.

Finally, an ambulance had come, after the sun had shined on Winifred for a long time. The men from the ambulance had wrapped her up in a black thing, like wrapping up leftovers at the table to put into the freezer, and had taken her away. The rope was left there, hoisted up from the ground a couple of feet on little posts, circling the spot where she had lain, and blocking off part of the cement walk that went past the hen house and down the hedge to the driveway.

All the policemen had left, finally, and nobody was there but Frank and his old red truck. Then Kim had gone out and talked to him. He couldn't hear their voices. The house was big and silent around him, closing him away from them and the whole world but leaving him a narrow view of them, the barn, and the dark and rolling river that he could glimpse in slices beyond the trees that lined it, like slices of a nightmare that didn't quite join.

The house seemed even bigger and emptier now that Sara was gone.

He hadn't seen Sara much since they had come to this big house, but he remembered things from their other life back in the apartment. Things he was sorry about now.

He remembered when she was born. He had had a big birthday party, and he was three years old. He was the baby in the family and everybody paid a lot of attention to him. His mom and dad, and his big sister, Kim. They had gone to McDonald's for the birthday party, and there were special treats and hats to wear and funny horns that blew streamers of papers that tickled. His mama had a big belly, and he had been told there was going to be a little baby, soon, but he hadn't really expected what happened. They, his mom and dad, had even told him the baby might come on his birthday.

Before he went to sleep that night he listened for the baby, but it hadn't come yet. He was a little disappointed that it hadn't come.

Then one day his mama went to the hospital, and a babysitter came to stay with him and his sister. He remembered her well, because she had made him be quiet while she watched a soap opera on television in the middle of the day. Kim was gone to school, and for the first time in his life he had gotten afraid. He was at home, yet he felt as if he were in a strange place, surrounded by strangers who didn't even know he was there. He had crawled under the bed to cry in the darkness against the wall, and he had gone to sleep there.

The babysitter never came back again.

His mama came home, and his daddy, too, and they were carrying the little baby. It was all smothered in blankets, and they let him hold her. She was sleeping the whole time.

It wasn't much fun having a new baby sister. She cried at night and woke him up. And during the day it seemed that every time he wanted his mother to hold him, she was already holding the baby.

Then the baby got big enough to move around on the floor and play with the toys. When he objected, so did his mother. But his mother was always after him, not the baby "Leave her alone. Let her play, too, Kevin. Kevin!" It was always him, not her, who was getting scolded, and so sometimes, when their mother wasn't looking, he shoved the baby over. He got a kick out of hearing her cry, sometimes, even though he usually got in trouble for it.

Then she began to walk and was even easier to topple over. All he had to do was run past her, brush her shoulder or arm lightly, and over she'd go. He'd have to run on in a hurry and make sure he was already in the hall, or the bedroom, or living room, when Mom caught up with him. He learned to look at her with blank eyes and say he hadn't even been close to Sara.

It was about then that she developed a name. First she was just the baby, then she became Sara. And there were times when he liked her. When somebody else made her cry, for instance, it made him mad, and he'd put his arms around her and comfort her the best he could.

It was one thing when he made her cry, but something else entirely when somebody else did.

She stopped trying to play with his toys when she was about three years old. She got more interested in her dolls, in the toys that were given to her. His monsters and guns and cars didn't interest her much. She stayed to herself a lot, too. And maybe the reason she did was because he had always shoved her around when no one was looking.

He was sorry now. It hurt to remember. He wished he had her back again.

He was going to get her back, too, as soon as he could. He'd go get her himself, since no one else was trying to find her.

They had searched the river for Carl's body; why did they not search for Sara's?

If they had looked for her today, before night fell, she might still be alive.

It was important to look before dark.

The sun was lowering in the west, going down behind the row of hills that edged the valley on the west, getting huge and orange, like a Halloween pumpkin. The tops of the trees at the river began to grow up into the sun, cutting large, dark chunks out of it.

Kim left Frank alone in the yard, and he got up into the back of his truck and began to move things around. There was a spare tire that he propped up on edge and fastened against the pickup bed. There were other things, tools and things, that he put in the tire or beside it.

Kevin waited, watching him.

Would he be able to sneak past without being seen?

He had to make sure he wouldn't be seen, for if he

were, he would be stopped. They were all against him now, against him and Sara. It was like they didn't really want to find her. If they had, they would have looked in the river.

As the day waned he heard Ivan crying somewhere faraway. Then he hushed, and Kevin knew that someone had come up to the nursery and gotten him.

He hadn't minded having Ivan born the way he had Sara. And that was another reason to be sorry that he hadn't been nicer to Sara.

When he got her back, he'd share all his things with her. He didn't have many toys left. They had been sold when they moved. But the few he was able to bring along—his robots and monsters—he'd share with her. He'd give them all to her, if she wanted them.

His door opened suddenly, unexpectedly. He pulled a curtain across his face, so that whoever came into the room would think he was gone and would go away.

"Kevin," Kim said. "Come on down to supper now."

Shhh. Quiet. Let her go away.

"Kevin, why are you hiding?"

She was seeing him, after all. Why did she enter his room without knocking? It wasn't fair. It didn't give him a chance to refuse to let her in.

He'd have to make them think that he wasn't going to search for Sara.

He pushed the curtain aside and stood up. Kim was staring at him in a strange way, and he avoided looking into her eyes. He walked past her and into the hall. It was almost dark here, like a tunnel that had no end, that got darker and darker as you went along it.

Kim walked beside him, and before they reached the stairways down, where light came in once more from the windows and open front door, she said, "Daddy's coming."

He felt no stirring of interest. It was like their daddy was gone forever and had become nothing but a name now. But he had to show some interest, because that was what she expected.

"When?" His voice sounded unnatural to his own ears. It was deeper and gruffer, as if he were changing from a little boy to something else.

"He's flying in from Chicago to Chico, and then he's renting a car to come on up here. So that Mama won't have to go after him. He'll get here sometime tomorrow. He called from a town in Missouri. The police had found him and told him about Sara being kidnapped and Aunt Winifred murdered. So he called Mama and told her he'd get here as soon as he could."

Shhh. Don't tell her where Sara is, because she doesn't believe you.

Their supper was a simple one, not like the kind Aunt Winifred and Mama had cooked before Aunt Winifred died. There was some fruit and cold cuts, and he tried to eat a sandwich, but it was like river weed in his throat.

While they were at the table his mother reached up and pulled on the light that hung over the table, and he grew ever more anxious, for the sun was going down and night would soon fall, and it would be too late to hunt for Sara.

He edged away from the table and went sideways toward the back door, keeping his eyes on his sister and mother. Ivan didn't count. Ivan didn't care what he was doing or where he was going.

He reached the door, finally, and pushed open the screen. His mother looked up, for the screen door made a sound, its spring stretching metallically.

"Are you going outside?" she asked.

"Yes."

She nodded, giving her attention again to the baby.

She looked funny, odd, like a stranger. For the first time in his life he noticed things about her: the way her eyebrows grew like bars over her eyes and the lump of a frown that was raised between them. Her eyes were smoky dark, shadowed, and looking faraway even as she took care of the baby in his high chair. The baby picked up his little bowl, leaned over and deliberately dropped it on the floor. Garden peas rolled everywhere, but their mother only bent down and began to pick it all up without really coming back, as if her spirit were gone.

Kim went into the utility room and got a broom and dustpan and began to sweep up the peas. It was the first time Kevin had noticed that Ivan had gotten peas for his supper, while the rest of them ate cold cuts.

Kevin slipped through the narrow opening that he allowed himself at the door. He looked back through the screen, peering through at the people in the kitchen, hidden by the fine wires between them. They weren't looking at him. His mother turned, as if she might glance up, and he jerked back out of sight and stood with his back pressed against the brick of the outside wall.

He waited, but no one called. He wouldn't have answered even if they had.

Ivan gave an abrupt scream, the kind that meant he wanted something, and the bowl went slamming against the floor again and rolled, as if it were alive and trying to get away from the monster baby. The baby's mother said something, and the sister replied, fetched up the bowl from the floor and took it screaming silently back to the little monster in the chair. Kevin heard it all and felt a strange kinship to the bowl. Then he slipped away, going in the direction of the setting sun.

He skimmed by the rope that was still hanging on its stakes surrounding the grounds where Aunt Winifred's blood had drained. He paused, seeing something there, half in the shadows and half out, something small and moving in the black seepage of blood. He stared. A wasp, he saw then, its wings rising and lowering slowly as it drank. The black kind of wasp that lived with hundreds of others in the peak of the barn at a nest that swarmed with their black bodies. Wasps that dipped toward his head and threatened with angry buzzing. Now one of them sat drinking Aunt Winifred's blood. Kevin backed away, turned and ran.

He ran along the fence, past post after post, all the way to the end of it. He wouldn't go through the barn lot. There was too much emptiness there, too much of a chance at being seen. He ran bent over, becoming part of the tall, brown weeds that grew in patches along the fence. Sometimes he threw a glance at the house. The light from the kitchen was beginning to splay out over the terrace, making long, pale bodies that reached toward the potted plants at the edge of the terrace. Light separating from dark. Ahead of him the sun had gone down, leaving a streak of red in the sky and sucking away the light from under the trees.

There were sounds: a car on the highway, a bird calling, the river moving in its banks. It was a softer, fainter sound, but he heard it in his head as if he were closely entwined with it.

The truck that was suddenly coming down the driveway past the house was more felt than heard. The ground beneath his feet vibrated faintly, and headlights swept his way without warning. Kevin ducked into the tall weeds at the end of the fence just in time.

Frank parked the truck and got out of the cab, pushing the door back. It made a long, metallic squeak. Kevin could feel Frank walking on the ground then as he went back and forth between the cab and the bed of the truck. The lights went out. The door slammed. In the silence the crickets chirped as if the noises had not disturbed them at all.

Kevin lifted himself slowly, pushing up with the palms of his hands, and peered over the weed heads. Frank was leaning against the front fender, looking toward the barn. He was sucking on a pipe, lighting it with a match flame that almost disappeared into the bowl of the pipe every time Frank sucked in.

Kevin swiveled his head and looked at the barn. The sunlight was still rosy on the tall, sharp roof peak and on the higher boards at the end. The old red paint looked almost as bright as new blood, not like

238

the ground now where Aunt Winifred had lain.

He ducked down again and began to crawl through the weeds, down the south end of the fence that made a large square around the barn lot. It seemed a long way to the river, and by now, hidden from the house by the other outbuildings and the trees, he could have stood up and run. But since Frank had come back, he had to keep down.

He raised up once more when he was several yards into the field and looked back. But now even Frank was out of view, hidden behind a tree that Kevin hadn't noticed before and the pig pen with its hovering fig tree.

Kevin stood up and ran through the weeds to the murmuring call of the river. He broke into the deep shadows beneath the trees and stopped. Beyond the tree trunks the river caught the last rays of light and held it like a wide, long ribbon that moved and writhed and sighed and murmured. Somewhere here was Sara, somewhere among the brush that grew in places to the river's edge, or in the trees, or maybe even in the water, waiting for him to help her out. He had to hurry before the dark fell and *it* came up from its lair beneath the tree.

He stumbled over a low bush almost into the river. The ground beneath his bare feet was cool and damp and slippery, as if the water had recently splashed upon it. He caught himself from falling by grabbing the bush.

"Sara!"

He listened and thought he heard her answer, and called again: "Sara! Sara! Sara!"

There. He heard it. Upstream. The darkness

beneath the trees was deeper now, but it didn't stop him. The light reflected from the surface of the river guided him, and the bushes he grasped kept him from losing balance and falling. *There*. Again he heard it, an answer, a call. Deeper than Sara's voice had been, but now she was scared, and he could feel her fear when she cried out so deeply and hoarsely.

"Sara, I'm coming. Sara, where are you?"

He dodged around a tree trunk, and the sound he had followed was gone. He stopped, gasping for breath, trying to penetrate what light was left with his eyes, listening with all his being for her to call him again.

Then it came, once, hesitantly, and again, and again, faster, faster, croak, croak, croak.

"Sara," he cried, and the croaking stopped, and a splash followed as a frog jumped into the water. A long, dark, silent body slipping away, taking with it the call that had sounded to him like Sara calling.

He turned back the way he had come, listening, listening, looking, searching. Behind him more frogs began to call: low, hoarse, medium, high, croaking, croaking, as he moved away from their territory. Ahead of them they hushed as he grew near. In the deepening night they were coming alive, singing their songs, calling their mates. Splashes ahead of him as he approached signaled their slipping into the water. He no longer listened to them or jumped when they splashed close by. His hearing went beyond them, beyond the sounds of the river, beyond the rustling of the wind in the tops of the trees. He began calling again.

"*Sara!*"

He came to a wider part of the river where the trees fell away and a sandbar came up to a bare spot that joined a narrow road that went off across a grape vineyard. He waded into the water and felt it curling cold and dark around his ankles.

"Sara!"

Upstream a treetop reached up against a sky that was beginning to show a few scattered stars. It was the tree whose roots bound the lair of the thing that had carried Sara away. Now he knew he would have to go there to get Sara. If she had been hiding in the bushes along the river she would have answered him. She couldn't answer because there was water all around her, holding her, filling her mouth. He had to get her before she drowned.

He ran back along the bank, the ground slippery beneath his wet feet, the sand gathering around his ankles, clinging, itching. His fingers reached down to scratch it away. His other hand reached out to push slashing branches out of his way. Darkness hid his progress through the underbrush. He stepped on something that writhed and slithered silently away, but he hardly noticed. Now that he knew for sure where Sara was he had to hurry. He had wasted too much time going up and down the riverbank. He should have gone straight to the tree while it was still light enough for him to see in the water. Now he would have to feel for her among the roots and the mud and the cold water.

He came to the tree at last. He could tell it was the right tree because its trunk was so big and so ghostly pale in the darkness. The light that was still captured by the surface of the river reflected back up its trunk for several feet where it leaned over the water.

He remembered that he was still wearing his clothes only after he had sat down on the bank and slid into the water. The cold came up around his ankles, his knees, then his hips, and he felt his pants grow heavy with the water. But it was too late to pull himself out and strip. His hands grasped the root that Carl's hands had held. He let himself down into the darkness of the water and felt it flow over his head and lie against his face like a huge blanket that shut out all air. He held his breath and lengthened his arms, unbending the elbows, and felt the water chill them and crawl toward his wrists. He let go of the root that was above waterline. He reached downward with his feet for the muddy bottom, but the water seemed swifter now, and his body was gently eased sideways. It didn't matter. He began to swim, inward, beneath the bank and the tree. He reached out, feeling for the smooth arm or leg of Sara, feeling for her face, her long, floating hair. He opened his mouth to call her name and water rushed into his mouth.

His reaching hands touched something. His fingers lost it, reached out, grasped it again. It was cold and smooth and thin. *Sara's wrist.* Sara's fingers reaching for his?

No. Only part of the roots.

His fingers entangled them. He used them to pull himself deeper among them, into its very lair where first he and Carl had found it. He felt among the roots for Sara, and his fingers touched something that moved away. He grabbed for it and found the chain again. He turned, swimming to the right, and once

242

again his fingers touched something, thin, cold, hard. Not Sara. It was too thin, too hard. There was no softness of flesh, no lingering warmth. But it wasn't a root this time, for suddenly it was wrenching violently, jerking him, loosening his hold on it.

He was not afraid. He was filled with a desperate mission, a cunning that was beyond it, for he knew he had come to its place of hiding, and he had grasped its leg, or its arm, and he was going to hold to it and show it that he was no longer afraid.

He reached out again, and his hand went into an opening that felt like bars, a rounded, small prison. His fingers closed around two of the bars, and as the thing again wrenched violently, the bars came away in his hand. He released them to drift away in the water.

But now he needed to breathe. His need for air was overpowering, the most important thing. He had to reach for the surface, and then, with air in his lungs again, he would come back.

He swam upward, and then suddenly, just before his face reached air, something jerked him back. He felt long, bony fingers cover his face and push him down, down into the mud in the bottom of the river.

13

"Where's Kevin?" Ronna asked, looking around the kitchen as if she had just come out of a dream. She had cleaned the floor, mopped the entire floor from the kitchen stove to the utility room door, even though Ivan had made a noticeable mess only under his chair; then she had turned around and brought him ice cream and spoon-fed him for a very long time. Kim had wandered around in the kitchen during the whole time, sometimes trying to help with the cleaning, sometimes just sitting. Then, seeing that the ice cream was not really appealing but something to do, she had slowly downed not only one dish but two.

The hour of dinnertime had passed, and then another hour, and still they were alone. The phone did not ring bringing news of Sara; and the back door did not open bringing Daniel. Of course she didn't really expect Daniel for another day or two.

Kim looked around the large kitchen, too, as if she might find Kevin sitting in a corner again. She said,

"I don't know. Probably up in his room," she added. "Would you go up and see, please?"

Ronna took Ivan out of his chair for the third time. This time she put him down on the floor. On hands and knees he went in a hurry for the open door of the utility room. Ronna sat with a long sigh and simply watched him. He had disappeared through the door before she got up to follow him.

In the utility room, in the cabinet doors which he loved to open, were all kinds of no-nos, Kim was thinking as she left the kitchen. The bleaches and cleansers. There also were mops and brushes and dustpans here and there in the room: Ivan's favorite playthings. Kim had seen him playing with the brushes on days when Ronna was doing laundry. But now Ronna brought him out and closed the door. Kim could still hear him crying when she was almost to the front stairs.

She turned on the lights as she went, but only the lights that Aunt Winifred would have turned on. The hall was long and dimly lighted and very quiet when Ivan's cries were finally left behind. Kim climbed the stairs in silence.

When she came to Sara's room she paused. The dim light from the hallway barely made a track in the darkness of the room, but she could see the soft pink of the bedspread pulled up so neatly over the narrow bed and the matching draperies on the closed window. She pulled the door shut softly, as if putting a kind of finality on life. She couldn't bear looking at the room where Sara had slept. Although she had just been there a little while, the room was Sara. Sara's personality was stamped on the room indelibly. It was so much like Sara: pretty, pink and white, and small.

Kim thought of the other room, Charlene's room. It was pink and white, too. She wondered if Charlene had decorated this room, but knew, of course, that she hadn't. This room was much older. The pink had faded, the outer gathers in the spread and drapery a duller, lighter color than the inner gathers. As if it were two-toned. Kim thought it must have been that way for a long, long time.

She went on down the hall to the end. The door to the dark, steep stairs was standing slightly open and she paused, very much aware of the darkness there. She closed that door also, easing it shut as silently as she had Sara's door.

She looked into Kevin's room and wasn't surprised that no light burned there. He had been staying in the dark a lot, sitting at the window, staring out, looking for something that didn't exist. Poor Kevin.

She leaned in and looked, using only the light that filtered down from the bulb at the far end of the hallway. She could see the window and saw that he was not there, not even hiding behind the drapes as he had been when she came up after him before dinner. Nor was he in any of the corners, for they seemed lighter in contrast to the figured drapes and were obviously empty. But the bed, mussed, rumpled, the blanket and bedspread in a roll in the center, looked occupied after a moment of staring. He was well covered there. He had come up and gone to bed without saying good night, but that wasn't surprising. He was acting so odd. But of course, everyone was, in a way.

"Kevin?" she said it softly, wanting an answer, an affirmation that he was really there, and yet not wanting to wake him.

When he didn't answer she remained for a few more moments in the doorway, looking at the hump of bedding. But she felt strongly that he was there, curled into a little heap in the middle of the bedding, sleeping with his head covered as he often did; and at last she drew away and closed his door, again softly and slowly to avoid disturbing him.

When she returned to the kitchen she went hurriedly, wanting to get out of the unending silence of the heart of the house. Sometimes she enjoyed wandering about the many rooms and sometimes she was frightened by them. She came into the bright kitchen with an audible sigh of relief.

Ivan was still on the floor, heading now for the sun room, even though a light had not been turned on there and Ronna was following slowly behind. She looked at Kim expectantly.

"He's sleeping," Kim said. "I didn't disturb him."

Ronna nodded. "Good." She caught Ivan just as he reached the door to the sun room and turned him around. He started to scream his frustration when he realized he was free again. This time he went for the nearest cabinet doors, sat back and pulled them open. Ronna added, "Maybe I should have given him an aspirin, or acetaminophen, to keep his fever down. I didn't check it again this evening, did I? I don't think I did. Maybe I should go up and see if he still has a fever. Watch Ivan, will you, Kim?"

Ivan was pulling pots and pans out of the cabinet, and Kim started to pull him away and return the utensils to their proper places when Ronna stopped her.

"Let him play with them. It won't hurt anything."

Kim backed off and sat down at the table.

Ronna paused in the doorway. "Maybe I shouldn't disturb him. If he's sleeping, he might get more benefit from that."

Kim said nothing. Ronna had been talking mainly to herself.

After a longer hesitation she came back and sat at the table, too, staring at the wall behind Kim, clasping her hands and unclasping them. Sometimes she looked at the phone. But she said nothing. There was only the noise of Ivan with the pots and pans.

Kim got up after a long while and went to the door. She could see the outline of the truck bed of Frank's pickup beyond the hen house and the trees, but that was all.

"Frank is going to stay all night," she said. "He's going to stay awake and watch."

"Watch? What for?"

Kim didn't know what to answer. Somehow it didn't seem appropriate to tell Frank's suspicions about Charlene, even to her mother; as if she knew in her heart that he was wrong. Why would Charlene run away and stay all these years and then come back and kidnap Sara? It wasn't logical. There was no reason. Charlene didn't even know Sara.

But then kidnappers usually didn't know their victims, did they? That is—sometimes they didn't.

Still, back to Charlene: It seemed more right to Kim that Charlene had probably been murdered a long time ago. But not by Daniel. Not by her daddy.

249

But if Charlene had not been killed, why would she have stayed away so long? And when she came back, why would she kill her mother and kidnap Sara?

Frank's theories seemed almost as ridiculous as Kevin's.

She got around at last to answering Ronna. "He's just watching," she said. "To make sure the kidnapper doesn't come back."

Ronna made a sound that was almost a snort of derision. "Why on earth would he come back? That's the least of my worries." She added vehemently, "I wish he would. I just wish he would!"

"Do you think it was a man?"

"Well, of course I think it was a man."

There, Kim thought. Even her mother would never consider Frank's theory as being correct. She was glad she hadn't told her. "But I'm glad he's here, aren't you? I mean until Daddy gets here."

"Yes, I guess I am. I think I might go upstairs and rest better just knowing that someone is outside. Someone we can trust."

It was past Ivan's bedtime. He paused occasionally, rubbed his eyes and whimpered. And after a few more minutes he crawled to Ronna's knees and began to whimper in earnest. Ronna picked him up.

"It's time to go upstairs," she said. "There's no reason to keep waiting here, I guess. If the phone rings at night—I don't know if there's a phone upstairs, do you, Kim?"

"No."

"Well, he probably won't call anyway, again. He'll probably just drive in. There isn't much chance he'll get here tonight. He said tomorrow. Maybe you

250

should go on to your room and try to sleep, Kim. Sleep is restorative."

"Can't I wait awhile?"

"Of course. But I think I'll go to my room. Ivan is ready to go to bed."

Kim heard her mother and baby brother leave the room. She stood looking out the screen door into the darkness, and then she remembered the lights beside the walk, and she almost turned them on. She hesitated, her fingers on the switch, something keeping her from lighting up the back yard. After a few minutes she stepped away from the door, leaving the back yard dark and the door open.

She turned out the light when she left the kitchen.

Milton Phillips sat in the old swivel chair with the cracked leather arms in the small office of his service station. He was leaning back, newspaper wide open in his hands, his feet on the desk. The electric clock on the wall indicated the time was approaching eleven, and he had closed the station at seven, but there was nothing special to go home for. His wife had gone to visit relatives in Washington and wouldn't be home for another two or three days. The house without her was too empty and quiet. He'd go home when he got sleepy. Last night he had gone home around nine, after eating dinner in a cafe out on the highway. But tonight he was reading the newspaper account of the murder of Winifred Childress and the kidnapping of a little girl, Sara, age six. Sara Childress, grandniece of Winifred. Daniel's daughter. There was a picture of the little girl, and she had the face of an angel. Of course, most six-year-olds do, Milton thought. The changes came in later years. Noses grew, chins lengthened, jaws broadened. Sometimes the face stayed like the face of an angel, and sometimes it didn't. In his observation the girl was just as well off if it didn't. Girls who were too pretty had trouble. Maybe it was because they expected too much of life. So sometimes their beauty paid off, and sometimes it didn't. He'd known more than one girl who'd ended up in worse circumstances than her plainer sisters.

No clues, no trace of the little girl, Sara. The newspaper didn't say much about it, but the people who had come by the station had picked up information from various parts of the law that had been out there, and the consensus seemed to be that there was nothing much to go on yet. The woman had been slashed and stabbed a number of times, a really brutal undertaking, and left lying on the grass. The little girl was simply gone. No one even had any good ideas. Of course there were no tracks, either of killer or car. But there wouldn't be. The driveway was mostly blacktop pavement, and the ground was dry.

Milton lowered the paper and stared at the wall. His memory returned to another little Childress girl who'd had the face of an angel. Her eyes had been large and blue, as clear and unblemished as the sky from the top of Mount Shasta. Charlene. They had started school together at age six, though he thought she was a few months younger than he. He had fallen in love, as much as a six-year-old can. Charlene had worn the prettiest dresses of all the girls in school: full skirts that stood out over ruffled petticoats, shoes

252

and anklets that matched. Her hair was long and the color of a brand new penny. She left all the other girls in the class looking colorless. For years he thought the only color of hair that was pretty was copper red, with all the gold highlights. He could still remember how it looked in the sunshine, as if it were on fire. He had marveled at it then, until that day when they were nine years old and he had been invited to go home with her. After that he had seen her hair in a different light. It still looked like it was on fire, but— even now, thinking back, he was chilled and sickened. He had tried to put it all out of his mind. Nightmares during his teenage years had brought it back time after time, and now, remembering, he felt them returning.

There had been five of them going home from school with Charlene that day. She led the way down the road out of town, holding her head high. They trailed behind her like the subjects of a queen. He didn't know how many times the other four kids had been invited home to play with Charlene, but this was his first time.

He hardly ever saw her during the summer. He lived with his mother, dad, sister, and brother on the other side of town, on a farm, and didn't get to town very often. But once or twice he had been in town and seen Charlene with a boy about his own age. Some of the other kids had told him the boy was Daniel Childress, Charlene's cousin, and that he spent the whole summer with her. His envy of Daniel began when he heard that and was revived again many years later when they were teenagers and he came more in contact with Daniel; when he had managed to successfully put out of his mind that day in Charlene's barn.

When they first arrived at the Childress house, they went into the kitchen through the back door and stood around bashful and quiet while her mother gave them cupcakes and punch. When that was finished they went out to play.

There was a swing set in the back yard, but Charlene lost patience with him and another little boy when they stopped to play on the monkey bars. She put her hands on her waist and frowned at them and told them to come on. The other kids, three girls, stood meekly behind her.

So they followed Charlene. She took them through a gate into the barn lot. A couple of calves were in a pen there and watched them go by. Then they went into the barn: a big, dim, very interesting looking place, with rooms of harnesses, tools, and stuff he would have given all his marbles to look at. But Charlene led them on to a strange room in the central part of the barn, a small room with a bench against the wall and symbols painted on the floor and wall above the bench. She said it was her church, and the bench her altar. Then she made them all sit in a semicircle and told them to wait. She left and came back later, in just a couple of minutes, with a kitten. It was, she explained, their sacrifice to the master, the devil. And they, Milton and the other children, were to be initiated into the Devil's Club of which she was the high priestess. The devil had spoken to her, she said, and told her to bring these special children into the club.

From there on he couldn't bear the memory. The

little girls were crying, but all had sat still until he began to fight Charlene for the life of the kitten. It was too late for the poor little thing, but it wasn't too late for him. He ran, like the other kids. Like most of the other kids. Two of the girls, he remembered, were still in the room, standing against the wall, crying quietly, their hands to their faces, when he burst out of the room on the heels of the other boy.

But Charlene was swift and strong, almost as if she really were imbued with special strengths and powers, as she had said she was. She caught him and spun him back around to face her. And the face he had loved and thought so beautiful was still beautiful but stiffened with anger, the clear blue eyes revealing something now in their depths that chilled him to the bone. She literally hissed in his face, spewing him with tiny specks of saliva. "Don't you ever tell, or I'll kill you. The devil will come and torment you from now on. Don't you ever tell. If you do, I'll know, and I'll come after you."

He wrenched away from her. And her predictions came true, in a sense, for he was tormented, for years afterward, dreaming about it against his will. Seeing her face in hideous cruelty, watching her again and again make the so-called sacrifice. But, as with most of the other kids, he hadn't told. It was as though once he was away from the barn, from Charlene, he had simply tried so hard to put it out of his mind, to pretend to himself it hadn't happened, that it came back only in his dreams to haunt him.

He was never again friends with any of the other kids. Nor they with him. If any of them became members of her club, he didn't know of it and didn't want to know. One of the girls had drowned a few months later, and now he wondered about it. Perhaps the girl had become a member and then tried to pull out or something. Perhaps she had told someone, and Charlene had drowned her. And maybe that was just an old fear revived that made him think such a thing.

Anyway, after Charlene's disappearance, long after, he had finally told. He had told his wife, who had never met Charlene Childress. Why he even told Amy about it was a mystery to him now, for he had been probably thirty years old at the time. He had never talked about it before, and he hadn't talked about it since.

There was something oddly similar about the two disappearances though, as if in some way they were tied together. Yet how could that be? Charlene had been gone for more years than he knew, off hand, and long presumed dead. The rumor around town when she disappeared though, was that she had run off. Maybe she had. Maybe she was still alive, somewhere. But still, there was something odd about its happening twice in the family, even though this little girl certainly did not go off on her own.

There was a sudden thump against the wall at his back, and then another sound, as if something were being dragged a couple of feet along the wall.

Milton sat forward, dropping his feet silently to the floor, his heart beginning to pound. Burglars? They wouldn't know he was here. The little back office had no window, and the light would show nowhere, unless it showed under the door. The front of the station had its usual light on, burning solitarily in the ceiling night after night.

There was silence now. The town had gone to bed. There was no traffic, no one out walking at this time of night. Not even a dog barking.

Milton heard himself breathing, taking long, deep breaths, then quick, shallow, open-mouthed gasps. What was wrong with him? It was probably a stray dog out there right now, and he had probably just knocked something over.

The knob on the back door made a soft, barely audible sound, and Milton stared at it, watching it turn slowly to the left as far as it would go and then reverse and turn to the right.

It was locked. He always kept it locked.

The knob slipped back to its former position and stopped.

No dog, not trying to open his back door.

Ha. Funny.

Some kid, no doubt. Thinking he'd get in and take some candy bars and pop and whatever spare change there might be in the cash register. And there was spare change. Milton took out the bigger bills, but sometimes he even left a pile of ones and fives in the cash register. He had gotten complacent over the years. The one burglary he'd had took only tires. Whoever it was hadn't even bothered the cash register. Kids, he thought, who needed a couple of new tires for their car.

He ought to get up, open the door, and surprise whoever it was out there. He tried to visualize a face, a young, smooth face that was just beginning to grow some fuzz, but it wouldn't come true. He couldn't even come up with a body. And the fear he was feeling just wouldn't go away. It was too intense. The first surprise was building, his heart making him feel weak with its pounding. His muscles were tense and aching, and his fingers gripped the arms of the chair as if his life were ebbing away.

Go away, just go away. That was all he asked. Just do your thing and go away. Don't try to open this door.

He half expected an ax, or something of equal strength, to shatter the wood of the door; but all was silent now. He sat tense in his chair and waited, listening for sounds beyond the sounds of his own body. There was nothing.

It began to seem like a standoff. It was still out there, he could feel it. Whoever it was hadn't given up yet. But perhaps they saw the light under the door and knew someone was still in the office. Maybe they had settled down under the trees at the back of the lot to wait for Milton to leave.

Of course, of course! His pickup truck was sitting out in the driveway beside the station, just as it always was. There was no way the visitor would think he was gone when his automobile was still there.

That made it even worse. Whoever had tried to open the door knew that Milton was in there all the time.

Now he felt trapped. If he went out the front, as he always did, through the lighted front office with the glass around the front and sides, he would be in full view of the guy in the shadows behind the station. When he crossed the short distance to his truck he would be in the light from the front office, and in full view for whatever the guy wanted to do.

There was one way out of this dilemma. He could get up, go whistling out through the front, go to his pickup without even looking toward the back of the station, get in his truck—*lock the goddamned door*—and take off. And let the burglar tear the place down, if he had a mind to.

He could call the police from down the street.

He could drive right to the police station, which was in a corner of the city hall, and since the murder and kidnapping yesterday, he might even find someone in. The town marshal, at least. The sheriff and all his deputies were in another town a few miles away. He could drive there, if he took a notion. Or he could go home, take a cold shower, eat a snack and try to get some sleep.

He could reach out to the black hunk of telephone on his desk, he realized belatedly, call the police and tell them there was a prowler behind his station. But when he leaned forward in his chair it squeaked, like a gunshot, and he paused, arm in midair, chair poised. It was the first time he had ever noticed that his chair squeaked like that. He sat still, drew his arm back slowly. There was no sound at all, and there had been no sound for quite awhile. Maybe whoever it was had realized, also belatedly, after he tried the locked door, that the owner of the pickup was still in there somewhere, and so he had snuck away in the night just as he had arrived.

Minutes passed. The little digital clock on the desk flicked silently from one set of numbers to the next, and Milton's heart and nerves settled down.

He'd just go, he decided, after fifteen minutes of listening and hearing nothing. Now he could just get up, let his chair squeak, and go out the front, locking the door behind him as he always did. He was ashamed that he had nearly panicked over a sound and the turning of his doorknob. That was one experience he'd certainly never tell anyone. Not even his understanding wife.

When he went through the glass-walled, brightly lit front office, he felt only slightly more vulnerable than usual. He didn't look out toward the shadows that hovered just beyond the light. He opened the door, stood on the step outside and locked it as usual. He walked around the cement pathway that edged the building, just as usual, toward his pickup that was half illuminated by the light from the office, but he added a little something: a whistle, tuneless and not very loud.

He started to get into his pickup. With the door open and one foot poised for the step up, he raised his eyes and looked into the shadows at the back of the small building and froze in horror.

It stood in the shadows at the corner of the building facing toward him. The bones of its body seemed to glow faintly. The large sockets where the eyes had been were black; the triangular nostril was black, but the teeth looked large, white and glowing in its perpetual grin. The ribs stuck out, ballooning above the column of the spine that was attached to the pelvic bones, but still it looked slightly lopsided. Then he saw, remembering from his days in biology class, that part of the ribs was gone. Two of them at least. The skeleton stood at the corner of the building, its right arm raised as if supporting itself there.

After his first shock, Milton grew suddenly and irrationally angry. Some dumb, suckin', bastard kids had stolen the school's skeleton and were holding it up at the back of his place just to scare him. The little sons-a-bitches didn't have anything better to do and had been given this idea by the recent murder, probably.

"All right," he yelled as he stepped around the door of his pickup and headed toward the skeleton. "All right, you little bastards, what do you think you're doing?"

If it had been Halloween he might have been able to laugh. If it had been any time of year but tonight.

"All right, come out of—"

He stopped, perhaps six feet to the side of the skeleton at the corner of the building. He hadn't been looking at it; he'd been looking for the shadowy figures of the kids who were hunched somewhere within reach of the skeleton, but he had a distinct feeling that the skeleton had turned its head. And he could see now that its head was turned. It had kept pace with him, and although he now stood at a forty degree angle to the skeleton's left, its face still looked directly at him.

The hideous grin was unnerving. He felt a faint shiver, cold and snaky, start on his thighs and move upward, raising the hair as it went. He tore his stare away from the skeleton's face. If the kids could drag it over here without losing more than two of its ribs, then they probably had rigged up a way to turn its head.

He looked for the bulk of their shadows at the corner of the building, just around the corner, within

261

reach of the door whose knob had turned. He thought he saw one, hunched down low, but then he remembered there was a small shrub there. So there was no one there? His eyes were adjusting to the darkness, and the shadows lay in degrees of deep black to deep gray, and he could see the shrubs, the back of the building, and the tree limbs that didn't quite touch it. How were they controlling the skeleton? They must have gone to great efforts to rig it up there at the corner, with strings attached to it which reached back into the impenetrable shadows beneath the trees.

"All right, you kids," he said, but his voice was losing its conviction. He was beginning to wish he had just gotten into the pickup and gone on, and spoiled their little joke by not responding to it at all. He wished he'd had the forethought to just tip his hat at the skeleton and say howdy—if he'd had a hat. That would have ruined their fun for sure. His eyes searched the darkness under the trees, with no satisfaction.

There was a movement to his left, a stirring of grass, an almost silent turning.

His gaze jerked to the skeleton and he stared open-mouthed. It had moved away from the corner and was facing him bodily, the right arm rising higher, coming out toward him even as he watched. Something was in the hand. He could see—a glint from the light, a long, pointed blade outlined— He couldn't move, he couldn't speak. His mouth came open wider, and his throat closed on an attempt at a scream. The thing was still six feet away from him. If he could make himself move, he could get to his pickup and lock the door.

He jerked sideways, and abruptly it jumped and was between him and the pickup. His whole body was covered now in cold waves that radiated through his blood and over his skin, making him stiff and slow.

It had leaped and was now between him and the safety of his truck, as if it knew where he was headed. He whirled to run in the other direction. It didn't matter where. It was the hopeless kind of run that he had encountered in nightmares when he was a child, but he had a feeling that he wouldn't be waking up from this one.

As if his own back yard were against him, he stumbled over a row of rocks at the edge of his driveway and fell. There was no sound as the thing with the knife came down upon him. Oddly, he thought, there was no odor either, except a faint, muddy smell of the river. Then, a more cloying stink, of rotting fish and worms and . . .

14

Frank sat on the ground leaning back against the fat bole of a tree. He had a fair view of the whole of the barn, on the south and east side. And when he turned his neck and bent forward a bit he had a pretty good view of this end of the driveway. The major part of the driveway was heavily shadowed by the trees, but if any car light came down he would see it.

The night was dragging along. He still had sharp ears, and at times he could hear the rush of the water in the river where it passed over the boulders down where it widened and shallowed on one side. He could hear the wind in the trees, too, and the sleepy coo of the pigeons sometimes. And there were always the crickets in the grass.

Once, he had nearly jumped out of his overalls when the cat had come and rubbed up against him. He hadn't known he was nervous. He guessed he was, some. The company of the cat was welcome. But its purr had seemed uncommonly loud. After getting petted for awhile, the cat had ambled off, a long, yellow body that looked a bit lighter than the surrounding darkness. It disappeared beyond the hedge.

Frank took his pipe out of his pocket and began to tamp tobacco into it when he thought of what he was doing and stopped. If Charlene came sneaking up in the dark, she would see the flame of his match, and after the flame was gone, she would smell the smoke. He'd just have to wait without the comfort of his pipe.

He got up and strolled slowly through the grounds. He went down the driveway and along the path to the front door of the house. He stayed on the lawn, going around the house. All the downstairs lights were out, except a faint light beyond the twin insets of glass on each side of the front door. A hallway light, he reckoned.

He went on around the house, slowly, looking up at the dark windows on the second floor. All was quiet. Everybody asleep, he guessed, the mother, her baby, her other two children. The boy, the girl. Friendly girl. He liked her. The boy had been friendly, too, and loaded with curiosity, before the drowning of the neighbor boy. It would take him a long time to get over that, Frank thought. Too bad how some things happened to take the fun out of being a kid.

He went down the north side of the back yard, keeping fairly close to the fence. The almond orchard pressed close against the fence, a black world of shadows. Overhead the stars looked dim and faraway, as if the smog from Southern California were drifting up into the northern valley and throwing a veil above it.

He looked for the cat and didn't see him. He looked for the moon, too, and calculated that it was still a mite too early. The moon should rise around midnight or one o'clock. He hadn't paid much attention to his almanac the past few days.

He entered the barn lot and walked a circle around the barn. He could hear the creak and groan of the old boards settling a bit more into the earth. He thought of the room in the middle, that dark and dreadful little room that made him feel like setting fire to the barn that surrounded it. He thought of going through the barn with the police, just a light glancing around was all they seemed to want, as if they knew ahead of time that they would find nothing there but the kind of junk old barns contain. He had led them and chosen his own pathway. By that method he had kept the little room hidden. They hadn't seen it.

Now, he wasn't sure he had done the right thing.

Maybe he should have shown it to them and told them his ideas about Charlene coming back.

Yet something kept him from saying anything. Was it Miss Winifred? She wouldn't have wanted them to know. She would have died for her daughter—and indeed, she had, hadn't she?

But he was here to see that no one else did.

He came back at last to the tree under which his pickup was parked and sat down again. He fingered the bowl of his pipe, but he didn't light it.

He sat with his back to the house, knowing that she would more likely come back to the barn, to the room that was more hers than anything else.

Sleepiness began to overtake him, and he remembered that he hadn't been sleeping well lately. It was a new habit for him, something that he accounted to his age, which was closer to seventy than he liked to think about. For a few nights he'd only half sleep, and then, as if catching up, he'd start sleeping in his chair in front of the television. Then in the morning he'd almost sleep through his alarm. He lived alone, as he had since his parents died years ago. There was no one to wake him in the mornings or care when or if he slept at all.

He caught himself drooping, his chin almost touching his overalls' bib. He jerked his head up and gazed through his drowsiness at the barn. The moon was beginning to rise now, its light touching the high peak of the barn roof.

He was almost asleep again, though his eyes remained open and staring resolutely at the brightening barn roof, when something burst through the hedge and ran out of sight into the shadows beyond. Frank sat forward, his heart speeding, all vestiges of drowsiness gone. He had blinked and it was gone, whatever it was. Then he knew. It was the cat. Spooked at something.

Frank eased his pipe back into his shirt pocket, as if that subtle sound might be heard by whoever it was that had scared the cat. He got up, careful where he put his feet, careful of the gravel at the edge of the drive and the sounds it would make when one pebble struck another. He walked quietly around to his pickup, reached in through the open window and picked up the old rifle that lay on the seat.

At the rear of the pickup he had a fair view of the driveway, and even though it was shrouded in shadows of night, deep shadows of tree trunks and tree limbs heavy with leaves, he was quite sure that no automobile had entered. To be sure, he walked a ways down the driveway before he returned to his truck. The house was still dark. The night had settled into a deeper silence than before, as if the creatures that brought the night alive were themselves going to sleep. The moon eased up, a great, deep, muted ball of fire just beginning to shine through the trees.

Frank went back to his station at the tree and sat with the rifle across his legs. Within a minute his chin was touching the bib of his overalls again.

Kim lay on her stomach catty-cornered across her bed. She was propped up on her elbows, her chin supported in her hands. In the small pool of light from the bedside lamp spread the novel she was reading. She had gotten it from the library after she learned that she couldn't sleep. Her mother was sleeping—she had checked on her. But her mother had sleeping pills.

It was a Victorian novel, published in 1897. And it was kind of funny in the way it was written. Not funny ha-ha, just funny-different. The sentences were what her English teacher would have called complex. The movement of the story was slow. It was as if people had a lot more time then. As if their days were longer, their hours slower. Could it be that as time passed it speeded? Was the world going a little faster now, and would it keep going faster and faster until every living thing was compressed to a small degree of its former size? She could imagine herself, all squished down, half as tall as she was now. Then a third as tall. Then—

She heard something. *What?*

She closed the book and sat up, concentrating on sounds in the house, on trying to catch again the one sound that had diverted her attention.

The house seemed unnaturally quiet, as if her room were soundproofed. But her door was open, and she could see the shadows thrown by the pillars around the mezzanine. She could see the upper part of the stairs. There was nothing there, yet she had a growing feeling that someone was in the house, moving around.

There was a sudden hollow bonging, one, two, three, on and on, and she knew instantly that it was the grandfather clock in the hall downstairs striking the hour of midnight, but the first strike had scared her half to death. With her hand shaking she reached over and turned out her light.

When the clock had finished striking, its echo lingering and enhancing the silence that was left behind, the other sound came again. It was faint and faraway, but as she had recognized the clock, she now recognized this sound, too. The stairs in the old, rear stairway had creaked. The loose steps had given under the weight of someone. It was like Aunt Winifred climbing the stairs; and Kim's first vision was of her coming up the dark stairs again. Her second vision saw the body lying on the grass.

Who could it be on the stairs?

Someone who knew the house intimately.

Kim slid off her bed and crossed the few feet to her open door. She started to close it and then visualized

270

it from down the rear hall. The light would be reflected on it, and any movement would be seen immediately. Whoever it was entering the hall from the stairway would see her try to close her door.

Suddenly she knew who was using the back stairs. It was Kevin. Why hadn't she thought of him before?

She stepped boldly across her threshold and was surprised to see that her visualization of the rear hall had been all wrong. From her doorway she could see only partway down its length, and Kevin, coming up out of the stairwell, or anyone else, wouldn't be able to see her door at all.

But her fear had receded somewhat when it occurred to her that it was Kevin on the back stairs, and she walked out around the end of the mezzanine and toward the west hall. Frank was outside, keeping watch, she remembered. If any stranger came to the house he would see. And besides, a stranger would not have known about the enclosed stairs.

She would ask Kevin what he was doing up so late. Maybe he was like her and couldn't sleep. Maybe the two of them could talk some. Maybe they could come up with some kind of answer about Sara, if they talked about it.

The door to the back stairs was just beginning to open when Kim reached the highboy at the entry to the hall. She looked through the varnished lattice-work that winged out from the top, pausing there, hidden, though she knew not why she paused. She fully expected Kevin to come in sight through the open door, but the sight she saw made her gasp and stare.

It was pale, almost diaphanous, the blackness of

the stairwell behind it showing through its body. Its skull seemed to be filled with the blackness of perpetual night, and streaks of it oozed down over the frontal bones, like a different kind of blood. Its right arm hung down, but in its hand was a knife, a long-bladed knife that looked stained with something dark. It was just like Kevin had said, but she hadn't believed Kevin—because things like this weren't possible. She closed her eyes, then opened them again, and a terrible fear entered her. Was it going to Kevin's room? It was seeming to hesitate there at the end of the hall, where one door was open and the other door closed.

Oh God, Kevin don't come out of your room now.

It began to move, and the subtle sounds of its movement reached her ears. She pressed back between the wall and the highboy and watched it come step after step along the hall, closer to her moment by moment.

She had to take the chance and run, back to the safety of her room, the comparative safety. She had to gamble on the chance that it couldn't hear, or feel the vibration of the house caused by her running steps.

She looked toward her door, and it seemed so very faraway. She'd have to pass by the closed doors to the wing where Aunt Winifred's room was. She'd have to go around the corner of the balcony.

It was getting closer, too close now for her to take a chance. It might see her; it might feel her presence. Yet how could that be? It was a dead thing. And yet, there was something about it that was alive.

She pressed back between the wall and the highboy and waited, holding her breath, hoping that her still-

272

ness and the shadows of the dimly lighted halls would make her unnoticeable.

Where was it going?

It had passed Kevin's room.

Where was it going?

In a kind of shock she waited, afraid to move, afraid to breathe, praying without words that nobody awakened and came into the hall. That her mother's sleeping pill would keep her unconscious through this night. And Ivan would not choose this time to wake up.

The odor preceded it along the hall, the smell of stale, muddy water, and of mud soured, and of something else worse, much worse.

The sounds of its movements reached her in whispers.

A moment more and it was there, passing the highboy, within easy reach. She flattened herself even closer against the wall and watched it as it turned to the right away from her. When it went under the hall light she saw that a few strands of long hair adhered to the back of the skull. Tangled among the strands was the slimy green of moss. Mud stained the bones and collected in dark, wet gobs in every joint. She saw this all with only a portion of her mind. It was clear to her vision, yet rejected by her intellect. It was something that she would remember forever in her dreams, in her nightmares, but forget consciously.

As though even now in a nightmare from which she would awaken soon, she watched the skeleton pass the front stairs, go beyond the mezzanine, and to the closed doors that led to the south wing.

It hesitated there, and then the left hand jerked

upward and turned the knob that opened the doors. It pushed the doors open partway, and stepped through, and was gone from sight into the unlighted hall.

Kim waited, watching the doors. A calmness had settled over her, a suspension of feelings. Curiosity became foremost. Forgetting herself, forgetting the danger of coming face to face with the thing that seemed to know where it was going, she followed it.

At the double doors she stopped, peering into the dark hallway ahead. At first she saw nothing. But the door at the end was painted white, unlike all other doors in the house, and as her eyes adjusted she saw that it, too, was standing partway open.

The thing had gone into Charlene's room.

Charlene had come home.

She knew, she knew, and she wished she could run and tell Aunt Winifred. Then as swiftly she remembered that Aunt Winifred was dead. And now Kim knew who had killed her. Charlene. Her own daughter.

What had she done with Sara?

She glimpsed a movement beyond the door at the end, a brief flash of white in the blackness of the room. She turned and ran, back to her own room. She pushed the door almost shut and waited there, looking through the crack at the hall.

Within a few minutes it was back, coming through the doors. It came toward her, between the hallways, at the end of the mezzanine. Kim watched it, unable to move had it come on directly to her door. But it paused instead at the top of the stairs, then slowly it began to descend.

When it went out of sight down the stairs, Kim followed, staying far back, just barely keeping it in sight. It went along the lower hall and into the kitchen. Then, as Kim followed, it went out the screen door and across the porch.

Not until that moment did Kim realize she had left the back door open, the screen unlatched. She ran to the doors and locked them both. When she moved on to look out the kitchen window, it was gone.

She retraced her steps hurriedly, going up the front stairs and back along the hall to Kevin's room. She had to apologize to him, first of all. Beyond that she could not think.

When she opened his bedroom door she could see the outlines of furniture, his bed, and the lump in the blankets. Only a portion of her mind noted that no change in position had been made, which was odd for Kevin. Like Kim he was a sprawler, lying every which way on his bed.

"Kevin!" she hissed in a loud whisper. "You were right. I saw it. Kevin!" Her hands pressed on the hump in the bed and felt it sink to nothing.

She stood back, both hands pressed to her mouth. She stared over her fingers at the bed, at the blankets now flattened. Kevin was gone! Kevin had been gone the first time she came up to check on him after dinner. She had to find him.

She turned on the overhead light and dropped to her knees beside the bed. She looked under, hoping, losing hope. She started down the hall to her mother's room but stopped, both hands clamped over her mouth again as she thought swiftly ahead. Her mother was exhausted from the care of Ivan and the worry about Sara, to say nothing about Aunt

Winifred. She was worried, too, about Daniel, and all of that. Also, she'd had a sleeping pill, of that Kim was sure, even though she hadn't seen her mother take it. She had known when Ronna got them from the doctor in Chicago, and she knew when her mother went upstairs, her eyes circled with fatigue, her face looking so much older suddenly, that she would go to bed and then, unable to sleep, take something for it.

Besides that, Kim didn't want to burden her further now. She'd find Kevin on her own, because she knew —she hoped—he hadn't been taken—kidnapped— no, that was wrong. There was no kidnapper; there was just the thing, the horror that Kevin had been afraid of, and he was right. My God, he was right. But he had to be here. Hiding. *Hiding.*

That was it, of course. He had been so afraid that he hid in another room. That was it. That had to be it.

She began to search, quickly, quietly, looking first into the closet in Kevin's room, and from there into other rooms, other closets. She didn't call his name as she went but moved methodically and silently through the house.

Frank stood up and stretched. The moon had risen enough now that it was spilling a pale light over the tops of the trees and onto lower planes, a slanted light that was more than welcome even though tonight it seemed inadequate and spooky. He had never noticed before how dark it could be among the trees. He had never noticed that the countryside was so filled with dark and shadowy groves of walnut trees or that even the lower vineyards cast so many shadows.

A wind worked in the tops of the trees, making so much noise that he wanted to tell it to hush, to listen. Maybe it was the hour, that strange time of silence just after midnight, but he had a feeling that he would be able to hear something if the wind would just settle down and be quiet. Still, the leaves rustled, and the breeze touched his hot cheek with coolness. The barrel of his rifle was still warm, as if it had lain in the sun recently. But the heat had come from his body, where it had rested between his bent legs and his chest. He cradled it in the crook of his arm and started on his tour again.

He crossed onto the back yard grass at the end of the hedge, near the ropes that cordoned off the area around the murder site. The light of the moon had reached the barn lot now, and the shadow thrown by the barn was huge, spilling over into the edge of his garden, past the pig pen, the fig trees. His glance over the barn lot was swift and almost missed seeing the movement.

He stopped, his hands instinctively raising the rifle, pointing it at the corner of the barn where he had seen something. From the corner of his eyes he had seen someone step out of sight around the barn, toward one of the doors that led into the interior. He was sure of it. Only a glimpse, but that was enough.

He hurried back to the pickup, his arthritic knee making him limp. He didn't try to be quiet now. She was far enough away there at the barn that she wouldn't be able to hear him. Still, when the door squealed rustily, he winced. Then he left it standing open to avoid repeating the sound. A sound such as that carried on the air better than the sounds of footsteps on gravel. He got his flashlight off the seat and whirled away from his pickup, limping as fast as he could toward the barn.

When he reached the corner he became cautious. He was dealing with a murderer here, he reminded himself. She was no longer the young girl he had dragged out of the barn by one arm that time he had caught her at her terrible, satanic games. She wasn't the child that Daniel had tattled on.

Suddenly he was back in the scene as if it were happening again. Coming out of the garden with the sun warm and bright around him, with life lying serene and peaceful behind and ahead of him, the young boy, himself no bigger than the girl, if as big, came with his face twisted and his eyes looking like something out of a nightmare, and he whispered to him, beginning to cry as he talked, "Please, Mr. Frank, you have to make Charlene quit. She says you can't make her, because you're just a man, but you have to."

On questioning the boy he learned of Charlene's so-called dealings with the devil and her sacrifices to that belief. And maybe she was right, and she had invoked the devil. He wondered at the time how she had even learned of such things, at her age. But he was mad enough that he went after her with no fear of the devil, and no fear of her grandfolks or even her mother. He had hauled her out of the barn and turned her over his knee and made her squall for the first time in her life. She had cursed him venomously, spitting and spewing, but he hadn't given a damn.

He had been wondering where his chickens were disappearing to, and now he knew. Curses on the heartless brat. He had always considered her too spoiled to be liked and hadn't understood how her grandparents could stand her. Nor her mother, for that matter. But then, how could he know the feeling a person had for his kids? He was unmarried and had no plans to change it. And after that, he decided he didn't want any kids, either. A body never knew what would turn up in them.

So here she was back, of that he felt quite certain, but she had upped her sacrifices to humans now. And for all he knew she was carrying the little girl, Sara, with her right this minute.

He adjusted his rifle under his right arm with his index finger on the trigger. A swift, vague question passed through his mind: Would he be able to shoot or hit what he shot at? The only shooting he had ever done in his life was at tin cans, and that was a long time ago. He'd had too much heart to go after the wild animals in the mountains.

He set his flashlight on the ground while he opened the barn door that led into the closest floored area. She might have gone into the old milking part, with its cement floor and its trenches, but it wasn't the nearest way to the part she would want—the old devil's room.

For a moment, before he picked up the light, he was looking into a dungeon blackness, the interior of the room ahead, and the hair on the back of his neck stiffened. He bent for the light quickly and shined it through the door. He caught glimpses of eyes from dark corners before their owners departed into the

279

nearest cracks and holes. There was a scurry of tiny feet and one or two larger ones that tromped through the dark hall beyond like horses. The sound of them, both the mice and the rats, comforted him; and then made him wonder. If she had entered here, wouldn't the rodents have departed then?

Puzzled, he hesitated. There were other doors, of course. Maybe she had seen him coming and had slipped on around the barn.

He left the door standing open and went on around the barn slowly, his flashlight making a path of light through the shadows ahead. His knee bothered him more than it ever had, but he went on, letting it hurt. When he reached the second corner, the southwest corner where the barn made its own large shadow out across the grounds, he stopped, put his light down and rubbed his knee. He hadn't seen a thing. No movement at all. Nor had he heard anything out of the ordinary. But he could feel her presence as if it were a cloud. The barn seemed alive with her. He had to go in now, go to the room in the middle.

He could see a portion of the rear of the house from where he stood, and he glanced at it and then looked again. There was a light in a second floor room. Someone was unable to sleep.

He picked up the flashlight, went on to the small door in the south end of the barn and entered. Once again there was the patter of mice and the eyes back in the shadows that reflected for brief moments the beam of his light. The barn seemed filled with those small eyes everywhere he looked. Eyes that blinked at him and were gone, all in a flash.

His footsteps sounded loud and hollow on the old

board floors. The barn was beginning to rót down, he realized, as a board almost collapsed beneath his foot. It would be a good thing if it did, he thought. He would be glad to see it go, collapsing in a heap upon itself. He wondered if the room in the middle would fall, too, or if it would keep standing there, a tribute to evil. Or maybe it would go first, struck down by a higher power.

He shined the light into every dark corner, through every doorway, over the low wall into the milk stanchions, and everywhere the bright little eyes glared at him briefly before they disappeared into deeper hiding places.

When he came to the room he found the door closed, and he was forced to take his hand off the rifle so that he could hold the light while he opened the door. This time he didn't want to let go of the light, even for a moment. He hooked three of his fingers beneath the handle so that he could keep his index finger on the trigger, then with his left hand free he turned the white porcelain knob of the door and pushed it open, slamming it back so hard that it bounced off the wall and returned a few inches. At the same time he grabbed the flashlight into his left hand and steadied and aimed the rifle with his right.

The room was empty. There was the bench and the painting on the wall and on the floor. And there were the dolls, their clothes faded and colorless under the dust. But other than that, the room was empty.

Thank God.

He leaned against the doorjamb. Suddenly he was feeling drained of all energy. And now, too, he was wondering something. Even if he had found her,

281

would he have been able to fire his gun? Or was he just carrying it around for his own sense of safety?

He left the barn quickly, his feet clomping loudly on the boards, the sound seeming to echo back at him from deeper parts of the barn mockingly, no matter how quietly he tried to walk.

His breath expelled from his body in a great sense of relief when he came again into the moonlight. Now he could tell himself that maybe he hadn't seen anything at all. His nerves had been playing tricks on him. Or maybe it was just the cat again, going around the corner of the barn just as he looked its way.

He closed the gate in the stockade fence as he passed through. He was moving slower and slower now, his knee almost giving way beneath him. He used the butt of the rifle for support, for a cane of sorts.

Then again, he was seeing movement. A shadow at the back of the house, accompanied by the hollow slam of the screen door as the dark figure peeled away from the shadows and became a real person. When she came running into the moonlight he recognized the girl, Kim.

"Frank, Frank," she called in a hushed voice, running with her long, young legs bare and white in the moonlight, her little nightgown coming only to the tops of her thighs. "Frank," she cried, her voice quivering as she came to a stop about ten feet away. "My brother is missing. I can't find him!"

15

The fisherman's boat drifted along the river close to the bank. It had a small outboard motor, but he hadn't used it for the last half mile. The kind of fishing he was doing was considered illegal by some, but he had been doing it all his life. He'd caught a lot of big salmon and trout by dragging grappling hooks along behind his boat. Another reason he was staying as silent as he could and keeping to the undercover of trees along the bank was the fact that he had no fishing license at all. Had never had one. He'd lived on the river since he was a kid, since back in the days before the dam was built up in the mountains, back when the river flooded every winter without fail. His house was on stilts then, and it was still on stilts, even though the woman he had married had insisted that the unused area beneath be changed into a porch and carport.

He drifted along beneath the overhang of trees, occasionally using an oar to keep from being pulled into the current in the middle of the river. Shadows fell darkly over him and his boat and dappled into moonlight a few feet away. The moon had just broken away from the horizon, and the long streaks of light that it spread along the river kept him entranced. It wasn't only the fishing that he came out on the river this late at night for; he liked the sounds, the feeling of being completely alone in the world, and the moonlight on the water.

One of his hooks caught and held, easing the boat sideways. He had something. But it wasn't behaving like a big fish. A fish would now be flopping about in the water and swimming, trying to swim away from the hooks caught in its flesh. He'd had fish on his hooks that had dragged his boat a half mile or more before the fish became exhausted and gave up to the sharp, many-pronged grappling hooks.

But this time he had hooked something else. The boat eased on, dragging his catch. So it wasn't a root or a limb or an old tire, as it sometimes was. He twisted around, dropped his small anchor, and when the boat had steadied again, hauled up on the nylon rope that was attached to the hooks. When his burden reached the top of the water and became heavier, he turned on his flashlight.

Clothing. His breath stilled. He was almost afraid to look. Probably, though, it was only a bag of old clothes that somebody had dumped into the river. Probably.

Through the film of water that overlaid the part of the burden that hung away from the hooks in the clothes, he caught a glimpse of something fish white. It was floating upward, coming out to the surface of the water slowly. A small hand, an arm—

He almost dropped it. He thought of the little boy who had been drowned near here just a few days ago. And now another. Or he was having a nightmare, brought on by the story in the paper?

His hooks had caught only the clothes. He could drop the body back, run home and pretend he didn't know anything about it. Then he wouldn't have to explain what he was doing out on the river with this kind of hook in the first place.

He thought of it, a firefly thought that swept into his mind and was gone.

He got on his knees, reached over the side of the boat and lifted the small body in his arms. He laid it gently in the bottom of the boat and noted by the indirect beam of his flashlight that it was a boy nine or ten years old. And although he was beyond help, he hadn't been in the water long enough for it to bloat him.

He reached back and gave his motor a tug. When it began to chuckle, he aimed the boat for the nearest landing, thinking as he went about the houses along the road. The closest one was a small white house in the middle of an English walnut orchard about an eighth of a mile away from the river. He could pull his boat up on the sandbar there, go to the house and have them call the police.

Sara cringed in the silence of the cellar, listening for the footsteps. The lantern light flickered, at times almost going out. She spent a lot of time staring at it. A long time had passed before she noticed the other things on the rickety old table. Then, when she dared put her feet on the earthen floor, she ran to the table and climbed up. She was hungry and thirsty, and on the table, like a magic table in fairyland, there was food and water. Peanut butter sandwiches. Cookies. Beneath the table a small mouse came hesitantly from its hole and looked up at her, and Sara could see in the pale light the twitching of its little nose and whiskers. She leaned over the side of the table and dropped bread crumbs, and then watched it eat. Part of her fear was taken away by the mouse, and she laughed when she saw it rise up and sit almost like a human and hold the crumbs in its hands to eat. It chewed fast, a tiny bite at a time.

But that was a long time ago. She didn't know how long ago. Now the sandwiches were all gone, and the cookies, too. She had no more crumbs to give the mice that were growing used to her presence.

She stared at the trap door in the ceiling. The footsteps were gone. They weren't coming back. In the endless time she had spent in the cellar she had heard the footsteps only a few times. It was like Aunt Winifred came to walk across her ceiling just to remind her of the death that waited.

She hadn't climbed the ladder to the trap door. When she slept she lay on the table, her knees drawn up to her chest. When she was awake she watched the trap door or the flickering light. She had grown used to the animals that shared her cellar. The mice, and even the big rat that peeked out at her, made her feel less alone. At first the rat had scared her horribly. But more and more her fear was for the footsteps that came to walk slowly across her ceiling.

The lantern was going out. Its flame flickered and

dimmed, as if a strong, silent wind were blowing in its smoked globe. She gave in to weeping as she watched it. And finally she let herself down from the table and climbed the ladder to the trap door. She pushed up with all her strength, but it didn't move. After trying again and again she finally backed down from the ladder and went back to the table.

When the light went out she began to cry, *"Mama. Daddy. Mama, come and get me."*

Frank drove his pickup off the street and into the service station, wondering if Phillips was open. He needed to talk more than he needed gas. Too much had been happening for him to handle it without exploding. Now the little boy, Kevin, had been found. A fisherman at the river had called in, just minutes after he had called the police that Kevin was missing. That soon, and the police were there to take the boy's mother to identify the body. Frank had to talk to someone. Milton Phillips's service station was where he went to pass the time of day, but he'd never stopped in so early.

He parked at the pumps and waited. The lights were on, and Milton's pickup was parked in its usual spot, but Milton seemed to be gone. There was no one in the front room. He could see from stem to stern in it, with its three sides of window glass.

The feeling of being in another world was still with him. This world was filled with tragedies and horrors, a world of dark edges and black pits. And that, he told himself, was why he felt that something was wrong here, too.

He got out of the pickup and stood with his thumbs hooked in his overalls' pockets. The sun was just coming up, a red ball in the east, and the town was beginning to stir. Down the street one dog was barking toward another that was so far away it sounded like it might be out of town. Good, familiar, homey sounds. Yet with his state of mind, his sense of absolute horror, Frank felt they might be sounds of demons instead of family dogs. He shook himself and went to find Milton. He could talk to Milton. He could tell him his suspicions about Charlene and ask him what he thought about it. Milton knew Charlene. They were about the same age. They had gone to school together, and he could remember seeing Milton out at the ranch with other kids at least once. But they hadn't been friends.

"Hey!" he yelled in toward the front door. Might be in the back room, he decided, as he reached to open the door. When the knob failed to yield in his hand, he stared at it as if it were alive. Door locked? Yet Milton's pickup was parked in its usual place, and no one was in it.

Well, he thought, it could be the pickup wouldn't start last night and Milton had caught a ride home with someone else. Or he might have driven up this morning and decided to take a little nap in the truck, and was lying down out of sight.

Frank walked around the corner of the station and toward the pickup and stopped, staring.

Milton lay face down in the area beyond the pickup, his shirt shredded, his back covered with blood.

Frank's movements then became automatic, as if

his mind had clicked off and an inner computer had taken over. He returned to his own truck, got in and drove away. He drove down Main Street, turned left, drove two blocks, and turned right again. He wound up parking at the fire station. He got out, went in, and said to the only man on duty, "Call the police. Milton Phillips has been killed. Just like Miss Winifred. Tell them to come to the station. That's where he's at."

He returned to his truck, got in, drove back to the service station and waited there for the police. But when they came he couldn't tell them his suspicions: that Charlene Childress might have killed Milton, too, and before she was through she would kill everybody in town that she'd ever had a grudge against. And he would be one of them.

"Where will you be if we need to talk to you again, Frank?" the officer that was called Ray asked.

"At the ranch," Frank answered. He was beginning to feel he knew these boys; he had been seeing them so often lately. They were more than fresh young faces and neatly pressed uniforms; they were a couple of guys that came when you called, the first two to show up before the others were called in. The ones who led the way. First Winifred, then Sara, Kevin, and now Milton. Frank had to get away from this latest scene of blood and death. He went to his truck, then turned, adding, "The Childress Ranch. I'll be there beside my truck, or close by."

He drove back to the ranch feeling he was needed there. He couldn't leave that young mother and her two remaining children alone there with Charlene on the prowl.

Why, he wondered, his mind beginning to work again as he parked in his old place in the driveway at the ranch, hadn't he been able to tell the police his ideas about Charlene Childress? *Because,* an inner voice answered, in your soul *you know she's dead.* It couldn't have been Charlene.

Shocked, he considered that new thought.

Dead?

No. He had never thought that at all. Still, he needed to do some more thinking before he told the police. He figured they would only stare at him. After all, the girl had been gone nearly thirty years. She was hardly a girl anymore. They would say if she'd hated the people here that much and planned to kill them, she wouldn't have waited this long.

Also, the voice told him, what about Sara? What did Sara have to do with Charlene?

He shook his head, the confusion causing a dull pain around the scalp. Thinking just didn't seem to agree with him anymore.

Kim sat in the sun room. It was the first time she had done more than walk through it. But she was alone, and the sun room was like a beacon of hope. If she went there and sat on the bright floral pattern of the couch, she felt it might have a magic effect on her life. Perhaps, in allowing herself to sink into the brightness and cheerfulness of the room, she would leave the old, dark world behind, and all the bad things would be wiped away. Kevin wouldn't be dead. Sara wouldn't be gone. The thing that had walked the halls of the house last night would only be the remnants of a nightmare.

The police had come to the house just at dawn that morning, asking her mother if she would identify the body. Kim stayed with Ivan while their mother went with the police. After that, her mother had collapsed. There was a nurse upstairs now, a woman in white who was taking care of both Ronna and Ivan. It left Kim with nothing to do but think and chew her fingernails.

There was no magic after all. The soft yellow of the walls was looking dull with the shadows. The sun was lowering in the west, and long shadows stretched out across the lawn beyond the windows.

She relived the hours of her search for Kevin. When she had gone out to get Frank to help her, he did something she hadn't even thought of. He called the police and told them Kevin was missing now, too, just as Sara was. And because of that the body in the river was known to be Kevin's. There was another thing Frank had done that Kim hadn't thought of, or hadn't wanted to do. He had awakened her mother.

Now Kevin was at the funeral home, where Aunt Winifred was. His coffin would be small. The plot in the cemetery would be small.

It didn't seem possible.

Kevin couldn't be gone.

She heard a car in the driveway. Just another police car, she supposed. But then, after the door slammed, she heard Frank's voice taking on a quality she hadn't heard before, as if he were greeting someone he knew well. She remembered something she had almost forgotten: Daniel was coming. Daddy was coming.

She went to a window and looked out. The car was blue, unfamiliar. And she remembered also that he would be using a rented car. Then she saw him standing by the hedge, shaking hands with Frank. Her daddy. She instantly recognized the broad, straight shoulders, the hair that was like Kevin's, only a little darker. And she recognized the bony jaw that now had a short beard. She threw open the door and began to run.

She flung herself into his arms, and for the first time since she had learned that Kevin was drowned, she wept. Her tears stained his shirt. One of his big hands pressed her head against his chest.

"He's dead, Daddy," she sobbed. "Kevin is dead, too."

"I know, I know." His voice sounded gruff and choking. "I stopped at the police station. Where's your mother, Kim?"

"In her room. Upstairs. There's a nurse with her. She came this morning, after Mama went with the police to identify Kevin's body. I guess the police got her to help Mama. Daddy, I went up to his room right after dinner last night, and I thought I saw him there. I thought all the time that he was safe in his room. I don't know what happened. He was wearing his clothes. He wouldn't have gone swimming alone, at night."

He had released her, and she moved back and looked up at him. She saw that he was staring up at the second floor of the house, his eyes narrowed. In his cheek a nerve twitched.

"Daddy I have to talk to you," she said. "There's something else I have to tell you."

292

He patted her shoulder without looking at her, without really hearing what she had said. In the horror of knowing her brother was found dead, in the desperate search of the night, she had almost forgotten the *thing*, the skeleton that moved through the halls of the house, and she hadn't mentioned it to anyone. But she had to tell Daniel.

"Later, sweetheart," he said, walking away toward the house. "I have to go up and see your mother."

Kim watched him go to the porch, up the two steps, and across the brick floor. She watched him go into the kitchen and disappear there in the shadows of the house.

She slumped and sat down on the grass. She was tired. She hadn't slept last night at all. She searched among the short blades of grass and found a clover leaf, but it had only three leaves.

"He's changed a lot," Frank said. "Your dad. I hadn't seen him since he was a teenager. The muscles and the beard make a lot of difference. I might not have known him right off if I hadn't known he was coming."

Kim got up and brushed her skirt.

"Seems odd to have him come back after all this time," Frank said. "It's too bad he had to come back to—all of this. His son. His daughter. Too bad."

Kim had nothing to say. She was beginning to feel light-headed, as if she might faint. She hadn't eaten today either, she remembered, and although she wasn't hungry, she thought of making a sandwich to take to her room. There she could close out the world and sleep and sleep.

"I just wonder what will happen when they meet

again," Frank said. "It's beginning to seem like that was what she had in mind maybe. To get Daniel back here."

Kim wasn't sure what Frank was talking about. It was like he was using her as a kind of sounding board. Did he know Charlene was dead and her skeleton walked at night?

"I'm going up to my room," Kim said, feeling a need to explain to someone where she would be. Yet she didn't move. Her mind felt dulled. There was something—something she had to do before she could sleep.

"Lock your door," Frank said. "And get some sleep."

"You haven't slept either, have you, Frank?"

"Not since—I can't remember when just now."

"Then you have to sleep, too. But not in the back of your truck." She thought of the skeleton coming along by the side of the truck and sensing that he was there. The blade of the knife was sharp and long, as if it had just recently been sharpened, as if the part of Charlene that had kept her from total death had kept it also honed beyond its original sharpness. "Come into the house instead. There are plenty of empty rooms. But lock the doors." *Be sure to lock the doors.*

A pleased look crossed his face. There was a quick half smile that faded at its genesis, and a softening around his eyes in which the wrinkles seemed not so deeply set. "Why, Missy Kim," he said after a hesitation. "I've never even crossed the threshold of the kitchen door in all my life until I went in last night to wake up your mother. No Childress ever invited me into the house before. I thank ye."

294

Did that mean he was coming in to spend the night? She wasn't sure. A thought struggled for recognition in her tired, sad brain. He had set himself up as guardian of the family, and to come inside and make himself comfortable in one of the bedrooms, with the doors locked, would put him on the side of the family, no longer its guardian. Yet staying out here wasn't safe. Even while she was trying to think he turned away and was walking toward his pickup.

She ran after him. He stopped and looked down at her. The slanting rays of the setting sun reddened the side of his face. She clutched his arm, yet the flesh was so sparse that her fingers ended up pulling on his shirt sleeve.

"Then go home," she said. "Now that Daddy is here, you can go home, can't you?"

"I'll go home and get me a bite to eat."

She didn't offer to bring him food from the kitchen. She thought of it, and as quickly discarded the thought, for if he stayed for food, he would stay into the night.

"And sleep, too," she said. "You need to sleep. Stay home and sleep. Come back in the morning. After the sun is up. We'll be all right. Daddy's here." *And the house will be locked. I'll see to that.*

He touched the side of her head with his rough palm. "You're a good girl, missy. You run along to bed now."

She stood at the side of the driveway and watched him get into his old red pickup truck. The engine started, stopped, started again, uneasily, before it began a regular rhythm of coughing. He drove out of sight toward the barn and sheds, turned around somewhere there, and waved as he drove back by. She watched until the pickup was out of sight between the twin line of trees along the driveway. She heard it stop at the end of the driveway then speed up toward town. The sound drifted away, absorbed by the orchards and the distance.

The sun had dropped behind the trees and the hills to the west, leaving only its reflection in the sky. The shadows across the lawn were deepening. She went to the house and locked both the screen door and the heavy, windowless kitchen door.

She went on through the ground floor of the house, checking every window to make sure it was locked. She went into rooms she hadn't gone in before: a music room that might have been fascinating at another time, the dark, somber, soundless instruments speaking of music that once was plucked from the strings and keys. In the shadowed corner then, sitting on the bench of the baby grand piano, Kim saw the girl. She had a lovely but dissatisfied face, and long, copper-red hair that hung in ringlets as if someone had carefully curled it around a loving finger. The girl was no more than eleven or twelve years old, and she looked at Kim petulantly. The music became audible, slowly, gradually, as if it had lain silent among the piano keys. A note discordant, and a flinch of the pretty face, then a slam of the keys in which all the notes resounded discordantly, and the girl tossed her head angrily and was gone. Kim stared and saw nothing but the wall behind the piano. The noise of the slammed keys drifted way into the silence of the house, ringing only in echoes.

The room was darkening, and Kim felt cold. She could hear her teeth beginning to chatter. She looked around: into the shadowed corner by the base viol; into the corner where the opened door created a dark triangle; but the girl was gone. Kim stood alone in the quickly darkening room with her teeth chattering, the only sound that reached her ears.

Hastily she checked the one window. It was a deep, long window half covered by old, faintly musty draperies. She tried to push them aside to get more of the dying light into the room, but they swung stubbornly together again.

On her way out of the room she looked once more at the piano bench, but the vision had gone. She closed the door and knew she would never enter the music room again. It was haunted, as was, really, the whole Childress place.

After she was sure that all windows and doors of the first floor were locked she went back to the kitchen. She was so tired she dropped the knife twice as she smeared peanut butter on bread. She took a tray carrying sandwich and milk up to her room, leaving on behind her the light in the kitchen and the hallways, yet wondering, too, if the light might attract the thing that was now Charlene. Finally, after standing in her room and feeling uneasy about the burning lights, she retraced her steps and turned them out. She hurried back to her room, feeling behind her the reaching darkness that was tempered only by a reddish, lingering light from outdoors. On the second floor she left the night lights burning. She looked for a long time toward the closed doors of the nursery and the master bedroom, and fought a wish to go there where her mom and dad and baby brother were, to gather into her soul the comfort of their existence. She looked toward the closed door at the end of the hall and felt a great hollow place inside her. Kevin's drowning had hurt her more than Sara's disappearance. With Sara there was hope.

At last she went into her own room and turned on all the lights. She saw the window, open to the growing darkness, and closed the blinds, and even took away the ties that held back the sheer curtains, as if that would help hide the lights and her presence in the room. But she took only one bite of her sandwich before she crumpled onto her pillows and went deeply and dreamlessly to sleep.

Daniel sat by the side of Ronna's bed. He had pulled a straight chair up from its place against the wall and waited in silence for her to wake up. He had met the nurse, a woman who introduced herself as Margie Whitmore, a pleasant-faced woman of indeterminate middle age. He had held wiggly, warm, living—blessedly living—Ivan for a few minutes, but then, glad that Margie Whitmore was there to look after him, had given the baby back to her. He had seen that a rollaway bed had been moved into the nursery for the nurse to sleep on, and now through the closed door between the rooms he could hear faintly the sounds of Ivan as he played. He waited patiently for Ronna to waken, his mind back at the funeral home where he had seen the lifeless body of his son.

He'd had to go there and see for himself. He had stopped at the police station to get any latest news about Sara and had been hit by the news of Kevin. Incapable of believing until he had seen for himself, he had gone to the funeral home, which was serving as a kind of morgue. The cause of death had already been determined. Kevin had drowned.

The guilt and the sorrow was almost unbearable. He had sent his family here, thinking they would be safe. But there was another reason he had sent them here, a reason that lay beneath his soul and would haunt him forever: He wanted them out of his way so there would be nothing to hold him in any one place. There had been a brief romance, but he had put that aside as too confining. He was running, he now knew, from the past. He had meant never to return to Childress. He hadn't realized that until he saw the beautiful, still face of his son. And now he hurt so desperately he couldn't even cry. The hurt was a knot in his throat threatening to choke him, and there was a part of him that wished it would and put him out of his misery. But he was needed here, by the others. By Ivan, by Kim and Ronna. For once in his life he had to stick around, stand up and be counted. If he managed to run this time he had to take them with him.

He reached over to the bedside lamp and turned it on. Ronna moved, disturbed by the light, or the movement of Daniel, or perhaps merely the wearing off of the sedative Margie Whitmore said she had given her this morning.

Ronna turned onto her back, raised one arm and put it across her forehead, then opened her eyes and saw Daniel.

He leaned across the edge of the bed and took her hand, pulling her arm away from her face. "Ronna."

As if suddenly remembering, she cried out and reached for him, burying her face against his chest. He held her, feeling her body tremble as she wept, glad she could find the comfort of tears. She raised her face to his after awhile, and her tears dampened his cheek and chin.

"Daniel, Kevin is dead. Our little son. Our first-born. I didn't even get to hold him again, Daniel. I'll never get to hold him again. The police came and said the body of a ten-year-old boy had been found by a fisherman and wanted me to identify it. *It*. Not him. He's still my baby, Daniel. Why haven't I held him lately? Why didn't I think to stop and take him in my arms and hug him?"

Daniel held her, his arms tightening, aching with the pressure, while his heart echoed her words, her grief. Where had he been all these months? At least Ronna had stayed with Kevin, while he hadn't. He had been searching and searching for something away from them, and now he was beginning to see he had been searching for freedom from himself.

"I've got to get you and Kim and Ivan out of here, Ronna," he said. "I shouldn't have sent you here."

As if she hadn't heard him, she said, "What was he doing down at the river at night? I don't understand why he went down there. In the dark. Why? He was at supper. When I sent Kim up to see if he had gone to his room, she said he was in his bed. Then in the middle of the night, at three or four maybe, Frank and Kim woke me up and said Kevin was gone. We thought he had been kidnapped, too, and Frank called the police. And just an hour later—or maybe it was only a few minutes, I don't know, the time is so mixed up—the police came and told me about the body found—and took me—"

He held her even tighter. "Hush, hush. Try to put it out of your mind. Maybe you should start packing now. I'll help you."

She shook her head. "Kevin's funeral."

"That's only two days away. As soon as it's over we can leave. We can get ready tonight, and tomorrow."

Hurry. *Get away from this place.* The urgent cry came from somewhere deep in his mind.

Ronna pulled back from him. Her eyes were red and sunken. He realized she had lost a lot of weight since he had last seen her.

"What about Sara?" she asked.

"Sara." For the first time he realized also that he had been thinking of Sara as being dead, too. All of his children were dying, would die if he didn't get them away from here.

Ronna's back stiffened. She slid her legs off the bed. Her thin jaw took on a stubborn set that he had never seen before. The tears were gone, and he had a feeling they would not be coming back soon. They would clog her throat, the way they did his, and make her feel she was choking. She would be unable to eat, to swallow more than a few drops of water or coffee. The caffeine in the coffee would keep her going. But then, he thought, maybe she had felt this way for a long time. Since he had put her and their children out of his life. Maybe that was why she had grown so thin.

301

"I'm not going anywhere without Sara," she said. "If you want to leave again, you go ahead, Daniel. I've made it through a lot of our marriage without you, and I can make it through this. I'm waiting here for Sara, even if it takes a lifetime."

He knew she would. This was a new Ronna sitting before him. The decisiveness in her voice made him all the more aware of his own weaknesses. She had given him a choice. He could stay, or he could go.

He wondered if he were capable of staying.

In the darkness something slithered along the tabletop toward Sara. She could hear it: a soft, sliding sound beneath the other sounds, the creaks of the wood, the loud cracks that came from far above somewhere in the top of the barn, the faint patter of the mice feet as they crossed the floor. The slithering had started where the table leaned against the dirt wall at one corner. Sara could remember seeing it when there still was light, and she had worried that something would come out from the earth behind the widely spaced boards and come onto the table with her. But nothing had, until now. She held her own breath and listened for its breathing, but there was none. There was a pause, as if it knew she was listening, as if it listened, too, then it came nearer, sliding, slithering. It touched her leg, cold, thin, like a nylon rope. And now she knew what it was, and she forgot that Aunt Winifred might hear her and come back to kill her. She screamed. Her voice high and thin, it filled the dark cellar. She jerked away from the snake and scrambled on her hands and knees, forgetting there was an end to the tabletop. She fell, knocking the lamp down with her. The globe shattered, and pieces of the glass embedded in her hands and knees as she crawled over it.

In her search for a place of safety she came up against the dirt wall. She whirled and crossed the floor still on her hands and knees, her screaming voice still pounding in her ears, thrown back at her from the cellar walls and ceiling. Her hands touched the ladder, and she grasped it and climbed. She clung sobbing to it, her head pressed against the ceiling, the floor above, the trap door that wouldn't open.

16

Kim woke and lay disoriented. The blue curtains, hanging still, their folds highlighted by the soft glow of the lamps, looked only vaguely familiar. Then abruptly she remembered where she was, and she sat up, and all that had happened crashed down upon her.

She sat for awhile with her feet hanging off the side of her bed, listening. The house was silent, but as she listened the big grandfather clock in the foyer below began to strike. She followed the deep-toned, mellow notes as if she were climbing a stair. She ended at number twelve and listened as the mellow, penetrating sound drifted away as if to a great distance that finally claimed it altogether.

Her daddy had arrived. He was here, at this minute, somewhere in the house. Maybe he was with Mama, or maybe he had left her sleeping and had gone on into another room. His old room, perhaps. But then she remembered that Aunt Winifred had said Daniel's old room was the room that had been given to Kevin. Daniel would not go there to sleep. Seeing Kevin's things in the room might make him too painfully aware that Kevin would not be coming back to it. Glancing into the room and seeing Kevin's things, one could almost feel that he would return. Tomorrow, perhaps, or next week when he came back from summer camp.

That was the way she would look at it. The only way she could. She thought of Kevin as being away at camp. She had to. It was the only way she could keep from coming apart in all her body: her bones from her flesh, her heart from her soul.

Yet she wondered: If she had let him talk to her about the *thing*, the skeleton that walked, if she had gone with him to find it, would he be alive now? She thought that he might.

She left her room and went out onto the balcony. There was no one in sight. She felt relieved. It would be better if they slept tonight, if they stayed in their rooms. And especially if they stayed in the house.

She went quietly past the stairways and to the closed doors of the south wing. She hesitated, remembering the last time she had stood here. A strong feeling of dread washed over her and then settled across her shoulders like a weight that would drag her down. She felt smothered and forced to take longer, deeper breaths. She pushed the doors open. They folded at their center seams and moved silently back against the walls, then edged half closed again. She left them in that position. There was plenty of room for her to pass through.

Her hand slid along the shadowed wall until she found a light switch. She pressed it, and a single light halfway along the ceiling came on. A portion of the deeper shadows in the hall were laid to rest. Kim moved on, not knowing exactly why she was going into this closed wing, except that her destination was the room at the end. The room that Charlene, in her present form, had returned to. The room that she would return to again, if she were to find access to the house.

Perhaps she had, even now, as Kim walked toward her. Perhaps first she should have gone downstairs and checked again the doors and windows she had locked. Someone might have gone out and left the door open, as Kim herself had done just—was it only last night? It seemed eons ago. Ages and ages into another kind of world. A world where only the expected happened. Where the laws of nature were not broken. This was a different world. One they had stumbled onto accidentally. Charlene's world.

The door at the end of the hall was still standing open, just as she—*it*—had left it last night.

The room was dark. Kim hesitated on the threshold. The odor reached her, faint but seeming to grow, fetid, old and rotting, coming from the dark, deep places beyond the earth. It repelled her, and she took a step backward. Then she stood, determined, looking into the room. The shadows were waning, giving in to the meager light from the hallway. Her eyes were adjusting. She could see the foot of the bed and the bulky darkness of an unidentified piece of furniture across by the wall. She could see the white throw rugs on the carpet, pale splotches she couldn't have identified if she hadn't seen them before. This was the room she had thought so beautiful, and she was going to enter it now, look deeper into it and try to find an answer to Charlene.

A river of fear played up and down her back until she felt that if she turned her head she would see the thing that was Charlene standing in the hall behind her. She listened with all her might, but there was no sound in the hall. Courage returned, and she glanced back. The hall was empty except for the furniture. The doors to the hall, that folded back, stood half open just as she had left them. Beyond, she could see the banister by the stairway, and although it was beyond the corner she knew the master bedroom was not far away. She wasn't alone.

She crossed the threshold into the bedroom and pressed the switch for the overhead light. Darkness remained, unbroken except for the light from the hall. Her courage almost failed. Then she thought about it. The bulb in the ceiling was probably years and years old. It had burned out a long time ago.

The room seemed less dark now. She could see shadowy objects around the room that had to be lamps. There were two by the bed, one on each side. There was one on the desk, and another one on a round table by the boudoir chair in front of the double windows. In one of them a light would work, maybe.

She went around the room trying lights, and all of them worked except the one by the chair. But even with the room beautifully lighted, she remained uneasy. The odor was less noticeable now, as if part of it had escaped through the door; or perhaps it was only that she had grown more used to it.

She sat down at the desk and began to go through

the drawers.

Charlene's handwriting was uneven and careless, almost awkward, Kim saw, as she examined the few papers that had writing on them. Most of the school papers that had been left in the desk were typed. When Kim left the desk and went into the closet she found a small portable typewriter on the floor in its case.

The clothing didn't look as if it had ever been touched. It was all new looking and very neat on the hangers. Charlene had been quite' a big girl, Kim saw, full busted, trim waisted. The dresses were tight-bodiced with a lot of skirt, full, gathered. There were dozens of petticoats layered with lace and stiffened panels that would hold the skirts out. Almost like the dresses of the nineteenth century, except these were shorter. Dresses of the fifties. Shoes, dozens of pairs, were arranged neatly in shelves. Kim checked the size. Eight, mostly, although there were a few that were seven and a half. There was also a fine layer of dust, Kim noticed. It had come away on her fingers. She wiped her hands on her shirt, feeling faintly nauseated and revolted, as if the dust were a film from what was now Charlene.

She backed out and stood on the threshold of the closet. Everything was so neat that it fairly shouted the tender care of someone other than its owner. What fifteen-year-old girl would keep her room so neat? None that Kim knew. This room said in deep silence that Aunt Winifred had put things away before she had closed the door forever.

Kim wandered around the room touching nothing, just looking, trying to think, trying desperately to pull from it the answers she needed. Answers? She didn't even know the questions. Yet she had a persistent feeling that if there were a question and an answer, it would either be here or in the room in the barn.

Kim stopped at a tall chest of drawers, and after hesitating, remembering suddenly the orders from Aunt Winifred to stay out of the room, she began to go through the drawers. She put aside her feeling of guilt. Aunt Winifred was dead now, the victim of her own daughter. Kim had to keep searching.

Clothing. A small treasure box of jewelry. Satin sheets for the bed. Kim arranged it all exactly as she had found it and closed the drawers quietly.

She was ready to give up and leave the room when she looked again at the bed. Now she knew what she was looking for. Every girl kept a diary. Perhaps Aunt Winifred had found it and took it to another room, to her own room perhaps, or even to the library.

But if it were the kind of diary that Charlene didn't want her mother to see, she would have tucked it into a hiding place.

Kim searched the small chests on each side of the bed, but there were no secret compartments, no diary taped to the back. She felt under each pillow. And finally she pulled up the satin spread and felt beneath the mattress.

Her fingers touched pitted leather, the narrow spine of a small book. She pulled it out. The leather was still soft. Dark brown alligator. The pages were edged in gold. The first page was dated October 12, 1958. "This diary belongs to Charlene Childress." A familiar scrawl read, "Keep out. Private. It was given to me on my fifteenth birthday. Keep out. Private property. Charlene. Charlene. Charlene Childress, aged fifteen."

Kim tucked the diary out of sight beneath her shirt and patted the bedspread back in place. After turning out all the lights, she closed the door and hurried down the hall.

At the entrance to the hall she pulled the double doors together and stood against them, looking into the soft lighting and the silences of the house. She wondered if they were sleeping, her mother, her dad. She wanted to take the diary directly to Daniel, as if by giving it to him all their problems would go away, and Kevin and Sara would be with them again.

She went downstairs instead and to a corner of the sun room where she sat on a stack of big, soft cushions. She pulled beside her a floor lamp and turned it on low. The windows reflected back the light, but after a long glance at them, she settled down, protected by the end of the sofa and a large potted plant that sat on the floor by the sofa.

She began to read.

During Charlene's fifteenth winter nothing beyond school seemed to be happening. Boredom was her major emotion, it seemed, with almost every page crying out, "There's nothing to do here. It rains every day. I can hardly wait for summer." Then, at last, summer came, and with it, Daniel; and the tone of the diary changed.

The first kiss was chronicled, and her intensely growing passion. Kim read with burning cheeks, and at times folded the pages together and laid the diary aside. She felt embarrassed and guilty for reading something that wasn't meant for her eyes. But then she picked it up again and read hastily, skipping lurid passages. She began to frown, slowing her reading, trying to absorb the meaning.

"I am pregnant. And now it is time to make the ultimate sacrifice to my lord and master, and in return we will receive life beyond life, love beyond love, never ending. We will be together forever, Daniel and I, in our mutual sacrifice to my lord, Prince of Darkness. Tomorrow we will die together, in the ecstasy of our passion, and thereby be transported forever to life beyond life. The knife is sharp. I honed it well, while my lover slept. I will kiss his lips once more, and I will ravage him. He is so beautiful. He will be mine forever. There will be no more long winters apart. This life will be left behind. And the ecstasy that awaits us will be more than we have ever known. We're coming, master, we're coming, netherworld. We will fly forever through the dark nights."

Kim was shivering. She felt cold, exposed to the night outside the windows. She crept farther behind the sofa and sat with her knees bent, her arms hugging her legs, and her chin thoughtfully resting in the dip between her knees.

What kind of power had that strange girl possessed? Kim no longer felt safe behind locked doors.

She watched for the pink light that meant the sun was rising. She prayed for it to come soon, soon. She heard a sound at the end of the room, a faint scraping along the outer wall. There was the merest shadow of a skeleton face outside the glass, looking in at her, and she realized there was no place in the room to hide from the windows. But as she stared at the glass she saw the face was merely the tracings of a shrub, parts of its woody structure highlighted by the light in the room.

Fear was crushing her, bearing her down, down beneath its weight. She could give in to it or rise against it. The burden of fear was too great, and she sensed her own destruction in the face of it.

She reached up and turned off the light. Faint angles of moonlight fell across the floor, separating window from window. As she waited the room seemed to grow lighter. She stood up, and though the fear was still her major emotion, she began to feel stronger.

Out the east windows she could see the lawn, the shrubs, and the dark orchard. A shadow moved into view on the lawn. She recognized the cat. It was ambling along, coming closer, going on around the corner of the house. Its naturalness, its lack of fear, helped stabilize her. The cat was not afraid. That meant that nothing alien roamed the yard on this late, moonlit night.

Kim watched it come onto the terrace outside the french doors of the sun room and sit there in the moonlight washing its face. She watched it get up and stretch, and leap down from the terrace. It became a low, moving shadow going beyond the hedge toward the pickup, and disappeared there in the silence of the night.

A taller, larger shadow moved at the end of the pickup bed. It was Frank, walking slowly to the end of the pickup and back again toward the front, out of sight. The night was still, the moon pale and steady.

Where was Charlene tonight?

A movement down at the northern end of the barn drew Kim's attention abruptly. She couldn't be sure if she had seen movement. A door there stood open, outlined by the moonlight. Had it stood open before?

Her blood ran cold as she stared at the barn, sensing the presence that had gone into the room. That was where Charlene belonged. She was connected to that room, by her beliefs and practices. Or maybe by something beyond Kim's understanding.

The door of the barn closed. Drawn inward by an unseen hand or pushed by a gust of wind.

Kim moved backward until she came to a chair. She turned it so that she would be able to watch the end of the barn, and sat, pulling her feet up from the floor. She stared at the end of the barn, where she had seen the door close, until it blurred into one great moon-touched, faded ball. She blinked to bring it back into focus. The door remained closed.

An idea began a formless growth in her mind. If she could approach the—the remains of Charlene, if she could talk to her, maybe the human part of Charlene would listen. She would ask her to please let Daniel go now. Hadn't she destroyed enough of him? She had taken Sara, and Kevin, too, she was sure, though he had drowned.

If she only had the courage to confront her, to face her.

She pushed instead into the soft protection of the wing chair and stared and stared at the barn until the pink light of coming day she had prayed for pushed the moonlight away.

*　　*　　*

He found her in the chair asleep, her head resting on her shoulder like a child, only a child, could rest. He could feel the stiffness of his own spine, the ache of his backbone just by looking at her. She looked so uncomfortable. How long had she been sleeping in the chair?

"Kim. Kimmy."

There was something in her lap, he saw, a small brown book with pages edged in gold. She was holding it tightly under her arm, protecting it even as she slept. A memory fluttered in the back of his mind. He had seen that small book before, sometime, far-away in the past. He tried to push the memory away. He wanted nothing of the past, and especially the memories. But a scene unfolded unbidden in his mind: "A birthday present," she had said. "But it's very private. No one shall ever read it, not even you." She had taunted him, tried to arouse his interest.

What was Kim doing with Charlene's diary?

A terrible dread settled over him like a foreboding of death. He was afraid Kim had already read too much of the diary, and he didn't want any of his family touched by Charlene in any way. She had been dead so long that it had seemed safe to send them here. He hadn't remembered much of Charlene in these many years, as if even his subconscious had tried to block her from his mind.

"Kim?" He touched her shoulder and shook her gently, and then tried to loosen the diary from her grasp. She woke instantly, her eyes round and frightened, her arm clamping even more tightly to the diary.

When she saw that it was Daniel she began to sob. She stood up and wrapped her arms around his body and wept against his chest. He patted her.

"Oh Daddy," she whispered, "I knew you didn't kill her. I knew you didn't, even though Aunt Winifred said you did. And I'm so glad, Daddy, that you didn't die with her."

He stood tense, staring down at her. She leaned away from him and looked up into his face.

"She's still—alive, Daddy. Not really alive, but—not dead. Do you believe that could be true? I didn't, when Kevin first told me. But she is. I've seen her."

17

Yes, he believed.

He stood on the terrace and looked at the great, faded red bulk of the barn. The trees scattered through the grounds among the farm buildings and the rear lawn of the house only partly hid its mass. It was long deserted now except for the pigeons and the rodents that surely had taken advantage of the empty space, but he could remember when there were cows and calves in the barnyard, and horses. There had even been a few well-petted goats, kept by Frank and grandfather Childress. There were fowl then, too: not only the ordinary chickens but peacocks and peahens, ducks, geese, even a covey of quail that had been found after the alfalfa was mown one early summer and the mother killed accidentally. The babies had been brought up to the barn and turned over to a bantam hen who raised them as if they were bantams like herself.

He remembered the playroom in the barn. At first it had contained a small housekeeping set of furniture: table, chairs, cabinet, even a tiny stove. Child size, not miniatures. He and Charlene had played there many times, with her directing the play. "You're my husband and you go to work every day, and these are our children. I cook and clean when you're gone and feed the—uh—I don't like this game anymore, Daniel. Let's get rid of this stuff and do something else." He had asked, "What?" He hadn't minded the game. Since he was the husband and went to work, that left him free to climb into the hay loft and play cops and robbers around the stacks of hay, even if his playmates were imaginary. Otherwise, he was subject to Charlene's rule, and at times deeply resented that they played only the games she liked.

"Well, something," she said. "I'll think of something. Come on, let's carry this junk out. I've got an idea already. Something I read about in a book." She looked at him slyly. "Do you know what the book is called? I'll tell you, if you'll promise never to tell anyone. It's called *The Occult, Strange Worlds of Darkness*. If you do certain things, you have enormous powers. You can even fly. At night, you can turn yourself into anything you want to be. So let's move this stuff out."

It was still stacked, so far as he knew, in a dark corner of one of the sheds on the river side of the barn.

Yes, he believed the incredible story Kim had told him. Once again he was thrown into Charlene's world: a frightening place that he had thought was left behind, forever.

Kim had given him the diary. It was in his hip pocket even now, waiting for its sentence. He had thought of burning it, but that seemed so inadequate, as if fire would only disperse it into the air to live on. A burial, then. Deep in the heavy earth, where the worms could digest it and turn it back to the earth from which it came in the beginning.

He walked with his head down, past the place where his aunt had been murdered. Kim's theory seemed incredible in a part of his mind, yet gruesomely acceptable deeper in, in the place that was ready to accept what had happened to Charlene. She had played with powers beyond decency. She had opened herself to it—whatever it was. Satan. The devil. The ultimate of evil. She had begun when she was a child. She had tried to drag him in, and others, but none of them wanted to play her dangerous games. Did he believe that she had remained, all these years, in a world between the living and the dead? Yes, he believed. She had sought powers that he had not believed in when they were young lovers. But now, haunted for these many years, running from the past for what seemed to be lifetimes, he realized that his nightmares had in some way known and tried to tell him that she existed yet, that she had, in fact, waited for him just as she had said she would; that she intended to take him into her world. She had not found the freedom she had reached for. Perhaps she was capable of feeling hate, such intense hate that it gave her the powers she had gained. Or, more likely, her actions were mindless and automatic, impelled simply from being the thing she had become.

Yes, he believed that she walked at night, fleshless, sightless, killing whatever she touched. Drawn, in some way he didn't understand, and didn't want to

319

understand, back to the places she had known. Back to the living people.

Why Kevin? his heart cried out. *Why Sara? Why my children, Charlene? If I gave you myself, could you give back my children?*

No.

He came around the end of the hedge and saw Frank leaning against the fender of his truck, smoking. Small puffs of gray smoke were rising from the bowl of his pipe, making tiny clouds in the air before they dispersed. His eyes looked sunken and misted. The flesh beneath his eyes was hollow and blue. He was an old man, and leaning beside him was a gun just as old. Daniel visualized this old guy, who had set himself up as guardian, trying to defend himself even against the phantom that Kim had described to him. What good would one of those tiny bullets do?

Thank God that she had not found this pickup and this old man in her nightly wanderings.

How could he send Frank home, permanently, without hurting his feelings?

"I appreciate your standing by, Frank, but I think you can give it up now and go get some rest."

Frank blew out a mouthful of smoke and told an obvious lie. "I'm not a bit tired. There's not much work to just standing around."

"I'm going to move my family out just as soon as my wife will go," Daniel said. "So you just go ahead and catch up on your sleep. And I guess there won't be any reason to come back every day, at least until this is settled and we're out of here. I'll need you to see after the place, if you don't mind, just like you always have, until I can get it sold."

"You're selling the Childress Ranch?" Frank cried, as if the news had struck him deeper than he would have admitted.

Daniel looked toward the river. "There comes a time—a time for an end. To everything, I guess. I've lost two children here, Frank. I could never live here."

"No, I reckon not. But it seems a shame to let it go. You've got another son who might want it someday."

Daniel shook his head.

Frank cleared his throat and tapped out the bowl of his pipe against the pickup bumper. "I've—uh—I've got this idea about who killed Miss Winifred and kidnapped your little girl, Daniel. I haven't told the police because I didn't have any proof, and I understand you got to have proof. There's just one thing that makes me wonder if I'm wrong. That's the killing in town of that filling station man, Milton Phillips." He waited. He looked into the bowl of his pipe and tapped it again on the car. Then he put it into his pocket and looked off across the fields.

"Milton Phillips?" A redheaded kid, as Daniel remembered, a little fat but with a good strong pitching arm. He'd played pretty good ball.

"Did you hear about him? I found him myself yesterday morning at sunrise outside his station, knifed just like Miss Winifred. But what would she want to kill him for? They never played together much that I know of. If Milton ever even mentioned her name to me I don't recollect it."

"She?"

"It's my idea, Daniel; that Charlene ran off back there when she disappeared. I don't mean to be speaking ill of your relatives, but if you'll admit it, and if you'd known her as well as I did, watching her grow up and all—well, that girl was pure evil, in most ways. She was spoiled rotten, in the first place, by her mother and her grandmother. The old gentleman spoiled her, too, though when she began that devil work in the barn, he didn't make excuses for her like the women did. They—or at least her mother—blamed you, even though you weren't here most of the time. I know very well you had nothing to do with any of that."

"No, I—" *Sick.* He had never, in all his life, been so sick as then. So torn in his heart and stomach.

"You came and told me, and I never saw anybody so pale. Lost your food, right there." Frank pointed to a spot that Daniel didn't want to see again. "But anyway, though we changed all of that, took all the animals away and kept a close eye on her the best we could, that girl was a strange one. You could see it in her eyes. She was restless. I thought at the time, she's got to be watched. So when she up and left I just knew that she'd show up again someday. And that's what's happened. The first thing that happened was the little pig. Winifred called and told me to come over, in the middle of the night. And there it was, on that dirty old bench in the barn room, dead. I was afraid that wasn't the end of it, and sure enough, it wasn't. She came back, killed her mother and kidnapped the little girl. The only thing I can't figure out is why she killed Milton Phillips unless there was more than I know about. I wondered if she might have a grudge against him. But I don't know. You don't either, I don't suppose."

Daniel had no answer for him.

"I was wondering if I ought to tell the police what I think."

Instinct. Deep intelligence that isn't derived from obvious sources. Without seeing Charlene, Frank had known, instinctively, that she had returned. But he had to be discouraged. The police couldn't help this time.

"Like you said, why would she kill Phillips?"

"Maybe she was at the station for some reason and he recognized her?"

The station was only a short distance away, Daniel was thinking, a quarter of a mile maybe, maybe less, the first place around the bend in the edge of town. Perhaps she had gone there in an aimless wandering. Or perhaps as Frank suggested, there was something long in the past between Charlene and Milton Phillips that neither he nor Frank had ever known about. He had only spent his summers with her, after all. Perhaps her wanderings and killings were not so mindless as he had thought.

Which was worse, he wondered. What were they facing? The whole town might soon be in danger from this thing that had to be stopped.

"How easy it would be," he said, thinking aloud, "to turn it over to the police and let them catch a living killer."

"Huh?"

Daniel clasped Frank's arm in an affectionate squeeze. He was appalled at the thinness. "Frank, go home, get some rest. Don't come back tonight. Come tomorrow if you want to. Let the thing about Charlene go for awhile. We'll talk it over in a few days if the police don't come up with any answers. If you stop and think it over, you'll see it's pretty far-fetched that she would have disappeared for all these years only to show up now. Go home and rest."

"Well—"

"I insist. I appreciate your help. But there's no need for you to be here tonight."

Frank nodded. "The funerals?"

"The day after tomorrow. Both of them."

Frank nodded and turned away, picking up his gun as he went by it.

"I'll keep in mind your theory, Frank," Daniel said.

Frank nodded again.

As he drove away Daniel could see the further sagging of the old face, as if he had allowed himself to relax finally, the burden passed on to someone else.

Alone, Daniel stood in the stillness of the morning. In the peak of the barn roof the pigeons cooed and quarreled. A low wind rustled the tops of the trees, a soft sound like whispers. Daniel felt his hip pocket. The diary was still there. It needed burying now, while he was alone. It had no information that would help anyone.

He went through a gate into the barnyard and carefully latched it behind him. He looked back toward the house but saw only small portions of it. That was the way he wanted it. He didn't want eyes watching him. Kim had wanted to walk with him, but he had sent her to her room. Like Frank, her eyes looked hollow, the skin beneath blue and thin. She had been awake too much of the recent nights and days, too worried, too disturbed and saddened.

Youth should be happy and carefree, but was it ever?

He wasn't worried that Kim would follow him. She was an obedient girl. He seldom gave her orders, but when he did he knew she would obey them the best she could.

In the shed at the back of the barn he found a shovel. Without leaving the protection of the shed he began to dig. The soil was soft and black, containing yet the manures of the animals that once had roamed freely through the open shed.

The soil made a soft sound as he shoveled it out of the growing pit into the little pile at the side. Grains of it slid down, whispering. His senses seemed highly attuned to every sound and movement around him: the sliding of the grains of soil, the separating of each small shovelful as it was lifted out. At a distant farm a peacock cried out, a raucous squawk that was softened by the rows of orchards between. And it seemed he could hear the river, too, pushing against the bank, twirling, splashing, gurgling; sounds he hadn't heard since—then.

He placed the diary in the bottom of the hole and scooped the pile of soil back in again, tamping it tightly with the back of the shovel, then smoothing it until there was no sign that the soil had ever been disturbed.

He put the shovel away and turned his face toward the river.

He climbed the fence and crossed the field, keeping the barn between him and the house. His steps were slow and the memories strong, tearing at him like talons from the past. In all the intervening years he had not allowed himself a conscious thought of Charlene and their last day together. Now he realized he should have gone immediately to the police. He should have gone to Frank and told him what had happened. The body should have had a proper burial.

Aunt Winifred should have known what had happened to her daughter. Grandmother and Grandfather Childress should have known.

He entered the space beneath the willow trees and beneath the ancient sycamore that leaned over the river, whose roots still held up the bank just as it had then. The place beneath the trees seemed not to have changed at all.

He sat down, leaned his arms on his knees and stared at the gently swirling water that splashed against the exposed roots.

The boys had freed her, Kim had said. They had found a skeleton chained beneath the tree and had broken the chain and freed it.

They hadn't known what they were doing.

Nor had he, when he was fifteen and horrified at what had happened.

"I'm here, Charlene," he said. "I've come back."

He watched the water, expecting it to be sliced by the rising of the spectre that Kim had described, but the soft ripples against the bank remained unbroken. He stared at the water until it was a solid glaze, with only misty colors, no shape, no form. At last he raised his eyes to the opposite bank where the trees grew as they did here, shading the bank deeply, drooping their branches to play in the water at times.

Kim had said she saw something go into the barn last night. Perhaps that was where she had gone. No longer chained in her watery grave, she had returned to the room in the central barn. From there? Where would she go from there? Her old room in the house?

He remained sitting as if he hadn't the energy or the heart to rise. It was here, somewhere along this bank, that Kevin had last walked. Oh God, why had he come to the river at night?

Daniel remembered the last time he had held the little boy in his arms. So long ago. Two years, three. When Kevin had passed the age of five he had stopped picking him up for a hug. Why? He tried to remember how it felt to hold Kevin, whose body now lay cold in its small coffin. The memory was gone, and his arms ached with loneliness. He lowered his head to rest on his arms and wept.

In the afternoon he rose from his seat beside the river and walked slowly back through the field to the barn. There was no activity near the house. They, Ronna, Kim, the nurse, Ivan, were waiting, as he was waiting. But were they waiting for the same things? The funerals tomorrow—and after that—what?

Tonight he would look for Charlene. Today he would look for her, in the barn.

A touch of sanity stopped him as if he had come up against a wall. *This can't be true. None of this is happening. It's some monstrous nightmare that I have fallen into.*

But then—

She's waiting for you, just as you always knew she was. All your running and running has done no good. She is capable of waiting forever.

The answer he had been seeking and had not found came to him as if spoken from the walls of the barn. It would end with his death. As she had planned, he, too, must die.

He closed the barn door behind him, sealing in the shadows and the gloom and the silences. He didn't try to quiet his steps. The wide boards beneath his feet squeaked, at times sounding as if they were splitting with his weight. He paused. The barn floor had been far more stable the last time he had walked here. As if the weaknesses traveled from the boards under his feet, to the walls, and to the ceiling, timbers cracked and popped far overhead. When the barn grew quiet again, he walked on, picking his path more carefully, trying to step on the supported sections of the floor. Then, deeper into the barn, as darkness gathered, relieved only by points of light coming through distant windows and cracks in the outside walls, he walked close to the wall where he knew the support was stronger. Still the sounds of weakness went with him, the boards groaned, the walls made faint cracking sounds, and far overhead in the peaked roof a shifting came, board grinding against board.

He paused again, waiting, and the sounds died away.

When he moved on, the barn was quiet, as if it rested. He began to feel that in some way it, too, lived and reported his entry.

The door to the room was closed. He stood quietly, listening, and it seemed he heard a cry, soft and far-away. Or near and subdued. Beyond the door, perhaps. She was here, he thought, in the room, and she had something—or someone—with her.

He turned the knob and threw the door open. It struck the wall and bounced back against his out-thrust hand, and the wall trembled. The darkness in the room seemed total. Yet when the silence returned and as he waited on the threshold, there was no movement in the room. The cry, if that was what he had heard, was not here.

His eyes adjusted, and he began to see the outline of the sacrificial bench. Even the ax that stood beside it. And the old red outline on the wall, the devil's head, still looking toward the doorway. The corners of the room came out of the darkness, faint, but light enough for him to see that nothing, no one, was there. He took one step across the threshold. The dolls were dark little lumps on the floor, the only occupants other than himself. There was a smell of dankness and something more, something that made him feel nauseated. Was it the smell that Kim had told him about? Lingering here, marking her recent presence?

A sudden, loud crack exploded somewhere in the barn, and small explosions of sounds raced away from it and died away, and when those sounds were gone it seemed to Daniel that he felt the floor beneath his feet shift slightly, a subtle movement that made him feel the earth beneath the barn had grown un-stable. Following the sounds of timbers moving came the cry again.

Daniel stepped away from the room, his attention captured by the cry, trying to bring it back after it was gone, trying to make sense of it. But now he knew— he thought he knew it had definitely been a human voice.

He hurried deeper into the barn, unheeding of where he stepped, even as some of the boards gave beneath his feet. He came into the largest room, where sacks of grain still sat in gray lumps, holes in the bottom eaten by mice or rats and spilling the contents onto the floor.

There was more light here. To his left a six foot high partition was the only wall between the grain room and the milk stanchions beneath the shed roof at the side of the barn. And above, cracks and knotholes in the ceiling allowed in light from the loft. He stopped in the middle of the room and looked around. There seemed to be no one here, but the stacks of feed were piled high near the corners, and hiding places were everywhere.

He could hear a whimper now. A low cry, as of an animal or—*a child.*

"My God," he said to the emptiness, and then shouted, "Sara? Sara!"

The whimper stopped, and for a heartbeat there was total silence, then he heard her voice, muffled, faraway, as if she were in another dimension.

He began to run about in the room, looking desperately behind every sack of feed. He could hear her, but he couldn't find her. Wherever he went in the room her cry followed him, tauntingly. He picked up single sacks of feed and threw them, and they split, their material rotten, and the grain flowed out onto the floor. He was calling hysterically, he finally realized, and forced himself to pause and listen again.

"Sara! Listen to Daddy. Listen, baby. Tell me where you are. Where are you, Sara?"

Her voice answered him, but it was too far away for him to make sense of it. And then he realized that the cry was coming from beneath the floor.

"Keep calling, Sara. Where are you?"

He followed the sound of her voice until at last she was directly beneath him. He still couldn't distinguish the words. She sounded as if she were in a well and had grown so weak she was hardly able to speak at all.

He pushed aside another sack of feed and put his ear to the floor. There were cracks between the boards, narrow, filled with darkness.

"Sara, are you down there?" he cried frantically.

"Daddy. *Daddy* . . ."

He began to run his hands over the boards, and suddenly he found a depression in the wood, and then the outline of the trap door was clear. He lifted the heavy lid and leaned it back. A perpendicular ladder went straight down into the dark and musty hole beneath him, but he could see the dark lump at the bottom of the ladder that was Sara. She lifted her face toward him, a pale oval of whiteness, ghostly in the dark cellar.

"Daddy," she said faintly, "Don't let Aunt Winifred hurt me."

"Nobody will hurt you, baby."

A moment more and he was down the ladder and had Sara in his arms. She seemed smaller and lighter than she had since she was a baby, and her weakness was so extreme that her head lolled against him. She collapsed as he carried her to the sunlight, only partly conscious.

He ran with her, shouting, "Kim. Get your mother. I've found Sara."

Instead, Kim met him on the porch, her hands pressed to her cheeks. "She's—she's—she's dead, too." She looked too crushed even to cry. "Was she drowned?" The tears began to gush forth and her face crumpled, her mouth opening as if she were getting ready to scream hysterically.

"No!" Daniel said, his voice harsh, to jolt Kim out of her approaching hysteria. "She's alive. She was in an abandoned cellar of the barn. I think Aunt Winifred put her there, for some reason we'll probably never know. But she's all right. We have to take her to a hospital, though. Kim, would you call for your mother?"

Kim blinked and used the backs of her hands to wipe the tears off her cheeks. She whirled to go back into the house, but at that instant Ronna came hurrying through the door, her eyes on Sara, her mouth working in silence.

"She's alive," Daniel said again.

He changed direction and went toward the rented car in the driveway, with Ronna at his side.

18

Kim played with Ivan on the floor of the nursery.
The nurse worked at something in the bathroom.
Washing the sink, perhaps. Kim could hear her
movements and the occasional run of water. She told
Ivan again, for the hundredth time, "Sara has been
found, Ivan. She's going to be all right. Mama and
Daddy have taken her to the hospital. You'll be all
right with me and your nursey."

Still, Ivan grew tired of the game and went back to
his fussing. He wanted his mama, Kim knew. She
had spent the last two or three hours trying to make
him happy. She wasn't sure what time it had happened—her dad running toward the house with little
Sara. But it seemed like hours and hours since the
three of them had gotten into the car and rushed off
toward the hospital.

The nurse came into the room smiling. Ivan
allowed her to pick him up, though he looked over
her shoulder and whimpered for his mother.

"I'll rock him awhile," the nurse said, "and give

him a bottle of milk. It's close to his bedtime anyway."

The sun was still shining but with a weakened light. Kim stood up and looked out the windows, but they faced the east, and she couldn't see how far down the sun had gone.

She dreaded the coming of night. The sun would become a huge red ball at the top of the western mountains, and then it would drop suddenly out of sight, and night would follow soon, too soon.

She went downstairs feeling lonely and frightened. The house seemed so empty now that her mother was gone. Yet she was glad they were gone, safely away. She wished they had taken Ivan, too. They had wanted her to go, but she had given the excuse of wanting to stay with Ivan.

She went outside half expecting to see Frank's truck parked at the end of the driveway. But there was no car at all.

An overpowering loneliness took possession of her. She might have been alone in the world, in her feelings of isolation and creeping panic. She wished Frank were here, and at the same time she was glad that he wasn't.

At the barn fence she stopped and stood against the boards, her hands gripping the top. At five feet three inches she could barely see over the top board. She was looking westward toward the river, and the last rays of the sun slanted across the field and at times blinded her. Its light was golden now and losing warmth. She felt chilled, and goose bumps stood out on her arms. Long shivers rippled over her body as if the river were overflowing upon her.

In the barn a series of sounds commenced and grew, as if someone were hammering on an inner wall. It became deafeningly loud, so that Kim put her hands against her ears and involuntarily turned to run, fear driving her away from her mission. Then as suddenly as it had begun it was gone, and the twilight was silent.

Kim gripped the fence again and looked into shadows. The sun was gone. There was only the merest light left in the sky. Above, a deep blue had fallen over the sky like a veil, and stars, cold, far-away, winked through, only to increase her sense of isolation.

The growing darkness meant it wouldn't be long now.

Kim climbed over the fence into the barnyard. An isolated clump of grass to her left, between her and the barn, looked at first glance like someone crouching. She stared at it until it took the shape of a weed clump. The darkness in the shadow of the barn seemed total, until she stepped up across the threshold of the barn and looked into the darkness there. She tried to swallow the fear in her throat.

It would stand out in the darkness, she thought, pale, thin, like a ghost. So pale it could hardly be seen at all. It would be there in front of her somewhere, in the unrelieved darkness of the barn. Perhaps it would make sounds when it moved, like the sounds she was hearing.

"C-Charlene," she said aloud, her voice sounding hollow and amplified. "I've come to talk to you."

Something leaped with a thud somewhere ahead of her, followed by lighter sounds of tiny feet.

"Eh—uh—" She couldn't speak, she was so frightened. She stood still, her mouth closed, both hands clasped over her heart. The running footsteps of mice and rats ceased, and the barn was quiet.

"I've come to talk to you," she tried again, her voice stronger. "You don't know me. But my daddy is D-Daniel. Please—what—"

A loud banging came suddenly from deep in the barn. It trailed away into mere pecks, as if the sound had raced up an interior wall and died away in the unpartitioned barn loft. Kim stepped backward instinctively and almost fell out the barn door. She caught herself on the outward swinging door, and something outside the barn, to her left, moved. A pale sliver of light, a thread, jointed, nearly invisible.

When Kim's feet touched the ground she faced the apparition, the ghostly figure that seemed suddenly much closer than it had been a brief thought ago. A gust of wind moved the door away from her, and Kim backed toward the fence.

It was moving toward her, the head a round, grinning entity that seemed in the darkness to be floating detached in the air. As it grew nearer she could make out the fleshless arms and legs; and the right arm was reaching forward, the knife blade catching a particle of remaining light and glinting in the air.

Kim tried to scream, but at this crucial moment her voice failed her entirely.

He had an appointment with death.

Daniel kissed Ronna and Sara and whispered to Ronna that he was leaving. He glanced again at Sara, asleep now, her face almost as pale as the pillow. An IV flowed into the vein of one small wrist. They would be feeding her intravenously for two or three days the doctor had said. She was dangerously dehydrated and in shock. But in a few days she would be as good as new. Cheerful, comforting words. They, her parents, had to believe he was right. But Ronna's face, now, looked desperate again.

"Why are you leaving?" she asked.

"Kim and Ivan are there alone," he reminded her. "You stay with Sara tonight. You'll both feel better. But I'd better go back to the ranch to stay with Kim and the baby."

She nodded.

He kissed her one last time, wishing that he had never put her away from him, ever; that he could go back and live his life over.

"Ronna," he said from the doorway.

She looked up at him. Though her face was thin and her eyes sad, she was beautiful.

"I love you," he said.

Her mouth softened, and tears glistened in her eyes. She almost smiled.

He closed the door between them.

Darkness had fallen when he drove into the driveway of the ranch twenty minutes later. He parked the car near the side of the house. There was only one visible light in the house, in the nursery at the front. He had seen it when he came down the driveway. The rear of the house was dark. His foreboding increased. Where was Kim? He had told her to stay in the house with all doors and windows locked, and he had expected a light in the kitchen, a beacon of sorts to his arrival home.

He found the kitchen door open. He turned on the light and called her name, but there was no answer. Turning on lights as he went, he hurried upstairs and to the nursery.

"Have you seen Kim?" he asked the nurse.

She shook her head, her finger to her lips. The nursery was dimly lighted by a shaded lamp. The roll-away bed had a stack of pillows for back support and an open book face down on the sheets. Beside it a floor lamp, covered by a towel, angled a reading light down upon the pillows. The nurse ushered Daniel out into the hall and then spoke in a hushed voice.

"She went downstairs earlier this evening. The baby has been very fussy, wanting his mama, I suppose. But finally, he's asleep. Kim was sitting out on the terrace by the sun room when I went downstairs to make myself a sandwich and to fix the baby some formula. I fed him a little jar of baby food. I didn't bother Kim. I thought she's old enough to make her own dinner. How's the little girl?"

"She's going to be all right."

"Her mother stayed with her?"

"Yes." He had to get away, find Kim. Maybe she was in her room. Yet he doubted that she was. He was scared to death that she had disobeyed him, for some reason of her own.

Like the ghost of a sound he thought he heard something, coming from faraway, like the cries of Sara in the barn.

He ran, around the banister and down the stairs, leaving the nurse staring after him. If she had heard the cry it did not register on her face.

In the utility room he turned on the yard light and grabbed from the wall hook the flashlight that had hung there since he was a teenager. He remembered to test it and found it had fresh batteries. Its light was a round, strong, three-volt beam.

In the back yard he stood in the outer glow of the yard light, hesitating. The solid wall of night beyond the yard seemed preternaturally quiet now, as if stilled by a quality that didn't belong or by the cry he had heard.

He walked toward the barn, the light in his hand bouncing ahead of him, seeming now no more than a pinlight against this incredible darkness.

"Kim!" he shouted.

She cried out suddenly, somewhere not faraway in the darkness, a scream that was strangled by sobs, her words garbled by fear. *"Daddy!* Go back! Don't come—don't come here—" Her cries died away abruptly on a choking sound.

He covered the distance between them without a conscious thought beyond that of reaching her. His light touched the rails of the fence and almost threw him off balance. He had forgotten, in his desperation, that a fence stood there. He swept the light beam along the boards of the fence, searching for her. He called out, but there was no answer. He climbed the fence and leaped down into the barnyard. A whimper to his left brought him whirling toward it, and his light beam touched upon the figure huddled on the ground in the weeds, just beyond the bottom board of the fence. Near a post on the barnyard side stood something that at first seemed only an extension of the fence. Daniel threw the beam of his light directly upon it, and it turned slowly and faced him.

Shock repelled him. His imagination, drawn from Kim's description, had not begun to touch upon the effect it now had upon him. Standing in high light, looking strangely lopsided, was the skeleton, animated like something from a Halloween carnival, something pale and thin and faintly glowing in the dark. He stared into holes where eyes had been, where now globs of mud made them large and dark in the gray skeletal face. Its right arm was rising again, jerkily, and light glinted on the knife blade. No rust on the knife, he found himself thinking, as if like her it had been instilled with its own abnormal immortality.

The skeleton leaped suddenly, it seemed. Its movement was not toward him precisely, but to his right, so that he was forced to face the opposite direction. He realized suddenly why it stood lopsided. Several of the ribs were gone on one side. And immediately he realized something else: He had no weapon. Had he intended not to fight for his life at all? Perhaps. He had come knowing that he had a date with death, a long delayed date. But he was not alone here. Huddled unprotected, perhaps injured, was Kim. And in the house, only temporarily protected, was his nine-month-old son.

"Kim," he said, surprised at the calmness of his voice, "get up and go to the house."

From the corner of his eye he could see her on the ground, and he saw no movement now, and received no answer.

The skeleton was coming toward him, slowly, and he backed away, keeping the distance between them even.

340

"Kim," he said again, daring not to look directly at her, not to take his eyes off the thing in front of him. "Kim, go to the house."

At last he knew that Kim was not capable of responding. She was unconscious—or dead.

A knot swelled in his throat. He'd had some vague idea of trying to communicate with Charlene, but that was ridiculous. His only communication would be with death. She would kill him—and then would she continue to walk the earth through eternity?

The flashlight beam outlined each movement it made, and its approach toward him seemed deliberate, like a cat cornering a mouse. He wondered briefly why, and then he came up against something solid, and he knew. The barn. She wanted him in the barn. And he had no choice but back into the nearest opening, the door, one high step up, backward. The door was standing open, back against the outside of the barn. He might have been able to pull it shut between them, but there was Kim, still out there with it.

He stumbled backward into the darkness and mustiness of the barn, and suddenly it was there, too, leaping effortlessly across the threshold. Overhead, toward the peak of the roof, there was a sound like a gunshot, with repeated, softer crackings moving down the beams.

To his left was a door into a tack room, and from there an exit, if only he could reach it. He whirled to run, and as if she had anticipated his move, she was there before him, blocking the doorway. Panic seized him, and he whirled and ran into the narrow passage deeper into the barn. Instinct for survival was coming to the surface, drowning out all else. A thought sliced into his mind as if it had been thrown from the walls of the barn: *The ax*. In the sacrificial room, at the end of the bench, was the ax. Exactly where Charlene had left it years ago.

He ran desperately, feeling the presence within reach behind him. He wouldn't be stopped yet, he knew, for she wanted him to go precisely where he was going.

The threshold was a length of board raised two or three inches, and he caught his toe on it and fell hard, face down, into the room. His chance to slam the door between them was gone. The flashlight rolled out of his hands and came to rest against the wall. Its light flickered and then steadied, still burning, the beam racing along the floor at the edge of the room and climbing the wall, lighting the evil drawing there, and the handle of the ax.

He rose only to his hands and knees and scrambled across the floor like some amphibian creature. His fingers touched the handle of the ax and knocked it sideways. He lunged, grabbing for it. When his hands closed tightly around the handle he rolled against the wall and stood up.

It was standing in the middle of the room, the hideous grin glowing in the faint light that reached it. The right hand was still raised high, and the blade of the knife looked longer and sharper, more powerful than the rusted old ax in his hands. The room was filled with the sounds of his breathing. He stared at the skeleton, at *Charlene*, and his eyes misted as he saw her standing before him, laughing silently, her face beautiful but with a terrible evil he had not seen before. Her red hair caught the light and came alive like fire. She was communicating something telepathically, but he couldn't quite catch it. He trembled and saw her pleasure. Hadn't his trembling always delighted her?

The wall moved. At first it seemed only a continuation of his hallucinations, yet with another part of his mind he saw the light on the wall had changed. Where at first it had reached only halfway to the ceiling, it now touched the ceiling and edged out upon it, like a bright stain. There was a sound in the wall, too, an echoing of the pounding of his heart. It was swelling in the room, making his ears feel stuffed and expanded with the noise.

The flesh fell away, and once again he was facing the skeleton. Then, abruptly, it moved toward him, the grin perpetual, the eyes draining moisture from the mud in rivulets down the bony cheeks.

Instinctively he raised the ax and brought it down. It cracked into the skeleton's frame, breaking off the left arm. It fell to the floor, clattering faintly beneath the other sounds in the barn, the swelling, splintering, cracking of its frame.

The loss of the arm only jerked it sideways and caused the other arm to move, swiftly, the knife streaking toward him. He jerked aside and cut sideways with the ax. It caught the skeleton just beneath the skull, and it separated, the head falling to the floor and rolling beneath the bench.

Daniel stared. The skeleton lunged toward him, headless, the knife stabbing the air, and then he saw the wall by the light was falling, inward, the ceiling coming down, first at the rear, above the bench, the face of the devil on the wall crumbling and losing form.

There was only a crack left of the doorway, and the

roaring of the barn as it came falling down, sinking into the room, knocked him to the floor. The flashlight still beamed, through the dust that fogged, showing him the doorway just beyond his reach. And then with a falling board the light went out just as Daniel reached and felt the opening.

He pulled himself through and found that the passageway was still holding. He ran through the darkness, toward the rectangle of light at the far end, going through thick stifling dust clouds, his head bursting with the sounds of the collapsing barn.

Something grabbed him. A hand caught his shoulder and pulled him back. He twisted to free himself and heard, felt, his shirt rip. Cool air bathed his shoulder and back. Harsh fingers, like steel claws, cut into his shoulder, turning as he turned, pulling him back into the collapsing barn. He fell, rolled, and could see it above him, pale as a ghost in the darkness, headless, with only one arm. The knife had fallen somewhere in the depths of the barn, along with the ax. At least he was safe from the knife. But the clawlike hand was pulling him deeper and deeper into the barn like a creature with its prey.

He heard his own voice crying out in hoarse terror. He began to wrestle with what was left of the skeleton. With his hands sinking into the spaces between the ribs he grasped them and pried apart, and had the brief satisfaction of hearing them crack away. Still it followed him as he rose again and ran toward the door that was becoming almost invisible in the choking dust of the barn. A huge portion of the upper beams crashed down ahead of him, and he was forced to climb. He found himself free at the top and the doorway in sight again, still standing, like a beacon to life. He glanced back, and it was there, the column of the spine with one arm attached, still moving, reaching for him. With his voice mingling and dying in the sounds of the crashing barn, he fell forward over the pile of ceiling boards and rafters, and when he struck the floor he felt as if the rest of the barn had fallen with him. With his hand touching the threshold to safety, he lost consciousness, a heavy board across his legs.

Kim regained consciousness and sat up. A sharp pain sliced through her head, and she realized she had struck it against the lowest board of the fence. She pulled herself to her feet and stared in amazement at the barn. The central portion of the entire roof-line was sinking in, slowly, like something in a disaster movie. The sounds of the falling jarred her ears, throbbed in her head. The light from the yard outlined the edges of the barn, the ends still standing, the door upright just as it had been before.

"Daddy!" she screamed. He was in there, she knew he was. Had she heard him calling for her? Hadn't she heard his voice? It seemed that she had.

She ran to the door and stopped. Light filtered through the fallen ceiling, through boards that had separated and dislodged, and it seemed hopeless that anyone could have survived the destruction that was now within inches of the doorway.

Her eyes caught a movement in the edge of the light, and she saw a hand. "Daddy?" she cried, climbing into the doorway, on her knees, reaching for the hand. To her relief it was firm and warm, flesh and blood. She felt his large palm, his thick fingers. *"Daddy!"*

She began to dig, pushing away boards that had fallen across him, grasping his shoulders and pulling, straining him forward inch by inch. Boards shifted and settled, but the crashing sounds drifted away, and only the restless movements and settlings were left. The dust choked her, made her cough. He was dead, dead, killed by the skeleton, or the falling barn. Either way, Charlene had gotten him, taken him away.

"Daddy! You can't, you can't let her!"

She felt movement in his arms as she dragged him nearer and nearer to the door. He was still alive, after all. She stopped calling to him and doubled her efforts to get him away from the barn before it started falling again. At the threshold he began to help her. He rose to his knees and toppled over into the grass. With her arms around his chest, Kim pulled him to safety.

"It's all right now. It's all right."

She held him as the barn crumbled, as his strength returned and he sat up beside her.

The sounds of timbers falling died away, and at last the night was quiet. It was a soft, natural quiet in which the crickets began at last to sing. Daniel looked up at the roofline of the barn against the sky.

The outer ends were still there, but the center was crushed inward, a large, jagged hollow, sinking down to the room in the center of the barn.

It had buried the room and all it contained within itself.

EPILOGUE

The bulldozer worked on the south end of the barn, pushing over the standing timbers, slowly pushing it all toward the collapsed center. The real estate agent shouted over the noise happily, delighted with the possible quick sale of the Childress Ranch. This young couple was really interested. They had loved the house and the setting.

"We'll burn this old barn when the dozer gets it all in a heap and clear it out of here. That'll give you another two acres of land. It'll be the richest acreage on the place, what with that old barnyard soil. None richer than barnyard soil. A barn like that isn't needed these days, with the present kind of farming, the orchards and all. It was too rotten to ever consider repairing."

The buyer said, "There must have been a quake here to cause a barn like that to fall." He kicked at a two by eight support rafter that looked as strong as a log.

"No," the real estate agent said. "It was just rotten.

The whole middle just gave in. The barn was over a hundred years old."

The child moved away, looking at the heaped boards and planks, the shingles, even a window frame. All of it piled like huge toys that needed to be put back together. She could hear the real estate man's voice, shouting along with the roar of the big tractor. It moved like a giant robot, in slow motion, pushing the distant end of the barn closer and closer to the center. She bent down and looked into the darkness beneath piles of boards. And then she fell to her belly and scrambled inward, reaching. Her mother yelled.

"Shelly! You're getting yourself filthy dirty, Shelly, get out of there." She came walking closer, and the men followed, slower, together, talking in lower voices. "Besides," her mother said, "you might get bitten by a black widow spider."

Shelly drew back and squatted on her heels, looking at this funny thing she had pulled out from under the boards. It was crablike, with thin, segmented bones. Dirt clung to the joints, and Shelly blew on it, trying to dislodge the sandy grains. She stared at it, then stood up shouting at her mother.

"Mama, look! I found a skeleton!"

The mother didn't bother to look. "Oh, Shelly, don't be ridiculous." She had stopped and was watching the bulldozer again. The men had stopped, too, and were now turning back. The mother glanced over at her six-year-old daughter. She smiled to herself. Ah, the imagination of children! "Shelly, throw it down, for goodness sake." She could see the small thing in the child's hand and thought it might be a skeleton at that. A rat's skeleton. "Shelly! Yucky! Throw it down. Go to the hydrant and wash your hands."

Without waiting to see that her orders were carried out, the mother went walking back toward the men. The child stood staring at the bones she had first thought was something that some other kid might have dropped. But she could see now that it was a hand, a part of a hand. There were the bones of a short finger and two longer ones, and a funny looking larger bone that must have been the palm of the hand. Altogether it was twice as long as her own hand.

The little finger had curled, she saw, and as she turned the skeleton over in her hands the longer fingers curled also. A long shiver went over Shelly and she threw the skeleton hand to the ground, shuddering. It had moved while she was holding it. It had actually moved, curling its fingers around her own.

She stepped backward three steps and opened her mouth to yell for her mother again. But then she stood in silence and stared transfixed at the three-fingered hand.

It stood up, like a huge, white spider, and it went crawling back into the darkness beneath the boards. The sound it made as it scraped in beneath the wood was one she would never forget as long as she lived. Later, when she lay in her bed in the upstairs bedroom and heard that same sound in the walls in the deep of night when all the world was still, she knew what it was. And she listened—and listened—and heard the faint scrape of bone against board, the light tap, tap, tap of fingers walking, the almost soundless drag of the palm.

Tap, tap, tap, dr-ag.

Silence.

And it always seemed to stop at the head of her bed, so that nothing scparated her from it except the plaster of her wall.

THRILLERS & CHILLERS
from Zebra Books

DADDY'S LITTLE GIRL   (1606, $3.50)
by Daniel Ransom

Sweet, innocent Deirde was missing. But no one in the small quiet town of Burton wanted to find her. They had waited a long time for the perfect sacrifice. And now they had found it . . .

THE CHILDREN'S WARD   (1585, $3.50)
by Patricia Wallace

Abigail felt a sense of terror form the moment she was admitted to the hospital. And as her eyes took on the glow of those possessed and her frail body strengthened with the powers of evil, little Abigail — so sweet, so pure, so innocent — was ready to wreak a bloody revenge in the sterile corridors of THE CHILDREN'S WARD.

SWEET DREAMS   (1553, $3.50)
by William W. Johnstone

Innocent ten-year-old Heather sensed the chill of darkness in her schoolmates' vacant stares, the evil festering in their hearts. But no one listened to Heather's terrified screams as it was her turn to feed the hungry spirit — with her very soul!

THE NURSERY   (1566, $3.50)
by William W. Johnstone

Their fate had been planned, their master chosen. Sixty-six infants awaited birth to live forever under the rule of darkness — if all went according to plan in THE NURSERY.

SOUL-EATER   (1656, $3.50)
by Dana Brookins

The great old house stood empty, the rafter beams seemed to sigh, and the moon beamed eerily off the white paint. It seemed to reach out to Bobbie, wanting to get inside his mind as if to tell him something he didn't want to hear.

Available wherever paperbacks are sold, or order direct from the Publisher. Send cover price plus 50¢ per copy for mailing and handling to Zebra Books, Dept. 1857, 475 Park Avenue South, New York, N.Y. 10016. DO NOT SEND CASH.